11/7/2015

With love to
my friend John

BELONGING
IN
AFRICA

JO ALKEMADE

FOR JOE

DISCLAIMER

This story is a work of fiction. I went to a great deal of trouble to ensure that the backdrop against which the action takes place – the political, social, and geographic realities of East Africa in the seventies - is as factually accurate as I could determine. Presidents Jomo Kenyatta and Idi Amin were real. Sam, Sara and the other characters sprouted from my own imagination, and should not be mistaken for any real person, living or dead.

CHAPTER ONE

I crawled onto the bed and sat on my knees, leaning forward until my nose touched the bug screen stretched across the open window. Night always fell so suddenly here. Every evening at 6:30 pm exactly, the blistering sun cooled to orange and sank low onto the horizon like an overripe mango. When it dropped from sight, the world turned instantly black. I took a deep breath and inhaled the smell of Africa: earth. Dust in the dry season and mud when it rained. I loved that smell.

A pack of Embassies lay hidden behind the socks in my nightstand. I shook out a cigarette, placed it between my lips, and pulled a lighter from the back pocket of my jeans. The spark wheel rolled smoothly beneath my thumb and I touched the flame to the cigarette and sucked deep, enjoying the bite of that first slow drag. My mouth grazed the screen as I leaned toward the open window and blew out a cloud of smoke. There was a small hole near the bottom of the fine metal mesh and I tore it wider, slid the cigarette through, and tapped ashes into the darkness. My parents had long given up trying to make me quit, but they would kill me if they caught me smoking in my bedroom.

"*Jambo, memsaab,*" a deep voice rumbled outside my window.

My hand twitched. A small circle of light danced on the grass and I realized it was the beam of a flashlight - our night watchman was walking his rounds. I grinned. Clearly I was suffering from a guilty conscience.

"*Jambo, Mwaura,*" I called out to him.

1

The beam of light moved away. I scraped my cigarette back and forth on the brick sill outside the window until it was dead, flicked the butt into the garden, and waved the last wisps of smoke out with my hands. I drew the curtains shut. The lighter felt cool and smooth in my hand, and I held it under the bedside lamp to admire it, again. Today's date was engraved in tiny black letters along the side - October 6, 1978 - and my name in curlicues on the front.

"Sara, where are you?" my mother called.

I hopped off the bed and ran to the door to stop her from coming in. My mother had a sensitive nose.

"*Ja, ik kom*," I yelled.

I stepped into the living room where I knew I would find my parents at this hour. My father sat in a brown leather chair that was shiny with age and worn into the shape of his body. A floor lamp stood beside to him, almost touching his elbow where it lay on the armrest - light gleamed on his bald head, and down on the newspaper folded open on his lap. My mother nestled into the beige corduroy sofa across from him with her things scattered around her. She was leafing through a cookbook, probably planning tomorrow's menu. Her knitting lay by her side and the cat was purring in her lap. My parents were so predictable.

"*Hartelijk gefeliciteerd!* Happy, happy birthday, my daughter!"

My father projected the words in his best flamboyant theatrical manner, punctuating each one with an upward thrust of his arms. His round face creased into a million laugh lines. I grinned. My father treated the world like it was a stage and humankind his adoring public, always expecting someone to be on hand to soak up whatever emotion he felt like projecting. It looked like we were in for some light-hearted entertainment today, maybe a comedy.

He stood up, clutched me by the shoulders and kissed me firmly on both cheeks in the Dutch way. "My, my, my," he said, shaking his head as if he couldn't believe his eyes. "When did you grow to be so tall? Surely it was only yesterday you were running around the house on chubby marzipan legs, wearing nothing but your nappies. Mama?" he turned to my mother, "When did our only child suddenly become a young lady, can you tell me this?"

My mother smiled, knowing no reply was expected, though the question about my height was legitimate enough. I didn't much resemble either of my parents. They were well-rounded and many-chinned. My twiggy shape, on the other hand, was practically curve-free with only a hint of hips and an A cup barely filled, though my stomach was not quite as flat as I'd like. Also, they were short and I was the tallest girl in all of Kenya. My mother liked to tell me I did my growing because of the good food she fed me. If that was true, I wished she'd stop.

"Why don't you come over here and sit down… tell me, are you having a good birthday?" my father asked.

I smiled and handed him the lighter before I fell onto the sofa next to my mother. "A gift from my friends at school."

He turned it over in his hands and clucked approvingly. "A Ronson… a decent brand, certainly. Silver plated. They must think well of you."

This morning my friends had gathered in the school parking lot and howled *happy birthday to you* so loudly and horribly that I had jokingly covered my ears. My best friend Chloe stepped forward and handed me a little box and a card, signed by everybody who had chipped in, and inside was the engraved silver lighter displayed on a bed of cotton wool. It was beautiful, and unexpectedly extravagant, and I stood there mumbling my thanks, not finding the right words. The first bell rang and the group fell apart, some reaching out to give me a quick hug before making their way to the classrooms. I spent the rest of the day smiling.

"I trust this will not increase the number of cigarettes you consume," my father said.

"Of course not – why would a nice lighter make me smoke more?" *Good grief.* I changed the subject quickly to distract him from the lecture I already knew by heart. "And then after school Chloe and Tazim came home with me. We listened to records in my room."

"Ah, yes. The decibels were quite high, I understand from your mother."

I grinned at the understatement. As soon as my friends and I arrived at the house, we sprinted to my bedroom and closed the door behind us. I dropped a record on the turntable and cranked up the volume, not just because we preferred our music loud, but to cover up talk and laughter about things that should never reach parents' ears.

"The girls couldn't even hear me," my mother complained. Apparently she had stood outside my door for minutes, trying to knock with one hand while balancing a tray in the other, and we never heard a thing. She finally thumped the door with the pointy toe of her pumps until we noticed it shuddering in its hinges and Chloe ran to open up. There stood my flustered mother, kicking at the door, trying not to spill mugs of tea, or snuff out the eighteen burning candles on my birthday *chocoladetaart*. My mother's chocolate cake, baked with her secret ingredient: a slosh of dark beer. We moaned with delight at each gooey, delicious bite.

"Did you make a wish, or are you now too grown up for such things?" my father asked.

"I made a wish."

He winked at my mother and said, "I expect it was to perform especially well at school this final year, am I right?"

"You know very well I can't tell you what I wished for, papa, because then it won't come true," I said, teasing him. My father looked pleased. He liked me to joke with him.

4

Actually, I knew exactly what I wanted. I blew out the candles in a single whoosh, squeezed my eyes tight, and made the only real wish I had: that things would pretty much just keep going exactly as they were. Today had been another perfect day and the future looked excellent, and I never wanted a life other than the one I was living right here, right now in Kenya. All I needed was a little more freedom, a little more space between me and my overprotective parents - and with graduation around the corner, that wish would come true soon enough.

"Speaking of wishes - we have not yet had an opportunity to give you your gift," my father said.

I already knew what my present was, but that didn't spoil the anticipation in the least. My father handed me an envelope with the flap tucked under. I flicked it open and took out a sheet of paper, unfolded it and read the thick black letters on top: **Westlands Driving School**. My first lesson was scheduled for next Monday and the last one in two months' time. Two months and three days from now I would have my driving license. No more bargaining with my parents to drop me off at a movie, no more having them pick me up far too early from a party, no more sitting around school with nothing to do during lunch hour. *Independence, here I come!*

"Are we correct to conclude by that very large smile on your face that our gift pleases you?" my father asked.

"Papa, mama, thank you so much," I jumped up and kissed them both.

"Listen to me carefully," my father said. "You must take every lesson extremely seriously and pay proper attention to instruction. Traffic is a free-for-all in this city and things are crazy on the road, absolutely mad. As soon as any person in this country steps behind the wheel of a car, they lose their sanity altogether. If you are going to drive here, you must be very, very cautious and adjust to the way things are done," my father said.

I sat back down and nodded, not really listening.

"Such as, for example, the incident just now," my mother prompted.

"Ah, yes, you are absolutely right! That certainly is the perfect example of Nairobi driving insanity." My father chuckled at the prospect of the story he was about to tell. I recognized the signs. The chortling as though something was just too good to keep inside; the shaking of his head in disbelief at the bombshells life threw at him; the way he rubbed his cheeks up and down with both hands, as if warming them up for a long storytelling session. He looked at me and said, "Did you hear the commotion at the gate when your friend was picked up by her father this evening?"

"No, I didn't." The volume of the stereo was turned up so high, the windows rattled.

"Well," he said, "Listen closely, because you are not going to believe your ears. Imagine me on my way home from work, driving my normal route with nothing out of the ordinary going on. Which is to say, I *believed* nothing out of the ordinary was happening. But then I began to notice a car behind me, following me very closely. It was one of those Peugeots, you know, thousands of them on the road - but this one had an odd rusty color and it caught my eye. I grew suspicious when it kept close as if it had become attached to my bumper."

He took a slow sip of coffee, allowing time for suspense to build. He continued: "Twilight was setting in and soon the streets would be black as a demon's heart. I knew I would be easy pickings for this criminal element who had fixed its eye on me. It was time to take action. I took a sudden right – the car followed me. I took a sudden left - it followed me. I stomped on the accelerator and raced through a red light – it followed me. This is when I knew I was in deep, deep trouble. I would not be able to shake this car. I was about to be carjacked."

I lifted my eyebrows and asked, "What did you do?"

"What could I do?" My father shrugged his shoulders as if it was obvious. "I flew through the streets of the neighborhood like

I had my own set of wings. When I got close enough to home, I leaned with my full weight on the horn and kept it screaming like a banshee, and prayed Mwaura had arrived for his evening shift. And so he had: Mwaura - our excellent, reliable *askari* - he heard my car approaching at unusual speed, and understood something was terribly wrong. He threw open the gates and I drove through like a Formula 1 race car driver – I did not touch the brakes until I almost rammed through the front door of the house. And Mwaura slammed the gates shut behind me."

I glanced at my mother, trying to gauge by the expression on her face whether this could possibly be true. She seemed to be listening attentively and didn't give anything away.

My father sensed my suspicion and said, "It happened exactly like that, like Mwaura and I had practiced these moves a hundred times and had them memorized precise as clockwork. As I was sitting there, thanking God in heaven for my escape and trying to catch my breath, the car that had been following me screeched to a halt just outside the gate."

"Are you serious? Carjackers followed you all the way to the house?"

My father threw back his head and burst into peals of laughter. Tears leaked from the corners of his eyes and he dabbed at them dramatically with his forearm, leaving round wet spots on his sleeve.

"*AHA, aha, ha, ha, ha,*" he chuckled, winding down. "Well... not exactly, as it turns out."

"What's so funny? Who was in the other car?" I asked.

"It was the father of your friend, on his way over to pick up his daughter. It appears he forgot the way to our house and had been wandering around helplessly for some time when suddenly, by sheer fluke, he saw me drive by. He thought this was his lucky break and he would simply follow me to his child, but instead, I forced him to participate in a high-speed chase."

"Tazim's father?" I asked in horror.

"Yes, indeed, it was your friend Tazim's father, Mr. Patel," my father said cheerfully. "And he was not a happy man, no, not happy in the least. He shook his fist at me and asked me why I behaved like such a lunatic, as if I had raced him around the city just for the fun of it. Of course, I hastened to apologize and told him I thought he was a carjacker, which somehow did not appear to improve matters."

Oh, man. I hoped Tazim wouldn't hold my father's craziness against me when I saw her back at school.

I glanced at the small cuckoo clock on the mantel over the fireplace. It was time to get ready for my date with Leander.

"Well, I guess I'm off to get dressed now," I said.

"Are you going somewhere?" my mother asked.

My birthday was not over yet... in a few hours my boyfriend would be picking me up for a surprise date. I hoped whatever he had planned would involve many sweaty hours on the disco floor with me caught in his strong arms in an embrace so close, my hot cheek would be glued against his and I'd feel his peppermint breath on my skin.

"Yes, Leander is taking me out for my birthday. He has something special planned. I told you."

My mother glanced at my father, and he answered for the both of them, "Of course, of course. Just do not forget to be home by midnight."

"Midnight? Come on, papa, it's my birthday!"

"Midnight. Some things will not change just like that, one, two, three, only because you are having a birthday, do I make myself clear?" He shook out his newspaper and opened it wide in front of his face. There would be no more discussion.

I rolled my eyes. I understood. Still, it was my birthday. I could probably stretch curfew by an hour or so without getting in too much trouble.

CHAPTER TWO

Leander. I met him three months ago when my parents let me throw a party to celebrate the end of the school year. Things quickly got out of hand. More gatecrashers showed up than invited kids and there was a lot of drinking. Someone vomited in the bathroom. I was worrying that I'd have to start policing the place to stop things from spinning even more out of control, when I caught sight of this guy. He was gorgeous. I watched him do his thing as he danced with one girl after another and flirted hard with each of them. He stroked arms, squeezed waists, and ran his fingers through long hair. His body swayed and flowed with the music and all the while he kept his eye locked on his partner as if she was the center of his universe. I imagined his hands and eyes on me, and a twinge of delight tickled up my spine.

"Who is that?" I whispered to Tazim.

"Let's see, the one dancing over there in the white t-shirt so tight you can see his nipples? The dude with the curly blond hair?"

"Do you know him?"

"I do, actually. He goes to the boy's school, you know, Saint John's. He's one of their top rugby players. Looks the part, doesn't he?"

"Oh, yes," I said.

"HEY," Tazim suddenly yelled loudly, making herself heard over the thumping music. "Hey, Leander! Don't you think you should be dancing with the party girl?"

I was mortified, but Leander beamed me a smile and bent his head toward the girl he was dancing with. He whispered into her ear, kissed her forehead, and left her. He came to me. His handsome face flushed golden by the sun, his eyes the color of the sea - indigo blue with flecks of silver - made me feel stupid and shy. He had an athlete's body, broad-shouldered and hard. He was the tiniest bit shorter than me. I bent a knee and leaned into my hip, and lost three centimeters.

Leander told me I looked pretty, congratulated me on throwing the best party of the summer, took my hand and drew me onto the space where the sofas had been pushed aside. We danced. He asked me out on a date. I was in love.

I leaned over the edge of the tub and turned on the tap - it was time to get ready for my birthday date. Carefully, I stepped into the bath and melted under the hot water. Steam floated up and my face glowed rosy and damp. My limbs relaxed, eyes shut, and my mind lazily fantasizing about the joys ahead. Leander was the best gift I could ever wish for.

When I felt the water cool, I roused myself. I foamed my legs, put a fresh blade in the razor, and shaved slowly, gliding lightly over the knob of my ankle and around the knee. My armpits felt smooth when I tested them with my fingers, but I shaved them anyway. I slipped underwater and soaked my hair until it was heavy with water and the waviness sagged out of it, and it fell below my shoulders. I wished it would grow long and sleek and reach down to my waist. I wished the sun would bleach it platinum blond instead of this ho-hum shade of pale brown I was born with. *Oh, well.* Nothing was going to ruin my mood today. I poured a double dose of green apple shampoo into the palm of my hand – tonight my hair would shine under the disco lights. I wrapped my toes around the silver chain and yanked the plug.

The hallway was clear when I peered around the corner, and I streaked to my bedroom and locked the door behind me. *What should I wear, what should I wear, what should I wear?* My favorite bell-bottoms had been washed but not ironed. Perfect. I stepped into the jeans, clutched the waistband and hopped up and down, yanking at the stiff denim to drag it over my hips. When they were on as high as they would go, I picked up a wire clothes hanger and pranced over to the foot of the bed, leaning back slowly until I landed flat on the mattress. I poked the hook of the hanger through the zipper, sucked in my stomach, and pulled hard with both hands. The zip crept up tooth by tooth until it closed at the top, and I forced the metal button through the buttonhole to lock it in place. My breath gushed out when I released my stomach.

I swung my legs to the floor and felt the denim bite into the back of my knees – these jeans fit tighter than a second skin. I felt sexy. I felt like the sexiest chick in the world. I felt like dancing. I stood up and hop-skipped small quick steps to the turntable, and when the needle hit the record the Bee Gees burst into my room and I wailed along with them: *My woman takes me HIGHER! You should be DANCING, yeah!* No doubt whatsoever about it, the Bee Gees were singing about me tonight. I swished my hair and swung my hips, bent my knees and plunged low, pushing into my jeans to stretch them out just a little, just so I could dance, free and wild as a gazelle.

The hands on my alarm clock pointed close to 8:30. Leander would be here any minute and I wasn't even dressed yet. I quickly pulled on a top I knew he liked: a cheesecloth blouse smocked snugly underneath my breasts, slightly see-through. I combed my hair, brushed on two thick layers of green mascara, drew kohl lines around my eyelids, and put on my glasses. The glasses were a bummer, but I couldn't see anything without them. I turned away from the mirror and pretended I wasn't wearing them.

9:00 o'clock came and went. I lay down on my bed and picked up a book and tried to read, but couldn't stop listening for

Leander's motorcycle. I put the book aside. The needle lifted at the end of another record and the room went quiet. I stared at the dead bugs trapped in the glass ceiling light. Leander was never on time for anything, I should be used to that by now.

Every so often a bike drove by on the main road and I willed each one of them to turn into our cul-de-sac. At last one did and stood idling while Mwaura walked up to it, making sure it was safe to open the gates. My cheeks flushed with relief – Leander had arrived. I lifted the curtain and peered out. Two headlights were pointed at our gate. Someone in a car was visiting my parents.

I heard a quiet knock on my door and my mother stepped into the room, her hand still on the knob. "It is getting awfully late, Sara. Do you think Leander may have forgotten? Soon it will be too late for you to go out at all."

Sometimes my mother had a knack for saying the exact wrong thing. I had spent hours getting ready and now I was lying foolishly on my bed in make-up and my tightest jeans. I flashed between feeling sorry for myself and worrying that something terrible had happened to Leander - maybe he had been in a wreck or come down suddenly with malaria. But I knew he would call as soon as he could get to a phone. He would call, I was sure of it.

I gritted my teeth and swallowed, willing myself to sound relaxed and ordinary, not wanting my mother to imagine I was about to be jilted on my birthday because even thinking such a thing would probably make it happen.

"Leander's running a little late, is all. He'll be here soon. Don't worry about it."

But he didn't come. And he didn't call, either.

CHAPTER THREE

I sat up, pressed a pillow to my face, and gave in one last time to the urge to howl. My eyes burned from catching only nightmare minutes of sleep and from the tears I cried all night.

I dried my face with the pillowcase, shook my head, and pulled myself together. Daylight glinted through the crack between the curtains, and the terrible night of waiting was over. I got up, pulled on my sneakers, washed the ruined make-up from my face and sneaked out of the house before my parents got up - I did not have the strength to face them. No doubt they'd be round-eyed with sympathy and tut-tut kindly, but they'd really be thinking I'd been stood up in the ugliest way, and I was not ready to accept that. There was a reasonable explanation for Leander not showing up last night and I was going to find out what it was. Lying awake, I had come up with a plan: I would go to Sam. He was Leander's friend and he would know what was going on.

I unlocked the front door, careful not to make any noise, and stepped out of the house into the cool morning air. The dark red patio tiles beneath my feet were misted with dew. Early birds sang, but there were no other sounds. The quiet comforted me and I felt my pounding heart slow - I stood for a moment to soak up the tranquility.

Mwaura had left his tray on the round wicker table. Every night, my mother made him a plate of sandwiches and fruit, and tea the way he liked it: hot and strong with lots of milk and sugar. All that was left were a few crumbs and a puddle in the

13

bottom of the mug. Mwaura had gone home. His shift ended at dawn.

I walked down the stone steps that cut through the flower beds. The pastel-colored pansies looked crisp this morning, though I knew in a few hours the sun would roll higher overhead and beat on them until they drooped and wilted. I placed a foot onto the gravel driveway at the bottom of the stairs and stepped lightly, walking the fifty steps or so to the tall front gate with as little noise as possible. The latch creaked when I lifted it and I slipped outside, reaching back through the bars to fasten the gate behind me. I walked quickly along the dirt road of Peponi Grove and turned right, down the paved main road that would take me to the small motel where Sam lived with his brother. I had visited them once with Leander and was pretty sure I remembered how to get there.

My mood improved now that I was taking action rather than just lying there anxiously waiting for something to happen. It felt good to walk. There was no sidewalk next to the road, just a narrow path worn through the grass by people who passed by all day. A woman came toward me with a round plastic tub balanced on her head, full of yellow bananas and ripe papayas. She adjusted it delicately with her hand but didn't break her stride. She wore a *kanga* wrapped around her hips; a rectangle of faded yellow and blue paisley patterns like a giant handkerchief, with the ends tucked under to make a skirt. A second *kanga* was slung around the baby on her hip and tied across her chest. The baby was asleep and his head bobbed with her every step. She was probably on her way to a busy street corner where she'd cut up her fruit and sell it to passers-by.

"Jambo," I greeted her as I walked around her, giving her right of way.

"Jambo," she answered. She smiled at me. She did not look at all tired, despite the load she carried.

The road stretched out far ahead, weaving downhill through

14

our Westlands suburb. Houses stood back from the road along both sides, half-hidden behind tall hedges and brick walls. Most of them were gray stone bungalows just like ours; older houses built by colonials to look like the cottages they had left behind in England, with casement windows and red tile roofs.

I hoped it was a good idea to go to Sam; I did not know him well. He and Leander both played on Saint John's rugby team and I'd sat in the bleachers many times to watch Leander play, though Sam was hard to ignore - he was fast, strong, and dominated the game. Up close, he was striking. His skin was dark, the color of unsweetened coffee, his eyes deep brown, and his hair cropped short in the shape of his skull. He stood fiercely upright. He always greeted me with the good manners of this country, shook my hand and spoke to me in his slightly formal African-style English, but did not seem particularly interested in being friendly. He was a tiny bit intimidating.

I crossed a shopping center parking lot to save time. The new Uchumi supermarket where my mother bought her groceries had not yet opened its doors, but the bakery on the corner was doing good business. With my back to the stores I hesitated, not sure which direction to take. I felt panic wash over me: I had to find Sam. I had to talk to him.

There were houses along the street on the left, and I turned in that direction because I remembered the motel stood in a busy neighborhood. I walked briskly, impatiently, and peered into every side street, looking for a driveway that dropped steeply downhill and ended in a dirt parking lot in front of the motel. I exhaled hard with relief when I found it.

The motel looked deserted. It was no more than a single row of rooms with identical brown doors and dark checkered curtains covering the windows. I had no idea which one was Sam's. Tears welled in my eyes. I had come so far, and now I had no idea what to do.

"Sara, is that you?" a voice called out.

I snapped my head around just in time to see Sam step out of a door at the far end of the building. It was clearly marked *Office.* An office; I'd missed that.

"Sam! I'm so glad to see you."

He walked toward me, carrying a styrofoam cup in one hand. He examined me with his head tilted slightly to one side. I didn't blame him for looking quizzical. I must have been the last person he expected to find on his doorstep at the crack of dawn on a Saturday morning. Sam carefully put his cup down on a metal folding chair next to one of the rooms. It leaned to one side where the rusted leg was bent and the cup slid slowly to the edge of the seat.

Sam walked toward me with his arm outstretched. "Jambo," he said.

"Jambo," I greeted him in return. I shook his hand.

"*Habari gani* - how are you? Are you well?" he asked.

"I... ah, yes. How are you?" I stammered. "I mean, actually... no, I'm not doing so well. Not really. I have a question, or more like a problem. I thought maybe you could help me, you know? That's why I came here."

"You walked?" he glanced around the almost empty parking lot.

I nodded my head slowly. Tears stung beneath my eyelids again and I tried not to give in to the fresh wave of self-pity that threatened to overwhelm me. Sam moved closer and wrapped his hand softly around my elbow. I was relieved to see kindness in his eyes.

"Why don't you tell me what's going on," he said.

"Oh, Sam," I blurted. "Yesterday was my birthday and Leander was supposed to take me out to celebrate, only he never showed up. I tried calling him last night and this morning, but he isn't answering the phone. I can't imagine what happened only I'm convinced it has to be something really bad..." I covered my face with my hands.

Sam was silent. I looked up. He was staring over my shoulder, his eyes squinting into the sun that was still hovering low over the horizon. He tightened his grip on my arm and pushed me firmly toward the door behind the metal chair. He called his brother's name. Dennis opened the door and looked out sleepily, his hair standing up in uncombed tufts, wearing nothing but a pair of striped pajama pants.

"Take her inside," Sam ordered. He let go of my arm and stalked off in the direction of the road. Dennis stepped aside to let me pass into the room, but I stood still and looked back over my shoulder.

A familiar motorcycle turned into the parking lot. Leander was driving. Sitting behind him - her arms laced around his chest, her body resting against his, her long ice blond hair floating in the breeze – was a beautiful girl.

CHAPTER FOUR

My heart was broken. All weekend long I wished and hoped and ached for a call from Leander. I wanted to hear him admit he'd made the worst mistake of his life and beg me to take him back, or at least explain what had happened and apologize for being such a piece of shit. I didn't hear a thing. A spear pierced my heart every time the phone rang and it wasn't him.

I cried until I thought I might finally be done, but then I'd remember the girl on the back of the motorcycle, sitting where I used to sit, replacing me, and I realized I'd probably never be able to stand it. I tried to stay in bed with the curtains closed and the door locked, but instead life decided to carry on.

Monday morning my mother dropped me off at school like it was any ordinary day. Chloe was waiting for me, sitting on the low fence near the picnic tables. I was relieved to see her because she was my best friend for good reason: I could always count on her to be by my side when disaster struck. Of course she knew what had happened, and so did everybody else - word of anything out of the ordinary spread like bush fire around our small school. Now I had to deal with my misery in public.

Chloe hugged me tight and gently patted my back. I strangled a small sob and she released me. She blinked sweetly while she adjusted her headband and tucked wisps of golden hair behind her ears. The big round amber bead in the center of her forehead looked like it was tied on too tightly; it had pressed a red dent into her skin. Chloe was the last of the living hippies, all about love-and-peace and flower-power long after the rest of the

18

world had given up on the whole idea. She said, "Come on, man," and walked up the path to the school, checking over her shoulder every few steps to make sure I was still following.

Bells rang at the start of classes and the end of them and I kept to myself. People talked behind my back and giggled, I could tell. I stayed quiet and pretended it was easy to ignore them.

"You look like you swallowed a chili pepper whole and it is burning you up from the inside," said Tazim. "Hop into my car. Chloe and I are taking you to the store."

"Is it lunchtime?" I asked.

"Yes, it is. Now settle down and let us put a smile on that gloomy face."

We stepped into her car and Chloe pushed a cassette into the dashboard player, turned up the volume, and soon we were belting out the song along with Gloria Gaynor: *I will survive, I will SUR-VIVE!* Chloe winked at me and I knew she had picked it especially for me.

We took the short dirt road from school onto the main road, and five minutes later Tazim parked in front of our store. It was open to the street and I sniffed the thick scent of herbs and spices that drifted from little bags folded from newspaper. The colors of the place were eye-popping: counters painted sky blue, walls grubby peach-pink, and the floor peeling shiny red paint on raw cement. A glass case like an aquarium stood on top of the counter, filled with silver-plated jewelry that turned your skin green in less than a day from the copper hiding just beneath the surface. Khaki-colored t-shirts with a picture of a lion or zebra and *Kenya* underneath them sagged from wire clothes-hangers on nails stuck in the walls. I wondered what tourist had ever come to this store to buy a souvenir t-shirt. The Indian owner, an iron-haired lady, sat rigidly on a tall backless stool behind the register. She bossed the African salespeople around, not trusting them to touch her money. She kept her eye on us, too.

Chloe held up a paperback. "Sara? Have you read this one?"

The title on the cover was printed in thick black flourishes: *Sweet Savage Love.* Beneath it, a cowboy with rippling arm muscles in a sleeveless flannel shirt was riding off into the sunset on a feisty brown horse. I hesitated. I did love a good romance novel, but right now stories about gorgeous hunks folding the women they loved in steamy embraces, and everybody living happily ever after, seemed far too hard to bear.

"No, thanks," I said.

Chloe and Tazim made their selections and we shuffled through the store single-file. My friends admired big hoop earrings with dangling glass rubies and ashtrays carved from pink soapstone with tiny lions along the rim. Finally they settled on bars of Cadbury's Fruit and Nut. They handed me one, and I unwrapped it and broke off a square. I took a nibble and found I was not hungry. I closed the foil and put the chocolate in my purse.

"Sara, you are taking this Leander thing far too hard," Tazim said. She was a girl who spoke her mind. I braced myself for what would come out of her mouth next.

"He broke my heart," I said, sounding more defensive than I intended.

"Leander is a player and everybody knows it – he's far too cute for his own good. What did you expect? He's the kind of guy you want to show off on the dance floor, even enjoy a date with now and again. But he'll never make a commitment to you or anybody else. Why would he? There are dozens of girls swooning at his feet everywhere he turns."

Chloe put her arm around my shoulder and looked sympathetic, but I noticed she didn't contradict any of this. What an idiot I was.

After school it was time for my first driving lesson. Just days ago I was sure getting a license was my ticket to freedom and doing my own thing; now I didn't have a boyfriend and I'd never be going out again, so what was the point? I went to the lesson because I didn't have the strength to tangle with my parents.

I walked into Westlands Driving School. It was a single large space with a receptionist sitting behind a long counter, facing the door. She looked at me over the top of her glasses without lifting her head.

"Who are you?" she asked.

"Sara Janssen," I said, stepping up to the counter and leaning my elbows on it. The lady glared at me disapprovingly. I stood up straight and stuck my hands in my pockets.

"Do you have an appointment?"

"Yes. For a driving lesson, that is."

She picked up some sheets of paper with typewritten names on it, stapled together in one corner. She looked through them slowly.

"I do not see your name," she said. "Is this your first time here?"

I nodded.

She looked at me accusingly and said, "Why did you not say so immediately?"

I had no idea what to tell her, or why it made any difference.

She put the papers down and told me to follow her. She walked quickly with her shiny black heels tapping the cement floor and led me to one of the four big blue boxes set up at even distance from each other. They looked like photo booths.

"You will start here," she said, and walked away.

The seat looked like it had been taken from a narrow car built for one. I sat down and looked around for a manual or instructions, but there were none. The steering wheel seemed the obvious place to start and I grabbed it with both hands and turned it first one way, then the other. Nothing happened. The dashboard looked like a toy version of the one in my father's car, with dials and numbers carefully painted on. Three pedals stood at an angle in front of my feet. Sticking out from the left side of the seat was a thin black rod with a knob on top that I recognized as a gear shift. What was I supposed to do next?

"I see you are quite prepared to take to the road," a voice said.

I looked up to see a man wearing a red polo shirt with *Instructor* embroidered on the pocket. A baseball cap with the name of the school dug into his afro.

"The road?" I asked, sounding as clueless as I felt.

The man smiled. "Yes. We start today with the one on your screen."

He handed me a key and told me to start the vehicle. I stuck it into the ignition, turned it, and the sound of an engine rumbled from the speaker standing on the dashboard. The screen in front of me lit up and a road with bends and turns rolled by. The instructor explained what each pedal was for, but it was hard to remember because pressing on the brakes did not slow this so-called car down and the accelerator did not make it go any faster. This experience was going to exist entirely in my imagination. I turned the wheel to the right and to the left and hoped I was keeping the car I was pretending to drive on the twisty road. Nothing I did made any difference.

After a few sessions, I graduated from the booth to one of the school's beat-up orange Toyotas. It had a big wooden triangular sign attached to the roof with Westlands Driving School painted in the middle and two fat red Ls on either side. The Ls warned everybody to keep their distance because here was a Learner on the road, as if they couldn't already tell. Driving did not come easily to me - it took me five lessons just to start the car and drive off without jerking and stalling half a dozen times. "Grasshopper fuel, I see," my instructor would tell me calmly, ignoring my despair.

Today I was supposed to drive along Uhuru Highway toward

downtown for the first time, and I had been breaking out in nervous sweats whenever I imagined being sucked along by insane Nairobi traffic as it screeched from one overflowing roundabout to the next. I took a deep breath. "I don't think I'm ready," I said to my instructor. "I don't think I can do this. I'll have an accident. We'll both be killed."

The instructor smiled. "I have never lost a student, and I do not plan on dying today."

He opened the door to the driver's seat and I hesitated. He gave me a gentle push behind my shoulder. I sighed. Too late to change my fate now. I sat down behind the steering wheel and started the car.

I plunged timidly onto Uhuru and pulled in behind a dirty green city bus that leaned to one side where passengers hung onto the door, forced out by the crowd inside. It belched clouds of exhaust so black I couldn't see a thing, never mind nearly fainting from the stench that wafted in through the window. I slowed to put some distance between us, and found myself alongside a *matatu*. Matatu vans, smaller and more limber than buses, thought nothing of cutting across four lanes of traffic, or slamming on the brakes without warning if someone flagged them down from the sidewalk. Only taxis were more reckless - cars of all shapes and sizes held together by bits of wire and plastic tape swooping through traffic like vultures hunting for prey. My eyes swept from side to side, alert for unexpected maneuvers while also keeping an eye out for people on bicycles and motorcycles and the vendor who was slowly pushing a wooden cart stacked with a mountain of coconuts, too wide to fit on the sidewalk.

I flowed onto the first roundabout easily together with the cars driving on either side of me, and exited neatly straight ahead. The second roundabout was just as straightforward. "You can relax now," my instructor said, tapping my pale knuckles, clutched around the steering wheel. "Take a right turn on the next roundabout." A right turn? But all these cars were going straight. I had to change lanes. I yanked at the steering wheel. The instructor stomped on his brakes and we squealed to a stop, missing the car next to us by a heartbeat. Traffic screeched to a halt. I braced for the explosion of cars smashing into us, but heard only honking horns and drivers yelling at me out their windows. Slowly the confusion evaporated as one car after the other pulled away, and I managed to drive us back to the school.

I had barely stopped shaking by the time I got home. I walked up the driveway to find my father sitting on the patio with a glass of after-work whiskey in his hand, swirling the drink; I could hear ice cubes clinking against the glass. He popped a handful of fat peanuts into his mouth and chewed energetically.

"Sara!" he called out after he emptied his mouth.

I looked up at him from the foot of the flowerbed that stretched uphill between us. He leaned his elbows on the low stone wall surrounding the patio. He looked like he was sitting in a box seat at the theater, or a bathtub.

"Sara, where did you just appear from? I thought you were in your bedroom, working on your homework like a good daughter." He chortled, like this was a really funny joke.

"I was at my driving lesson."

"Ah, yes, quite right, of course that is where you were. You have been learning how to operate a vehicle so that you might maneuver through Nairobi traffic doing a minimum of damage to the rest of us who are also on the road." He laughed some more. "So tell me, what did you learn today?"

"Three-point-turn," I said, in no mood to tell him my latest misadventures and having to defend my lack of driving ability from his so-called funny remarks. I had been through enough. But my father was feeling sociable and would not let the matter go.

"Three-point-turn, ah, excellent! I remember learning that

valuable technique myself back when I was preparing for my exam in Holland. We call it *driepuntskering*. I am delighted you are being taught such things, naturally I did not expect much from the quality of your instruction, what with the lackadaisical approach to things in this country. Just look around at the way people drive, as if they are possessed by evil spirits, it would appear none of them know a thing beyond how to ram an accelerator pedal to the floor. And why do they even bother to install indicators, I wonder? Nobody seems to know how to operate them. Now," my father said, switching his attention back to me. "Why don't you give me a little demonstration of this three-point-turn you have so recently mastered? So I can see with my own eyes whether all the hard-earned money I have been throwing at that driving school of yours has resulted in any worthwhile skills?" He stood up from his chair, dug the car keys from his trouser pocket and threw them down at me in a gentle lob. They plopped onto the gravel by my feet.

I looked at the keys. I did not want to demonstrate a three-point-turn for my father. He'd exaggerate even the smallest mistake until it ballooned into a huge, entertaining party story with me starring as the fool. But I couldn't come up with an excuse, at least not with my self-respect intact. I sighed, picked up the keys and dragged my feet to the white Volkswagen beetle. The car would be mine once I passed my test, so I supposed I should see this as useful practice.

My father had recently announced he preferred riding his motorcycle - he said it helped him squeeze through small gaps in choking rush hour traffic on his way to work and he'd shave half the time off his commute. He had done a trial run last week, sitting upright on his motorcycle in his office suit with his attaché case strapped to the passenger seat with purple bungee cords. A gleaming full-face helmet covered his head with the visor down so air pollution wouldn't leave a layer of grime on his face. His tie flapped over his shoulder when he rode off, as if it was waving goodbye. My mother and I waved back, laughing at this latest performance.

I started the engine of the Volkswagen and carefully backed up along the curve of the driveway until I was parked more or less beneath the patio. My father beamed happily, ready for the show.

I rolled the steering wheel as far to the right as it would go and slowly inched the car forward until it touched the edge of the driveway. I put the car in reverse, using both hands to budge the stiff gearshift. There was a nasty crunching sound when I let go of the clutch too soon, but probably my father hadn't heard from where he was sitting. I turned the steering wheel to the left and backed up until the car stopped. Had I reached the edge of the driveway? The car wasn't back far enough. I stepped on the accelerator and the rear wheel shot over the white grapefruit-size stones along the flowerbed. I put the car into first gear, turned again, and came to a stop facing the opposite direction. A perfect three-point-turn. I stepped out of the car, relieved I had pulled off my exhibition without a hitch and there would be no embarrassing stories to tell.

"What are you doing?" roared my father gleefully. "You plowed right into the flowerbed - you launched your mother's pansies through the air – look here, I am picking them out from between my teeth! Lumps of dirt are showering down all over the neighborhood! I thought for a minute you were going to back right into the house... *AHA, aha, ha, ha, ha.*"

"What? I did a three-point-turn, didn't I? The driveway isn't wide enough to do it any other way."

My father guffawed loudly and I could see his ribs bouncing up and down under his shirt and his face flushed dark pink. I stood there waiting, strangling my irritation - what was so damn funny? Finally he pulled himself together and told me, "No, no, no, you little idiot... if a street is too narrow, you must make more turns back and forth, five, seven, however many it takes to turn the car around without destroying the flowerbeds of innocent bystanders."

How the hell was I supposed to know that?

I did not have it in me to pretend to be civil one moment longer. I stomped past my father without looking at him and went straight to my bedroom and slammed the door behind me.

I did not join my parents' chit-chat over dinner. I was pissed off and wanted them to leave me alone.

"Sara," my father said, putting down his knife and fork. "Your mother and I have noticed you are - how to put this - you are not yourself. You are agitated and, frankly, bad tempered."

I rolled my eyes. I supposed it was too much to expect a little sympathy for my broken heart.

My father continued, "We are thinking a change of scenery might cheer you up and do you a world of good."

I frowned at him suspiciously. My father was going to arrange for me to have fun? It was hard to imagine how that could possibly end well.

"I'm OK, actually," I said.

"Of course, of course you are! I am not suggesting you are not OK. But..." he paused dramatically, "what would you say to a few days in Mombasa? Kenyatta Day is coming up and I am sure your education will not suffer too much from an extra day or two off from school. Now, what do you think?"

I'd been trying to get out of family vacations for years because it was unbearable to miss out on what was going on while I was away. Right now, though, Mombasa sounded very attractive. I imagined lying on the beach with a magazine, not giving a thought to what I was wearing, and especially not worrying about whether I was going to bump into Leander. A lot could change in a week, too. People would have forgotten all about the two of us by the time I got back.

CHAPTER FIVE

We packed the car and left early on Kenyatta Day. The founding father and president of Kenya had died less than two months ago, and this was the first time his national holiday would be celebrated without him. My father wondered briefly whether it would be safe for us to travel, but the power struggle everybody kept predicting would tear the country apart after Jomo Kenyatta's death never happened, and neither had any riots. The new president took over with a minimum of fuss and life continued as before. There was no reason to think things would suddenly fall apart today.

The sun rose behind thick clouds and shadows were soft and green - no hint yet of the heat we'd be driving into soon enough as we dropped altitude toward the coast. We left town and turned onto Mombasa Road. The drive would take six hours, longer if my father decided he needed to stretch his legs and stop for a smoke. He rolled his own cigarettes from loose-leaf tobacco my uncle sent him from Holland, and they looked exactly like joints. The surprised looks this triggered did not bother my father in the least. He insisted his cigarettes tasted better and were not at all bad for his health because rolling tobacco was natural, a plant product untreated by chemicals. I doubted the truth of this. The fumes were so vile they made my eyes water. I wished he'd just smoke filter cigarettes like everybody else.

The view from my backseat window changed as we drove away from the city. Fewer buildings stood along the road and finally even the brightly colored corrugated metal and plywood shacks of the shantytowns on the outskirts disappeared altogether. The land was flat and the tall grasses yellow and dry. Single thorn trees and low shrubs stood scattered in the grassland. In the distance, hills broke the horizon. I saw a baobab tree and remembered the legend of the playful god who pulled up the tree and plunked it back into the earth upside down, which was exactly what it looked like: as if the thin branches sprouting from the enormous trunk were really its roots dangling in the air.

The Mombasa Road was in terrible condition and my father cursed as he swerved to avoid potholes deep enough to break an axle or blow a tire. Accidents happened all the time along this road, especially at night when a driver could see only as far as his headlights reached. There was no other light - no streetlights or buildings – and the night was as dark as the inside of an elephant's mouth. Jam-packed buses roared up and down between Mombasa and Nairobi 24 hours a day, with drivers high from chewing *miraa* to stay awake. They earned their living carrying as many passengers as they could in the shortest possible time, and for them to sleep meant to lose money. Very slow buses swerved into oncoming traffic to overtake even slower buses, and got stuck there when neither would let the other pass. It was not unusual to see the rusted, dented carcass of some vehicle balancing on its roof beside the road.

Miraa. I heard people got very upbeat and talkative when they took it. Apparently chewing on the twigs gave an agreeable little rush - still, I was put off by the idea of chewing a mouthful of plant. I didn't even like sugarcane because it was so unpleasant to be left with a bunch of wet fiber on my tongue after all the sweetness had been sucked out. I'd spit and spit, trying to get it out of my mouth, but strands always stuck to the inside of my cheeks and between my teeth.

"Did I tell you about that family of Dutch tourists last week?"

29

my father caught my eye in the rear-view mirror.

"No, I don't think so," I answered.

"A tragic story, tragic." My father shook his head in dismay.

"What happened?"

"They were a family of four. Parents and two young children, boys, I don't think either of them had even ten years. For whatever reason - I believe their safari was canceled or overbooked, I'm not certain - they decided to rent a car and drive themselves down to Mombasa. Can you understand such recklessness? Direct off the airplane from Holland, not accustomed to driving on the left side of the road, and finding the steering wheel on the wrong side of the car. To drive at night, in pitch darkness along this miserable road... who takes such a risk? With two small children?"

I didn't know. I imagined they didn't have a clue what they were getting into.

"They made it almost halfway. Then they drove full speed into a giraffe crossing the road in the dark - didn't even have time to hit the brakes. The car slammed into the animal's legs and its neck jack-knifed down and smashed the car completely into the asphalt. *Ach*," my father said with a sigh. "The devastation was complete. They had to rip the car open like a can of peas to remove the bodies."

"Horrible," I said, shuddering at the image. I thought about it. "I'm surprised a giraffe would do such damage. They always look so delicate, you know, those long skinny legs and necks."

"They weigh many tons, actually."

It was disturbing how things could turn out to be not at all what they seemed.

"Sara, now that we are sitting here without any distractions, it seems like a good moment to discuss some things with you," my father said, changing the subject.

"Yes?"

"You are eighteen and soon you will have completed your

secondary education. This is an enormous achievement, to be sure, but in today's modern world it will not be enough. You must earn some additional qualifications to ensure your ability to find a proper job. Do you agree?"

"Yes, I think it would probably make sense to go to college or something."

"Very good, excellent. You must also understand you will not be able to continue your education in Kenya, for many practical reasons. You are a Dutch citizen, after all, and you will have opportunities back in your home country that are closed to you here because you lack the necessary papers. In Holland, you will be able to find a job and receive a student loan. And of course the quality of the schools is exceptional over there, far better than anything available here."

"Ah."

"Do not forget, we have our little apartment back in Holland, in Rijswijk, which will be a comfortable place for you to live. Did you know there is a world-class secretarial college within walking distance? You should consider this option seriously. It is excellent training for a woman, leading to many appropriate job opportunities. And do not worry about being lonely. Your aunties will be thrilled to have you back, and will look after you."

I couldn't imagine leaving Kenya, ever.

"Perhaps this is a new idea for you, and you need some time to become accustomed to it. After all, there is no need for haste quite yet. First you should focus your energies on studying hard for your exams. There is some time left before arrangements for your future must be made."

"OK, I'll think about it," I mumbled.

I didn't like anything about this plan of my father's. I didn't want to live in cold, wet Holland light-years away from my friends and my life, and I didn't particularly want to be a secretary, either. But if I said so, my father would undoubtedly ask me what better idea I had, and I hadn't come up with one yet.

I needed more time to figure things out.

My mother turned to me and asked, "Do you want a cup of coffee, and a cookie to go with it? Which would you prefer, chocolate cream or ginger snap?" A road trip of any length was an excuse for my mother to take her red and white striped beach bag and fill it to the brim with food and drink to keep us fed the entire journey, and today was no exception. I was groggy from eating too much, and from the sun that hit the side of my face through the window.

I sat up straighter when we drove past the baboons, because seeing them meant we didn't have far to go. For mysterious reasons they liked this particular stretch of road just outside of Mombasa town. They sat on the white kilometer markers on either side of the street with their knees pulled up to their chins, whether the day was burning hot or raindrops fat and hard as pebbles bounced off their heads. Sometimes they wandered around on the ground and snarled at each other irritably - baboons were notoriously bad-tempered - or went to nap in the shade of a nearby baobab. But mostly they scratched their itches and looked at traffic without much interest, their eyes unfocused and staring past the cars that roared by. One or two turned their backs on us and flashed their hideous puffy red butts.

I rolled down my window and took a deep breath of humid air, almost tasting the salt in it. A breeze cooled the sweat on my scalp and lifted my hair from my shoulders. My father squeezed the car on board the Likoni Ferry and we sailed the short distance across the harbor, and from there it was just a few miles to Diani Beach. Someone from the rental agency was waiting to unlock the doors of our cottage and we quickly unloaded the car, happy to have arrived.

I changed into my shorts and walked out of the house, straight onto the beach. The clean, white sand was warm beneath my bare feet. Kilometers of it, firm underfoot like pavement, stretched to the left and right. The tide was low. Dry ruffles of seaweed lay near the edge of the water. Tall, thick clouds like blobs of whipped cream skimmed the horizon. There was no more beautiful place on earth.

I swished my foot back and forth slowly and dug a shallow ditch with my toes. The warmth only reached down a few centimeters and as soon as I scraped below it, the sand felt cool and damp. I pushed my foot forward until it was covered and leaned my full weight onto my arch, liking the feeling of the earth pressing back, holding me up. I lifted my free leg high in the air behind me like a ballerina and lost my balance and jogged a few quick steps to stop from falling, and kept going, right into the sea. When my knees were underwater, I stood still and let the waves bump into me, low and gentle. The water was lukewarm and clear as air - I could see my feet standing on the bottom of the ocean. Schools of tiny white fish, almost transparent, darted around my legs. It looked like they might be touching me as they swirled by, but I couldn't feel their weightless bodies against my skin.

My arms were turning pink. The sun was so strong here at the coast, it was easy to burn even this late in the afternoon. I turned around and walked back to the cottage. My mother stood on the porch with her hand shading her eyes and when I came within earshot, she called my name and flapped her hands for me to come closer. Where else would I be going?

"*Ja?*" I called back.

"You are not wearing a hat. Did you put on sunscreen, at least? If you are not careful, you will get a sunburn and your vacation will be ruined."

I rolled my eyes. As if I hadn't noticed the sun beating down on me. "I can look after myself, you know," I said.

My mother looked at me critically and started to say something, but changed her mind. It was a moot point, anyway, because I was already inside.

The next morning I woke to the sound of gulls screeching outside my window. I lay still and listened, and heard waves slapping softly onto the beach. I took a deep breath, but exhaled hard when the muggy scent of my room hit my nose. Things quickly got smelly here with the humidity, and mold grew wherever it got a chance. On my last visit I had found proof of that when my shoes were hidden from sight under the bed for a few days. By the time I drew them out, they were furry with green and blue mold.

I got out of bed and went to the airy living area, with one side open to the beach and the sea. My mother stood in the kitchen, behind the breakfast counter, putting away dishes. She looked relaxed with her frosted hair burst loose from its normal tightly primped style; it had become frizzy and wild from the moisture in the air and the constant breeze. She wore a pair of navy blue Bermuda shorts over her conservative flowered bathing suit, keeping her knees carefully hidden because she said they were chubby and wrinkly. She looked pretty good for a middle-aged lady when she loosened up a little. I wandered over to her across the flagstone floor, cool beneath my feet. She poured me a cup of tea.

"Did you sleep well?" she asked.

I nodded. Unusually well, come to think of it. Nights at the cottage were sweaty with no air-conditioning, and I usually spent them floating in and out of restless sleep. Maybe I was making up for the hours I had lain awake torturing myself over Leander.

"Well, we have been up for some time. Papa is on the beach working on his fishing rod or whatever it's supposed to be."

I ate the sandwich my mother made for me quickly before the cheese turned sticky in the heat, and walked down to the beach to see what my father was up to. He stood near the water bent over a construction I couldn't quite see, dressed to protect himself from the sun. His skin was light and freckly and burned horribly

34

to actual blisters if he wasn't careful, especially on top of his hairless head. He was wearing an old long-sleeved office shirt, frayed at the cuffs and buttoned up to the neck, with gaps between the buttons where it stretched too tightly across his belly. A towel with faded orange polka dots covered his head and neck and was held in place by a cotton bucket hat, the rim already soaked with sweat. Dark sunglasses and baggy checkered swim shorts completed the outfit.

"Hello, papa, you look charming."

"Ah, daughter, you are awake! Excellent, excellent. Look at this fishing device I have constructed," he raised his arm in a swooping arch. "I've been thinking about this for days and am now certain the design has been perfected. Since you are here, you can help me step into the water so the lines don't tangle."

"And how is this supposed to work?"

"Yes, absolutely, let me explain it to you. Just look here, this belt goes around my waist. It is an old one that I used to wear to work, but mama replaced it when it started to look worn and the notches tore slightly, do you see? A pity. A comfortable belt. Exactly the right color of dark brown to match my good shoes." He shook his head sadly. "In any case, pay attention, this is how it works. I buckle the belt around my waist. These two strings go from both sides of the belt to the ends of the branch. And then, as you can see, I have tied six fishing lines at equal distance along the branch, with a hook at the end of each. It will be your job to keep the lines separated as I walk into the water to where it is deep enough to swim so I can tow the lines behind me. I suppose I should swim slowly or maybe float, and the fish will forget I'm there. I will catch six fish at the same time, easily. What do you think?"

What did I think? I gazed with disbelief at the contraption tied around my father's waist, a stick hitting the back of his knees with six fishing lines dropping onto the sand. It was the most hysterical thing I had seen in my life. A giggle bubbled in my stomach and I tried not to let it erupt, but when I opened my mouth, I laughed like I hadn't laughed in weeks. I started to calm down, but when my eyes dropped to the fishing apparatus attached to my father, I started all over again.

"Well," my father said, sounding somewhat pained. "It is obvious you don't think much of my idea. But I don't see why it shouldn't work, just look into that water, you can see the fish swimming right there and practically pick them out with your bare hands."

"No, no, papa, I'm sorry. I'm not laughing at you, really, I don't know what's so funny." I dried the corners of my eyes. "I'm done now, I promise." I wasn't. Laughing felt good.

I helped launch my father and his fishing lines into the sea. He stayed in the water for hours – my mother and I watched him from the veranda and saw him alternately swimming slowly and floating motionlessly on his stomach with his limbs spread out like a starfish, only lifting his head when he needed a breath of air. When he finally came out, the unprotected heels of his feet had burned bright red from sticking out of the water. He limped awkwardly up the beach, holding the belt over his head so the lines didn't drag through the sand. He had not experienced even the tiniest nibble from a curious fish. He was disappointed but not discouraged, sure there was nothing wrong with his theory even if it had not delivered in practice. And, he told us, he had already figured out how to improve matters for the next attempt. He would wear socks to protect his heels, and tie small rocks to the fishing lines so they would sag to the bottom where the fish would undoubtedly be biting. *Tomorrow's gonna be another day, hey, hey, hey, hey...* just like the old Monkees song said.

CHAPTER SIX

The rainy season started the day we arrived home and it felt like a sign: vacation was over and it was time to get back to the real world. I heard the first heavy drops smack on the roof of the house and walked into the front yard to see it come down with my own eyes. For weeks the rains had been trying to break through - clouds gathered but then the air would just sit there, pressing down on us like a heavy blanket, thick and choking, with bursts of thunder and lightning over the hills, and gusts of wind whipping dust up from the bone-dry earth. Each time only a little drizzle fell from the sky before the sun burned the clouds away again. Now, at long last, here was a real shower, and relief was instant. The air was washed clean and I inhaled the fragrance of wet earth. The temperature dropped as I stood there and I rubbed goose bumps that lifted the skin of my arms, smiling at the feeling of coolness. Enough rain fell to soak right into the earth, and the small flying ants that lived underground were roused and suddenly rose in thick clouds. They swarmed for a while, swooped in spirals around the garden lights, then dropped their wings and fell to earth in a sheet of writhing bodies. I took a step back - flying bugs were not my favorite thing - but here was another sign that the worst of the heat was behind us and more comfortable months were on the way.

Today was the day of my driving test, and I was on my way to the examination center with my instructor beside me. When I couldn't stand worrying in silence any longer, I asked him, "Do you think they'll ask me to do a three-point-turn?"

My instructor smiled and shrugged. "Anything is possible," he said.

We entered a small square room and he pointed to an empty chair standing against the wall. I sat down. He pushed through the low swinging door between the waiting area and office and greeted the people who stood there. They seemed to know each other well. They chatted and laughed, and lounged around a desk that was empty except for one old-fashioned black telephone standing in the corner. Nobody else was waiting to take the test and staff seemed to have nothing to do.

A man wearing a tag marked *Examiner* entered the room with a clipboard tucked under his arm. He glanced at me briefly and turned his attention to my instructor. They stood slightly apart from the others. After greeting each other warmly, they lowered their voices and leaned their heads more closely together. The instructor placed an envelope in the examiner's hand, and he slid it quickly into his pocket.

"Sara Janssen," the examiner said loudly.

I jumped at the volume of his voice and looked at him expectantly. I waited for him to tell me what to do.

"Please come here," the examiner said.

I walked over, my nerves fluttering. He picked up a pointing stick that looked like the antenna of a car and turned to face the wall. Five rows of large street signs covered it from floor to ceiling. I blinked. I hoped he wouldn't ask me anything that involved right of way, which still confused me, or expect me to explain the difference between round and triangular signs, which I didn't know. He pointed at a sign in the top row. It was a red-bordered triangle with the black silhouette of a giraffe in the middle. I'd never seen it before in my life.

I hesitated, then guessed: "Beware of giraffes?"

"Correct. This one?" He pointed at an eight-sided red sign

with the word STOP in the middle.

"Stop?" I said.

"Correct. Follow me."

We walked to the orange Toyota and I sat down behind the wheel. I demonstrated a hand signal by flapping my arm up and down through the open window. The examiner took place in the passenger seat. I made a show of adjusting mirrors so he could see I knew the rules, and started the car. I used my indicator when it was called for and followed the examiner's instructions precisely: turn left, change lanes, exit to the right on the next roundabout; all actions I had by now mastered, thank goodness. He coached me to a nearby industrial area. Traffic was light, and the roads were wide. We drove onto a deserted parking lot and I steered the car slowly into a slot, parking neatly between two lines. I reversed along the sidewalk and cringed when the back wheel screeched along the curb - I glanced at the examiner but he did not make a note on his clipboard. Ten minutes later we were back at the test center.

"You have passed," the examiner said. He quickly filled out a sheet of paper. "Take this inside to receive your interim license. Your permanent driving license will be sent to you by post within one month."

When I got home after the test, I had yelled for my mother, and she'd appeared quickly, wiping her hands on her apron. I raised my license above my head and announced the obvious: "I did it!"

She laughed, and kissed me on both cheeks. "This is wonderful news indeed. So, you are going to drive yourself to school in the morning? How very lovely, I will be able to sleep in from now on."

I smiled at her. "Yes, you can sleep in as long as you like."

I knew she would never do such a thing. Even without having to take me to school, my mother would be the first one up to make sure the breakfast table was set and eggs were cooked and tea brewed, and I was not surprised to find her sitting at the breakfast table as usual this morning. She was still wearing her nightgown and robe, and had not put on her makeup, which was probably her way of taking it easy.

I put my school books on the back seat of the Volkswagen, slid behind the wheel, adjusted the distance to the pedals, lowered the back of the seat a few notches, and leaned back comfortably. The engine started on the first turn of the key and I drove out of the gate and down the road, sure joy must be radiating from me like rays from the sun: here I was, driving myself to school, in my very own car, choosing my own direction. It didn't get any better than that.

The car behind me honked when the light jumped to green - I hadn't noticed because I was looking in the mirror, distracted by a flake of mascara stuck to the skin beneath my eye. I tried to drive off quickly, but it took me a couple of tries to force the stubborn gearshift into first. Down the road I stood still again, too long, while I gathered courage to launch myself onto the small roundabout in front of me. I waited anxiously for a gap to appear in bumper-to-bumper traffic while my heart pumped wildly. More cars honked behind me. By the time I pulled onto Caldwell's red dirt parking lot, I was damp with sweat and relieved to switch off the engine.

"Jambo, Sara!" Chloe called as soon as I stepped out of the car. She stood with a small group of smokers getting one last cigarette in before the first bell. "You got your license, man. Congratulations! How did it go?"

"Well, let's see. Yesterday, the test was so easy, I actually walked away pretty much convinced I was an ace driver ready to handle anything the road could throw at me. Today, reality set in and I nearly killed myself trying to get here in one piece." I laughed sourly.

Chloe squeezed my arm and made soothing sounds about

how things would get better with a little practice. She put a fresh cigarette in her mouth and sucked on it, holding the tip against her own half-smoked one until it glowed. She handed it to me.

"Your reward," she said.

"Thank you. You know I would go through it all again for a free smoke."

"I knoOow," Chloe said with a wink, in the way only she used those two words. I could pick her out of any crowd just by hearing her say *I knoOow.* She'd start low, ease into a high OOO, and then slide back down. It always made me grin.

"Did they test you on how to out-maneuver carjackers, in case you find yourself being followed by one?" Tazim said.

"Ouch," I said. "You mean my father driving like a maniac, trying to escape the so-called carjacker who turned out to be *your* father. And all the while you and me sitting in my bedroom innocently eating birthday cake without a care in the world."

Everybody laughed, the bush telegraph of gossip obviously having spread the story around.

I shook my head in exaggerated despair. "You know how expats get, the slightest thing throws them into a full-blown panic."

The ones in the group who came from expat families themselves knew what I was talking about - it was a favorite subject among us. We couldn't relate to the fears of our parents, and didn't understand why they thought danger lurked around every corner. They drove us crazy with their warnings to be on the alert for the thieves, rapists, kidnappers and hustlers who existed only in their imaginations. Oh, and carjackers.

We knew what Kenya was really like; this was where we went to school, and partied, and made friends. It was our parents - trapped in their expat bubbles, carrying on their European lives as if they had never left their northern homes - who had no clue what was going on in the world around them.

"It's their loss," I said. "They miss out by always keeping to their own kind, and living in Kenya as outsiders."

Everybody murmured their agreement. Soon stories flew about the fearfulness of all parents, regardless of their color.

"Did an envelope change hands, by the way?" Mike asked me. He had a loud voice and a cynical take on things.

"What?" I asked.

"Your drive test? You do know how these things work, don't you? The driving school slips some money into an envelope on your behalf. Actually, the amount was included in your lesson fees, though of course not specified as 'bribe for license'. Then, on test day, the school gives a nice, fat envelope to the examiner to make sure you pass."

"Why would they do that?" I asked.

"Isn't it obvious? The driving school keeps its perfect pass record, you get your license, and the testing guy earns some extra cash to pay his kid's school fees. Everybody happy."

I shrugged my shoulders as if I didn't believe him, but I knew he was right. I hadn't passed my driving test, I had bought it. *Shit.*

Chloe and I put out our cigarettes and walked the short distance to the school. Caldwell's Secondary School was a small place. An uneven path led to *the villas:* two large old houses in which bedrooms, kitchens and living rooms had been turned into classrooms and offices. Trees and overgrown gardens grew thick all around and gave the place a quiet that was unique even here, on the farthest outskirts of Nairobi. Our school did not have sports fields or much of a library or even a cafeteria - we ate the lunches we brought from home sitting at picnic tables on a square of grass next to the parking lot. It was the perfect oddball place for our mishmash of two hundred or so students; many had drifted here after not finding a place for themselves in mainstream schools, because they couldn't fit in.

My parents enrolled me in Caldwell's because other KIKS

expats had recommended it, and I thanked my stars I had ended up here instead of at one of the big shiny expat institutions. Where else would I have made friends with Africans and Asians and Europeans, and grown to feel at home with all of them?

Here in Kenya, schools were either mostly white or black. This kind of segregation was not because of any law, but because of tuition. Whites usually had much more money than blacks, and sent their kids to the more expensive schools. There were exceptions, though - some successful black Kenyans were richer than the Queen herself. Some white settlers who came over during the old colonial days to strike it rich had failed miserably, and were dirt poor to this very day.

Chloe and I stood on the narrow strip of weedy grass alongside the main villa. We joked that this was our "quad", the common man's version of the manicured lawns at posh schools, where students wore embroidered crests on their blazer pockets. Today, like schools everywhere in the country on a Friday morning, we would start the day by singing the Kenyan national anthem. Our headmaster, Mr. Caldwell himself, was already busy setting up the record player. We called him "Bobby" behind his back because his head bopped up and down all day as if it was attached to a spring, never missing a beat. Rumor had it he was shell-shocked from the war, but nobody knew for sure.

Bobby put the school's old-fashioned record player on a low stool in the grass and ran an extension cord to the outlet inside the dim building. It was an ancient portable model in a hard cream-colored case that closed like a handbag, with a wide strip of ribbed plastic for a handle, grimy with the prints of many hands.

Students and teachers stood together in a rough half-circle with their backs to the villa, facing the stubby flagpole. Bobby handed each of us a half sheet of paper with the Swahili text typed on one side and a translation in English on the back. The needle was carefully lowered onto the spinning record and after a few scratches and pops, the familiar choir burst into the opening words of the national anthem. *Ee Mungu nguvu yetu,* O God of all creation! *Ilete baraka kwetu,* Bless this our land and nation! I sang the rousing melody with all my might along with everybody else and inhaled deep, clean breaths of cool morning air between the lines. I felt my spirits rise, as they always did when I took part in this morning tradition. The flag hung quietly. Its black, red and green bands were visible, but the warrior shield was hidden in its folds.

After the needle lifted from the record, Bobby collected the sheets of paper to file them away for next week. He muttered something about the questionable memories of students who could not seem to remember three simple stanzas of Swahili from one week to the following, but we knew he wasn't really bad-tempered. Our headmaster was a man who bopped and mumbled; it was just his way. I walked into the cool building to find a seat in my math class, even the prospect of algebra not ruining my mood. Besides, the weekend was just a few short hours away.

CHAPTER SEVEN

The Flame Tree was my favorite place to hang out: a sidewalk café in the middle of the busiest part of downtown Nairobi, right where everything interesting always happened. The rush of traffic starting and stopping at the lights never stopped. Passengers hopped out of cars when they crept forward too slowly and made their way on foot instead, while drivers honked horns and shook their fists at whatever was blocking their way. The smell of fresh baked pastries, pizza, or tandoori chicken was thick in the air, depending on the direction of the breeze. Shop owners called for tourists to come in and buy their carved masks and woven baskets. Newspaper and fruit sellers who couldn't afford to rent a shop, set up their wares on blankets spread on the ground. And every Saturday, everybody I knew would show up at the Flame Tree, sooner or later.

I had arrived a little early and looked around, but didn't see my friends, and wandered over to the tall flame tree in the middle of the café. Legend had it the tree had been growing in this spot long before the city sprouted up around it. Back in those early days, settlers on their remote farms didn't have phones or real roads to help them stay in touch with each other, and they'd leave messages pinned to the tree trunk whenever they were in town. These days backpackers had taken over the system. The café had recently wrapped a screen around it for people to slip their notes and envelopes behind, because after years of being poked by nails and thumbtacks, the tree looked like it was about

45

to keel over dead. I turned my head sideways to read a scrap of paper through the mesh. It had been ripped from a spiral notebook and was covered in pink ink, the writing large and hasty: *John, I'm trying to find you! Where are you? I'll be in Mombasa one week then I fly back home. Please meet me!!! Janice.* It was dated more than six months ago. I wondered if John ever showed up. Trying to get in touch with someone using a tree seemed about as efficient as tossing a coin into a wishing well.

A group of chattering tourists walked by. They gathered in a cluster by the parking bay, waiting to board a sparkling white van. Apparently today was safari day. The tourists were dressed for adventure in brand new, crisply pressed khaki outfits, carrying enough gear and provisions to last a month in deepest bush. In reality, they would be spending a few hours in an air-conditioned van, driving safely along the trails of Nairobi National Park just outside town. Their guide would promise them leopards and lions, but most likely they'd have to settle for a herd of fat grazing warthogs or a pair of impala leaping away through the tall grass. They'd be back in time for sundowners at their hotel, sipping neon umbrella drinks and exchanging stories about the wildlife they'd seen from a distance. They'd never get any closer to Africa than the view through a rolled up window.

"Sara - hello - over here!"

I waved at Chloe and the friends who were settling down noisily on the street side of the café. Chairs were dragged squealing across the cement floor and seven of us crowded around a small square table meant for four. I sat next to a friend of Chloe's whose name I had forgotten, Mary or Marion, a petite, energetic Kenyan girl with a bright smile whose words gushed from her like a waterfall. Across from me sat two boys from school who were more comfortable tinkering with their motorcycles than sitting in a classroom. Skinny Liam, with his trademark lock of dark hair falling into his eyes, pulled his chair close to the table. His fine red felt-tip pen was out and he doodled, a tiny tree growing branch by branch in the notebook he always carried in his back pocket. Cynical Mike squeezed into a chair on the other side of me.

A waiter stood patiently as we decided what to order. The Flame Tree was crowded with customers on Saturdays, but waiters were easy-going and would let us sit as long as we liked while we made one round of soft drinks last most of the afternoon. Money was never evenly distributed among us, and those who had enough today might be dead broke next time. Coins were dug out of slim wallets and from the bottom of purses and jeans pockets until there was enough to buy each of us a drink. I paid for Chloe and me. The waiter returned with a tray loaded with colored bottles and glasses with ice cubes and I took a grateful sip of my soda, the big cool bubbles tingling my tongue.

Liam lowered his pen and pulled a pack of cards from his shirt pocket. He leaned back and performed a series of shuffling techniques as if it was a magic show, and finished by cutting the deck with one hand, sliding the top cards to the bottom with his long fingers.

"Who's in?" he said.

"Deal me in," I said. "What rules?"

"Lunchtime rules," he said. Arguments about what was the best way to play the game, or even the official way, were ongoing and never resolved. Rules changed all the time and different versions were passed along by word of mouth, and impossible to keep track of. Nobody even knew why the game was called *matatu* like the taxi vans that raced along the roads.

But today, for once, there was no argument and we agreed on lunchtime rules, which meant the way matatu was played at Caldwell's during lunch break. Liam skimmed the cards across the table until each player had seven. The game took off. Cards smacked onto the center pile, with yelps of frustration when punishment cards had to be drawn, and poker faces when a hand was good.

"Chloe!" Mike called out.

"What, man?" She said, taken aback.

"Pay attention already; it's your turn."

"Oh, right, sorry," Chloe said. "Wait, let me just..."

Chloe stared at the jumble of cards in her hand and tried to clasp them with one while she organized them with the other. Her cards dangled in plain view.

Players around the table groaned. Mike threw down his cards and said dramatically, "Chloe, what the hell? You've just destroyed my chance at playing a truly spectacular winning hand."

Chloe's smile faltered, and she said, "I was distracted, man, sorry."

I wondered what was bothering her. She didn't seem her usual Zen self at all. "Never mind, it doesn't matter, it's only matatu," I said, and reached across the table to touch my fingertips to her arm. Nobody had wanted to hurt her feelings - the guys were just messing around. I leaned closer and whispered, "You OK?"

Chloe nodded, but then she wasn't going to tell me anything personal right now - I'd ask her when we found ourselves alone. Liam swept up the cards and shuffled them again. We played and chatted, and our group shrank and grew as people left to do other things and new ones took their place. Finally talk slowed and became ragged until we grew tired of playing cards and ran out of things to say altogether. Chloe left when her mother showed up to collect her, and soon everybody else started to drift home. I felt sluggish from hours of sitting and doing nothing much except smoke too many cigarettes. When the last of my friends stood up to leave, I roused myself. I reached behind me for the brown patchwork bag I had looped across the back of my chair and unzipped it, plunging my arm in to search for car keys and sunglasses.

"Jambo, Sara. Long time no see. How are you?" said a familiar voice with an African accent.

I looked up to see Sam smiling at me. It really had been a while. Our paths didn't cross now that I was no longer dating Leander, and I was surprised to feel my cheeks grow hot.

"Sam, how's it going? What are you doing here?"

He lifted his hand, plastic bags dangling from his fingers. "I picked up some medicines for my brother Dennis. He isn't feeling well. And some things I needed from the bookstore, like that," he said.

"Right."

I didn't know what to say next, so I reached for a smoke. Sam beat me to it, and offered me an Embassy from his own pack. He leaned over and lit it for me.

"Thanks," I said.

He shook one from the box for himself and pointed at the chair across from mine. "Do you mind?" he said.

"No, please," I said. "Sit down. I mean, of course I don't mind." I was taken aback by his question. I didn't know anyone else who would ask for permission to sit.

Sam pushed empty chairs out of the way so he could arrange himself more comfortably at the table. He dropped his bags on the floor, sat down, and stretched his legs out straight in front of him, crossing them at the ankles.

"So, what have you been up to?" he asked.

"Nothing much. Busy at school, getting ready for exams. You know how it is."

"A-levels?"

I nodded my head.

"Me too," he said. "Though I'm not too worried about the exams, to be honest. I expect I'll do well enough. But it is beginning to dawn on me that I need a plan for what happens afterward. Do I go to university? Do I look for a job? Is there something better out there for me that I'm missing altogether? It's complicated," he said.

"I know what you mean. I have no clue what I'll be doing after exams, but I'll have to worry about that later - there's no room in my brain for it right now."

Sam nodded. He changed the subject: "I haven't seen you around these days, at the disco or that party of William's the other night. Everybody came. I was expecting to see you."

"I guess I haven't felt much like going out."

Sam hesitated. Then he frowned and clicked his tongue against the roof of his mouth in disgust. "That dude Leander. Did he really think nobody would notice, the way he flaunted his girls without any discretion? You should have dumped him months ago."

Sam's words stung me. What did he mean: the way Leander flaunted his *girls*? Had there been more than just the one blonde? I thought I'd put the Leander nightmare behind me, but now I felt a fresh flash of anger. *Stupid bastard.* If his cheating had been worse than I thought, I didn't want to know.

My cigarette had burned clear down to the filter. I reached for the small white ashtray and flicked the old butts aside, and ground the cigarette slowly into the tiny green flame tree in the middle.

I pulled myself together and changed the subject. "How is Dennis? Is he very sick?"

"It's nothing, only a cold, but he has a fever and won't stop moaning and coughing all night like a goat. I'm not getting any sleep. He's driving me crazy."

I remembered their set-up at the motel. One room with somber checkered curtains, closed tight because the window faced the street and every passer-by could peer straight in. Bed covers with big brown flowers and carpet in a dark speckled color. The room looked airless and cramped, with two narrow beds and a dresser that doubled as a desk, and a television. There was not much hope of getting away from each other even at the best of times.

Sam laughed his deep belly laugh, and shook his head a little from side to side. "Maybe I should take him to stay with his mother like the little boy he is right now, so at least I can get a good night's sleep."

His mother? Rumor had it Sam lived at the motel because he had nowhere else to stay with; because his family lived in Uganda and everyone knew that country had been in shambles since psycho dictator Idi Amin took power. They said Sam and Dennis had fled to Kenya to get the education they couldn't find back home.

My curiosity won out, though I was afraid I might sound like I was prying. "Your mother lives here in Nairobi? Aren't you Ugandan?" I asked hesitantly.

"I am. But my father has six wives. The youngest one is Kenyan and she lives here."

I was startled and Sam laughed at me.

"I am a true traditional African man, you understand. I have the honor of being the eldest son of the first wife," he said, smiling widely.

I wasn't sure what the significance of that might be, or even whether he was joking. I knew polygamy was legal in Uganda, but presumed it only happened in the bush these days; surely modern educated men and women no longer practiced it.

Sam continued, "Which means I am second in line after my father. Whenever he is not around, I am responsible for everything that happens in the family - the money and any affairs concerning his wives and children. *Every little thing*," he stressed the three words, tapping out their rhythm on the table. "Which has been pretty much keeping me busy full-time these days, I can assure you."

"Are you serious?"

"Absolutely."

"So, is Dennis your actual brother?"

"Yes, we have the same birth mother. We also have three full sisters living back home in Uganda. They are young enough still to attend decent schools there. The primary years are not too bad."

"Are all those wives like your mothers?" I asked. I shuddered mentally at the thought – one mother was more than enough for me.

"Technically, yes, we are all one family and the wives are mothers to each of the children. But there is a stronger bond between birth mother and full siblings, without a doubt."

"Don't you miss your family?"

He threw back his head and laughed again. "Miss them? *Hapana* – definitely not. There are hassles every single day with so many women in one house, competing for the attention of one man. Always some *shauri*, some trouble or other. All the time, there are arguments and fights about money and about the children. Every mother is convinced she and her kids are not getting their fair share." He shook his head while he looked me straight in the eye. "My own future will be very different, I assure you."

The air stirred in a cool breeze, and the sun started to drop below the horizon, the bottom of the orange ball already flat. Sam glanced at his watch. "Well, I'd better get going. Dennis is waiting for his miracle cure."

"Me, too. My mother expects me to show up for dinner."

"And what are your plans?"

"What?"

"Are you going somewhere tonight?"

"No, no plans."

"Me neither."

We pushed our chairs back from the table and picked up our belongings.

"It was really nice seeing you again," I said. "Tell Dennis I hope he feels better."

"Yes," Sam said. He hesitated before speaking again. "So... what do you think? Should we get together some time, eh? Maybe see a movie or go dancing?"

I wasn't sure if I was ready to date Sam or anyone else. On the other hand, going to see a movie with someone wasn't the same as starting a relationship. And not dancing all this time was beginning to feel like being on a starvation diet.

"Yes, I'd like that," I said.

I dug into my purse for a pen, wrote my phone number on a scrap of paper napkin and handed it to him.

I climbed into the VW, turned out of the small side street where I had parked, and swerved into a gap in main road traffic. My dislike of driving downtown hadn't gotten less over time – I hated the feeling of having to rely on quick thinking and reflexes I didn't trust I had. Friends told me I worried too much: *you only have to look at what's happening ahead of you - those behind you will fend for themselves.* What they meant was: rear-view mirrors, who needs them? Or indicators, for that matter? I supposed that explained Nairobi traffic. It was never easy, getting from one place to another without damage in this city.

I left town behind me and turned into the tame and familiar roads of our Westlands suburb. I relaxed and reached for the cassette deck on the floor of the passenger seat, confiscated from a shelf in the garage where the six-line fishing device and other long-forgotten experiments of my father's were stored. It had large pushbuttons so I could lean over while I was driving, keep one hand on the steering wheel and both eyes on the road, and press *play* using only my sense of touch. *Take it eeeeeeeeeeasy.* Eagles; how appropriate.

It had been nice to see Sam again. The more we talked, the more comfortable I felt with him, though he seemed to be leading a life I could not even imagine. I was flattered he wanted my number and maybe spend time with me. I wondered if he would call.

CHAPTER EIGHT

Weeks passed slowly, increasingly dominated by school work as exams drew closer. I was looking forward to going to Chloe's place after school today and spending the weekend with her – we hadn't had a good talk in forever and there were things I needed to tell her. Geography was my last class before lunch and Mr. Vasudeva was ready for us, standing by the blackboard, dressed impeccably as always. Every day he wore a neatly pressed olive-green or brown suit, with the jacket buttoned up tight across his round belly. He was the only teacher at Caldwell's to wear a tie; not even Bobby thought it was called for at our school. Mr. Vasudeva pasted his straight black hair down firmly with something that made it shine just like his patent leather shoes, and parted it on one side in a laser-sharp white line. He was a little pompous, but always in such a funny way that nobody disliked him for it, and he was our most popular teacher.

"Jangle your bangles, Chloe!" he cried in his dancing Indian accent as she entered his classroom, her arms stacked with tinkling glass bracelets. Chloe smiled and jangled her bangles, swiveling her hands and wrists above her head.

"Sit down, class! Silence, now, I say. Silence!" he said. We continued to scrape chairs along the floor, settling behind our desks, until finally we were quiet enough for the lesson to start. Mr. Vasudeva began his lecture and I stopped paying attention. Teachers had worn me out altogether today. One after another they had started their classes by scolding us that we should be doing a better job preparing for exams, and had to stop frittering away what precious time we had left. I promised myself I'd start doubling up on study time soon, but in the meantime, I was tired of hearing about it. Chalk screeched horribly on the blackboard and the class groaned. I looked up and saw Mr. Vasudeva's drawing of something that looked like hills with a river running between them.

"Settle down, settle down, now. Really, what a bunch of silly children you are," Mr. Vasudeva jiggled his head back and forth in mock despair and rolled his round eyes for extra effect. "Enough fooling about. Do you see this here?" He tapped his drawing with a piece of chalk. "This is called a *wee shep walley...*"

"I'm sorry, sir, could you repeat that?" One student asked the question, but all of us looked mystified.

"*Wee shep walley.*" A girl giggled. "*Wee shep walley; WEE SHEP WALLEY!* What is so difficult to understand?"

"Ah," someone in the back of the room said. He spoke in a loud stage whisper, articulating each syllable with exaggeration: "*V-shaped valley*". The translation buzzed around the classroom until all of us were shaking with laughter.

Mr. Vasudeva had put up with this kind of thing before, but today his patience ran out and he did not brush us off with his usual wave of a hand. His face crumpled in anger and he raised his double chin, drawing himself up to stand as tall as he could manage. He jabbed the air with a chubby finger and listed his many accomplishments in a stern voice: his degrees, the books he had published, the important schools he had taught at. We smiled at the round little man in the stiff suit, with his shiny shoes jammed tightly together, who stood there chiding us in his comical accent.

Mr. Vasudeva had had enough. When he spoke again, his voice was quiet. "You are ungrateful, unmannered youngsters. Do you think this kind of behavior is acceptable? Do not forget prejudice and lack of tolerance are equally abhorrent in such so-called insignificant incidents as they are in the explicit ones."

Those were his final words. He turned his back to us and wrote out the entire lesson on the blackboard in longhand. He did not speak another word and the classroom was still silent when the bell rang. We got up and filed out of the room. He did not turn around even then.

"Wow," I said to Chloe, glancing over my shoulder to make sure Mr. Vasudeva was out of earshot. "He has completely flipped out."

"I knoOow. Poor Mr. Vasudeva."

"Yeah."

I had never before been accused of being intolerant. Was Mr. Vasudeva right, and was I just another small-minded expat who secretly felt superior to anyone who had a different accent? I considered the idea seriously for a moment. *No.* I shook my head. It wasn't very nice of me to giggle at Mr. Vasudeva's pronunciation, but that did not make me a racist.

The final bell rang and I drove home to pick up some things on my way to spend the weekend with Chloe. I found my mother in the kitchen.

"Bye, I'm off," I said.

"You didn't forget to pack enough clean clothes? Do you have your school materials?"

"Yes, mama. Chloe and I have sworn to waste part of our precious weekend poring over our books."

"Very funny. Before you know it, it will be time for your exams and then the joke will be on you."

"Oh, mama," I said. "Don't start. I've been listening to this kind of thing all week at school – I'm worn out. I need a break." I kissed her cheek and waved as I left the house.

Chloe's family lived in Karen, a large suburb just south of Nairobi. Driving there felt like leaving the busy world where I lived behind altogether. Huge old estates stood far apart with rolling meadows between them. I passed a row of dilapidated stables by the side of the road, covered in vines, with shrubs pushing through crumbling walls. The upper class colonials who used to live out here in splendor had moved away after Kenya gained its independence fifteen years ago. Regular working-class people had taken their place. Times had changed and keeping horses didn't fit into the new way of life.

Chloe's place was an antique colonial house. The heavy wooden front door stood slightly open, and I leaned in and called *hodi* to let the family know I had arrived. Chloe's voice answered *karibu* from somewhere inside and I stepped into the house. I made my way to the living room. The walls were paneled from ceiling to floor with wood, deep brown and glossy with age. Small windows kept the house cool and dark. Rugs were thin and faded and chairs mismatched and threadbare, but the effect wasn't somber at all – the house felt cozy and much loved.

Chloe walked in and asked, "Would you like something to drink after your long drive?"

"Do you have Coke?"

"I think so."

"I'd love one," I said.

We went to the enormous kitchen. Half a dozen cooks probably bustled back and forth here in the old days, preparing fancy luncheons and six-course dinners without ever getting in each other's way. Now it was the domain of Gabriel, houseboy and cook both. He had been with the family for a generation and cooked simple meals served on trays in the living room. This family was not interested in pomp and circumstance.

Chloe and I decided to postpone the inevitable homework just a little longer by walking down to the *duka* to buy some sweets. The late afternoon sun blanketed everything in a golden glow. It was my favorite time of day, and I felt content and in tune with the world. We crossed the front lawn diagonally and stepped onto the red dirt road. The past few days had been rainy, and car wheels had sunk into the soft mud and churned it into hills and valleys with tread marks stamped in the middle. The top crust was almost dry, but we walked along the grassy shoulder anyway, where the ground was sturdier. Stiff grass tickled the soles of my bare feet.

The duka was just ten minutes from the house, on the corner where dirt road met main road. Four bent wooden poles balanced a sheet of corrugated metal on top for a roof. One side had been boarded up to make a wall, with two shelves attached on which the goods for sale were displayed. A few packs of cigarettes were neatly stacked, with the top one open for customers who wanted to buy just one or two singles if they couldn't afford a whole box. On the other shelf, five bags of sliced white bread were arranged in the shape of a pyramid. A large plastic bag of sweets - rock-hard sugar in bright red, greens and yellows - was torn open across the top. People sat in the shade around a wooden picnic table that was warped and sagging in the middle, and drank cups of tea with a few slices of plain bread, chatting with each other and whoever happened to be passing by.

"Jambo," Chloe and I said in chorus, as we bent our heads and stepped under the roof.

"Jambo," everybody replied. All faces turned toward us. Some looked curious.

"*Ni vipi naweza kukusaidia?*" a man asked from where he was sitting at the table.

I did not speak Swahili. I envied the kids who did, especially the white ones, who seemed to belong here much more completely than I did. Almost every Kenyan spoke English and I had never gotten around to learning more than a few words of pidgin, but Chloe, born and raised here, spoke fluent Swahili. She answered the man in English for my benefit.

"We would like to buy some sweets, please," she said, pointing at the bag.

He nodded and walked up to the shelf. "You are the one

staying there, in that house back there," he said, speaking with a strong accent, indicating the road we had just come with a tilt of his chin.

"Yes. With my parents."

"You have sisters also, is it not so? I have seen them before, they are grown, and have *watoto* of their own."

Chloe giggled at being recognized. "Yes, that's true! My sisters are married and have their own families now. They do still live around here, though."

"It is a good thing, to have family close by."

Chloe nodded.

"How many sweets are you wanting?" the man asked.

She looked at me, and I shrugged. "Ten, please."

The man took a square of newspaper and counted out ten sweets, making sure to evenly distribute the colors, though the taste was the same for all of them, and then added another one. "For good luck," he said, grinning at us, showing two rows of bad teeth. He folded the newspaper into a package and handed it to Chloe.

We both thanked him, feeling charmed and a little shy at his generosity. "How much do we owe you?" I asked.

"This here costs one shilling."

I handed him a ten shilling bill.

"*Eh, hmmmm.*" His brow creased and he looked worried. "Do you have perhaps something smaller, some coin instead?"

I shook my head and patted the pockets of my shorts to indicate they were empty.

He stood for a moment, thinking and waving the bill in his hand. He turned to the people at the picnic table who had been watching developments with interest. Some quick Swahili passed between them, and people started digging into their pockets and pulling out money - coins mostly, and one or two bills. A woman untied the knot in the corner of her *kanga* and dropped a small stack of coins into her hand. The man quickly counted the money after everything had been handed over to him and said, "It seems we are a little more than twenty-five cents short here."

"Oh, don't worry about it, it's OK, really." Twenty-five cents. Only here could you buy anything for less than a shilling. In the supermarket these exact sweets cost five times as much, and you had to buy the whole bag, too.

The man scooped the money from the table and held a small mountain of it out to me on both his hands. I stuffed it into my pockets as best I could and felt the waistband of my shorts sag from the weight.

"Thank you," I said.

"*Asante sana. Kwaheri!*" Chloe and I called out as we walked away.

"*Kwaheri,*" people answered, and waved at us.

We decided to take the long way home, stopping at the fence of a neighbor's home before turning back. Chloe unfolded the newspaper package and I picked out a neon yellow sweet, tore off the clear wrapper and popped it into my mouth.

"I have something to tell you," I said, pushing the candy into my cheek with my tongue and trying to speak without drooling.

Chloe looked at me. I grinned to see her scan my face, trying to gather what I was going to say from my expression.

"Out with it," she said. "Is it something juicy?"

"Last time we were at the Flame Tree, after you had already left, Sam sat down with me."

"Sam? Sam who?"

"You know, Sam, Leander's friend. The one who helped me after Leander stood me up on my birthday."

"Tall dude, very dark? The one they call arrogant?"

"He isn't arrogant at all."

"I've heard others say that about him, that's all. Though I remember once I saw him walk by this group of little kids when he came off the rugby pitch, and they scattered like antelope running from a lion. They seemed quite scared."

"That's probably just because he's an upperclassman. He's nice, Chloe."

"He does seem nice, not that I know him, really. So, what happened at the Flame Tree?"

"We sat and talked for a while and I gave him my phone number."

"You did? Has he called you?"

"A couple of times."

"Really?" Chloe said. "I didn't think you were ready to start this kind of thing all over again. With a guy, I mean."

"I'm not sure what I'm ready for, to tell you the truth."

"Just be careful. I don't want you to get hurt."

I blinked, touched by her concern. "You're a good friend, *rafiki*," I said, and gave her a quick hug. "What would I do without you?"

We stood quietly, looking out across the unkempt lawn, moist new green shoots poking through the old dry yellow grass. Crickets and small frogs chirped. I looked farther out across the land and saw the Ngong Hills clear and blue on the horizon.

"They named this place after Karen Blixen, didn't they? The one who wrote *Out of Africa*."

"I think so."

"Maybe she used to be your neighbor."

"I don't know where her fields used to be, only that they're not around anymore. Everyone knows coffee doesn't grow at this altitude, though she only found that out the hard way."

"She was looking at these exact same things, though," I said, raising my hand to the world around me. "It's what she describes in her book."

"Yeah, I suppose she did."

"She wanted to live her entire life here, but instead she lost her farm and was forced to go back to Denmark and was homesick for Kenya the rest of her life," I said.

"I knoOow."

I sympathized with what Karen must have gone through; it didn't look like I'd be able to stay here forever like I wanted to, either. One day my father would be transferred to another country and that'd be the end of it; I'd have no choice but to pack my bags and leave, though I had no idea where to, because I had no other home.

"I almost feel like I'm doomed to the same fate," I said.

Chloe kept her eyes fixed on the ground and said nothing.

"Are you alright?" I asked.

She nodded her head *yes*, but stayed silent, collecting her thoughts. She seemed unusually serious. "Maybe it's the price we pay, when we leave behind the places we come from and set out into the world. We have no choice but to accept the uncertainty – it's just part of the deal."

"Well, it's not a problem for you, is it? Your settler ancestors have been in this country forever; aren't you a legitimate Kenyan? Your roots are right here."

She shook her head and said, "British citizen. All of our family is. For the passport, in case we decide to leave one day - to keep our options open."

"Leave? Why would you want to leave?"

"Well, I don't want to leave... I feel just like you, man. But my parents, they're from a different generation and they worry. We used to have a farm, too, you know."

I had no idea and looked at her in surprise, wondering what else hid behind the mild expression on her face that never gave much away.

"They sold in '64, back when I was too little to remember."

"Right after independence."

Chloe nodded. "They were scared their land would be taken from them by the new African government and given to the Kenyans. It wasn't unthinkable; it happened to whites in other countries across the continent."

"So they sold to avoid trouble, in case it came to them."

"Exactly. And much as they love the house in Karen, even after all these years, they still seem to have one foot out the door. Almost as if they expect things to come apart at any moment."

I wished I'd been born on a farm. I'd never wear shoes again, and I would not let irrational fears get under my skin.

Chloe hopped on one leg a few paces and we stopped walking. She balanced herself with a hand on my shoulder and reached down to pull a thorn from the sole of her foot.

"Prickly shrub got you," I said. We admired the size of the thorn, easily two centimeters with a long thin point as sharp as a needle.

"Didn't step down on it with my full weight. It barely pierced the skin."

She threw the thorn as far as she could into the rustling high grass and smiled. She reached down and picked up a handful of pebbles, and threw them one by one in lazy arcs toward the horizon. "See who touches the sun first," she yelled, releasing a *whoomp* of air as she launched a smooth little rock, whipping the gloom of her earlier words away.

I joined her in the silly joy of skipping stones into tall grass, where they dropped from sight instantly, and barely made a ripple in the space that pushed endlessly out into the distance on all sides.

CHAPTER NINE

Our house only had one telephone, and it stood on the *howdah* in the hallway. The chair had been designed to straddle an elephant's back, and not for people to hang out in for hours on end, talking on the phone. I sat with my legs folded against my chest, squashed inside the wooden barrier that held the cushion in place. My knees throbbed, and I squirmed to try and find a comfortable position. Finally, I couldn't stand it any longer and rolled down to the floor, laying down flat on my back on the cool tiles, splaying my limbs in all directions. *Ahhh, what a relief.* I tugged at the coiled cable to drag the phone closer until I could place the receiver to my ear, careful not to pull the whole thing down on my head.

"What's going on over there?" Sam's voice asked. "What are you up to with the sighing and moaning?"

"Just lying on the floor, getting comfortable. Why? What did you think I was doing?" I said.

Sam whistled a low *whooee* and laughed softly. "Naughty chick, eh? Good to know."

I giggled.

"So, tell me more. What brought you to Kenya?" he said.

"My father's work, you know how these things go with expats."

"But you're originally from Holland, right?"

"Yes. Native of Rijswijk." I was born there just like my parents, and much of the rest of our family. Travel was never part of the Janssen family history.

"*Rayzw...* what? Where's that?"

I smiled. Only those of us born and raised Dutch could pronounce the word. "Rijswijk," I repeated. "It's a small town, not far from The Hague."

Silence greeted this statement. I tried again. "Amsterdam? Does that ring a bell?"

"Amsterdam! Ah, yes. Bicycles, tulips, windmills, wooden shoes and first-rate partying. I hear the best weed on the planet is to be had there."

I laughed at such an unlikely combination of Dutch stereotypes. "Well, that is what they say. I wouldn't know. I've never really been to Amsterdam, except to land at the airport and drive straight through to our old apartment whenever we go on home leave."

I was only two years old when our belongings were packed and we left the motherland to live abroad, and I had no memories of those days. The story went that one day my father got so fed up with the gray skies and the rain, and how small and crowded everything was, that he decided to leave it all behind and find out what else was out there in the world. My parents and I visited Holland every other year, in the summer, and each time the place felt stranger and stranger to me.

"What does your father do?"

"He works for KIKS."

"You mean those bikkies in the round red tin? Your father makes those?"

"He doesn't actually *bake* anything."

"Right." Sam paused, and an idea seemed to occur to him. "Hey, maybe you can pick me up some samples? Those things are delicious."

Our pantry was stocked with every possible combination of KIKS cookies in tins of many sizes, though we rarely ate them at home. A lifetime of the same treats, no matter how delicious, ruins them for you. My mother was generous in handing the tins out, but it seemed too soon for me to be making promises to Sam.

"It depends," I said.

"On what?"

"On how nice you are."

"*Sweets for my sweet, sugar for my honey,*" Sam sang the old tune.

I sat up. He used a song to say what he meant; I was always doing the same thing.

"That's exactly right," I said, smiling to myself. "Anyway, now my father says he doesn't ever want to go back to the tiny apartment and his boring old job in Rijswijk. KIKS has factories all over the world."

"Where else have you lived?"

"Holland-Peru-Italy-Thailand-Kenya."

Sam laughed and said, "And me, I've never been anywhere, just back and forth between Kenya and Uganda. There you have it: the traditional African man all over again."

"Mostly it's a huge pain in the ass to move around so much, let me tell you."

"What, you don't want to be here? And all the while I was thinking you were one of those who fit in well, like you belonged in Africa all along."

I was flattered and hastened to explain myself, though I heard a twinkle in his voice, and suspected he might be teasing me.

"No, that's not what I meant," I said. "Only, at first I was as miserable here as anywhere else, just because the beginnings are always terrible. I'd change places with you in a heartbeat. I'd never leave Kenya, if it was up to me."

"You're happy here?"

"For sure."

It was easy to talk to Sam. He was nothing like Leander: having a conversation with him had been like pulling out each word with pliers. I was beginning to suspect my obsession

Leander had not had a lot of substance.

"What are you doing tonight?" Sam asked.

"Nothing much."

"I'm thinking of going out to the disco - the Drive Range - with Dennis and some of the guys. What do you think?"

I didn't even blink. "Sounds great."

"See you inside, 9:30?"

"I'll be there." I hung up. It felt like I had known Sam for a long time, though I hadn't seen him since that afternoon at the Flame Tree.

I tried not to worry about walking into the Drive Range alone. Only sad, dorky chicks went to the disco without a date, or at least a girlfriend by their side, and I didn't want anyone thinking I was that chick.

I ran my fingers along the lotus flowers and elephants and curlicues carved into the dark wood of the elephant chair. The legs were an upside-down V, supposedly to fit onto an elephant's back. Maybe they did. Or maybe the guy in Thailand who had sold it to my parents knew foreigners would pay big bucks for authentic souvenirs, and insisted this was the real deal so he could crank up the price. It was always hard to know these things for sure.

I wanted to see Sam again, I knew that much.

The Drive Range was at least twenty minutes outside of town - remote and isolated. I drove carefully along the dark road, sliding my eyes to the left again and again, looking for the side street to turn into and breathing with relief when I saw the flashing lights of the disco in the distance. A wooden sign with "Drive Range" painted on it stood where the two roads met. Most of the nails had rusted through and the sign tilted to one side; it was unlit and practically impossible to see at night.

The road to the disco was in terrible shape, nothing more than earth topped with a layer of gravel that had been ground almost down to sand by years of rolling tires. Monster potholes were never filled, but grew larger and deeper with each car that bumped through them, and every rainy season that washed out another layer of soil. I maneuvered carefully, and jumped when a pickup truck came tearing up from behind. Its engine whined as it bounced and crashed straight ahead, forcing the rest of us off the road and onto the grass. Spinning wheels dug into the potholes and raised enough dust to cover every car within honking distance. *Asshole.*

I bought my ticket, walked into the building and looked around, trying to be inconspicuous, hoping it wasn't obvious I was trying to find someone. What would I do if Sam wasn't here? The place was packed. Wisps of smoke floated on the air and the smell of stale beer stung my nose. Cigarette butts littered the floor. This used to be the clubhouse for the golf course out back, but after independence there weren't many people left who wanted to play golf. Someone decided to change it into a discotheque, and soon the building lost its colonial dazzle and started showing signs of hard wear from the hordes of kids who mobbed the place every weekend. Outside, the only reminder of its former life was a handful of filthy numbered flags leaning crookedly on their poles. Nobody cared what the inside or outside looked like. On disco night the Drive Range throbbed with the latest hits and the best dancers in town, and that's all that mattered.

I walked to the edge of the dance floor and looked down at the crowd, inhaling the animal smell of sweating bodies. Spotlights circled from the corners of the ceiling and washed the dancers in reds and yellows. I felt the *thump thump thump* of music vibrate up my legs, and unlocked my knees, gently swishing my hips. Not quite dancing - I didn't want to make a spectacle of myself - but not quite resisting the pull of the music, either. I scanned the dance floor. It pulsed with people boogying, grooving, bellowing along with the songs. You could never hear yourself sing over the pounding music, but you had to open your mouth wide and try anyway.

I turned around and saw Sam and his friends sitting a few steps above the dance floor. They were grouped around a low wooden table with brown bottles of Tusker beer within reach. Sam's chair was pushed back a meter or so from the others and he sat with his legs spread wide and his elbows propped on his thighs; his head rested on his fists and he was looking straight at me, his gaze intense. He seemed taut, as if he might spring up at any moment. The ease with which we had talked on the phone a few hours ago had disappeared, and I briefly wondered if I had only imagined our chemistry.

Sam was not going to come to me. I didn't know what to do. His friends seemed to be watching us, waiting to see what would happen. For an instance I thought of turning around and leaving, but there were too many eyes on me for such a dramatic gesture. Besides, I wanted to see Sam, to find out how things were between us. I pulled myself together and went to him. He drew himself upright, slowly, and waved a hand at Dennis for him to make room in the booth. Dennis jumped up as if this was the cue he had been waiting for and greeted me enthusiastically, grinning widely and beckoning for me to come over.

"Eh, jambo, you are here now – sit down, sit down!"

I smiled back at him, grateful Dennis' noisy welcome distracted me from wondering why Sam was so distant. I sat down and Dennis scooted next to me. He talked directly into my ear to make himself heard and asked, "Are you drinking? Can I get you a beer, maybe?"

I nodded my thanks and reached for my purse. "No, no, put that away," Dennis said. He stretched out his hand to Sam, who was already drawing bills from his wallet. Dennis took the cash, examined it quickly and yelled at his brother, "I think maybe you have made a small miscalculation, eh? A few bucks for my beer seem to be missing, what do you say?" He ended his speech in a

70

toothy grin.

Sam raised one eyebrow and let his brother sweat a little, then reached back into his wallet and pulled out some more money. Dennis skipped off to the bar at the rear of the building. He was barely seventeen but that wasn't going to stop anyone from serving him whatever he ordered. Drive Range policy was: cash up front, no questions asked.

The music was too loud for much conversation and our heads turned to watch the dancers. I tried to relax. When a new song started, Sam caught my eye. He raised his chin in a question and I nodded OK in reply. I stood up, kicked off my sneakers, and followed him to the dance floor. We plunged into the crowd, meandering carefully around dancers, trying not to bump into them. We found a spot near the outer edge, not too close to the tall, thundering, vibrating speakers, and worked the space to make room for ourselves. The reggae song felt awkward to me - too slow, or not slow enough, and I felt off balance as Bob Marley cried: *is this love, is this love, is this love that I'm feeling*. Sam did not falter, but snapped up the rhythms in sultry, flowing movements. When the song ended and a disco beat drummed through the air - *get up and BOOGIE* - Sam's energy exploded and I matched his moves, and we danced like we'd been out on this floor together all our lives. Drops of sweat rolled down my neck and my armpits turned damp. I stopped thinking about what I was doing and trusted my body, and my insecurities melted away. I smiled at the pumping legs and swaying hips around us, at dancers gazing hazily at their partners. Dancing was not a solo affair.

The DJ lifted the needle from the record and broke the spell, chattering in a fake American drawl, as if anybody cared what he had to say. Sam and I walked back to the table and he placed his hand low on my back, attaching himself lightly to me. I dropped into the booth and Sam slipped beside me. We smiled at each other, still floating on a disco high, and lit up some smokes. I rinsed my dry throat with a few deep pulls of beer straight from the bottle and pushed a damp strand of hair behind my ear.

"We move well together!" Sam yelled into my ear, grinning like a kid. "What do you think, eh?" he said, his thumb pointing at himself.

I wasn't sure what he meant.

"I saw you checking out my ass earlier," he said cheerfully. Apparently I hadn't been as subtle as I thought - I *had* checked out his ass. It wasn't easy to ignore anything about his body. His high-waisted trousers were made from slithery fabric that fit snugly around his tight hips and thighs. The legs flared wide and dragged on the floor, the toes of his polished shoes barely peeping out from beneath them. The top three buttons of his shirt were undone. He dressed differently from most guys I knew, who rarely changed out of their one pair of tattered jeans and faded t-shirt.

"Eh?" Sam was waiting for an answer.

"Yes," I said with a smile, not sure what to say.

"I knew I had to work it, so I wouldn't fade into nothingness next to you." Sam threw back his head and belted out his deep-throat guffaw.

I wondered what he meant. Was that supposed to be a compliment?

Sam took another swallow from his beer and put the bottle back down. He let his eyes drop to my bare feet, already black-soled and grimy. "What's this all about, do you always dance like that? One of these days some dude will stomp on you. Break your foot."

I hesitated, not wanting to sound weird. I decided to try to explain, and hoped he wouldn't laugh at me. "Because when I dance, sometimes shoes slide away or brake when that's not what I want. And because... I need to feel the floor to feel the music. Everything is better without shoes."

Sam looked at me seriously for a moment, considering what I'd said. Then he nodded. "I get that." Another pause. He brought his face very close to mine. "Also," he said, his lips stirring the air near my ear. "It is incredibly sexy."

Did he just say I was sexy?

I looked away from Sam's face, flustered. My eyes drifted over his shoulder, then stopped, shocked, when I realized what I was looking at. Leander and the blonde, snuggling together just two tables away. I snapped my head around quickly, afraid my eyes would accidentally lock with theirs.

Sam followed my line of vision and saw the couple. He leaned in and said, "Dance?"

I nodded. He took my hand and we walked down to the floor. A slow song was playing and the blacklight concealed me. Couples rotated gently in almost total darkness. I stood close to Sam, facing him, my eyes resting on his shoulder. I drew my arms around his waist, laced my fingers together and let them slide into the hollow of his back. I rested my body against his. My heart stopped thudding and I took a deep breath. I closed my eyes and leaned my head against his shoulder. His skin smelled faintly of musk.

We stayed until the slow set was over and the pace picked up. We stood still while people pulled apart and started gyrating and pounding their limbs. I felt the softest of kisses brush my neck, and wished everything could be as easy as a slow dance with an understanding partner.

CHAPTER TEN

Chloe stood in front of the old yellowed building where we had been taking our A-level exams. Today was English Lit, our last exam. She leaned against the massive trunk of a shady tree, looking calm. I grinned as I walked toward her, and called out: "Do you realize there's only ninety minutes between us and absolute freedom? No more exams, no more school, nobody chasing us down to spend every single minute studying. Wow. I almost can't believe we made it."

"I knoOow," Chloe said, smiling. She was wearing her good-luck red suede jacket, with the long fringes dangling from the sleeves making her look like a parrot about to spread her wings and fly away.

The doors to the test center hadn't opened yet, and clusters of students hung around, waiting. A few had their books open, some were clearly not worried and chatted and joked with friends, and others stood off on their own looking stressed. Last night I had lain awake in bed long past midnight, stomping facts into my brain until my arms grew too tired to hold a book over my head and my eyelids too heavy to carry on reading. I had to do well today. Geography had been a disaster. I don't know why I had expected anything different after Mr. Vasudeva's terrible silent classes these past few months, but it had been awful to sit there staring at exam questions with a mind as empty as the notebook in which I should have taken notes. I felt a stab of shame when I read a question about V-shaped valleys and realized I had no idea what to answer.

"It feels weird, doesn't it, standing here without our school stuff? No books or notebooks, not even my coffee thermos. Like that part of life is already over."

"It just about is," Chloe said.

"Are you ready for this one?" I asked. The doors of the building opened, and we merged with the tail end of the ragged stream of students flowing inside.

Chloe nodded. She was good at English, and despite a weakness for romance novels, she studied hard.

"Sara, where do you want to meet up afterward?"

I hesitated. I had known this was coming but hadn't figured out what to say. I was going to come off like a miserable friend no matter what.

"I can't, Chloe."

She glanced at me and I could see her quickly figuring out why I wouldn't be going with her for French fries and Cokes today like I had after all the other exams.

"I see. OK."

"I'm sorry, Chloe."

"It's just, because this is the last exam, I presumed we'd go. To celebrate. No worries, I'll phone mum - she'll come and collect me," Chloe said.

I felt worse because she was being so sweet, and because I hadn't even realized my plans would leave her stranded without a ride. We walked into the building and looked for places to sit. The square room was bare and silent, with small desks and chairs carefully placed exactly two meters apart.

"Good luck, *rafiki*," I whispered to her, hoping she would forgive me.

She nodded back, but her smile looked thin, and she didn't say anything.

By the time I walked out of the building, Chloe was gone. I wondered if it wouldn't have made me happier to celebrate the end of my Caldwell days with her, and regretted my decision not to. Chloe had been my friend since the first day I set foot in the school as the new girl, still trying to pull myself together in this new country. She had walked right up to me and made me feel welcome and part of the gang. I shook my head: *too late now*. I drove to Sam's place and pulled up in front of his motel room. He sauntered out as soon as I yanked up the handbrake.

Sam leaned close to my open window and said, "How did it go?"

"I think I did OK. I can't tell you how relieved I am that it's all over."

I got out of the car and Sam wrapped me in a bear hug probably meant as congratulations, but I took comfort from it. He tapped my butt and released me.

Dennis came out of the room, followed by his Pakistani friend. Rashid was tall and slender, dressed in sloppy jeans and a t-shirt that had probably once been black but was now a muddy gray. His thick black hair was mussed, as usual, and he looked like someone who had just walked in from a storm. All of which made Rashid not very typical. Pakistani men were generally slickly groomed, especially their hair, which was worn pasted down so firmly not even a monsoon would budge their pompadours.

I noticed Rashid's light blue Peugeot parked near my car. He had done things to it to make it go faster than anything else on the road, and it made such a racket that people clamped their hands over their ears to protect their hearing when he came near. It was probably just as well. No doubt lives had been saved because bystanders had enough advance warning to dive out of the way as he roared toward them. He sped through town overtaking everything in front of him, shooting through almost-red lights and flying around roundabouts so fast the inside wheels actually lifted from the street. Passengers were thrown from left to right and back, then launched forward when Rashid stomped on the brakes if a traffic light was too red even for him to ignore. His brakes developed a distinctive squeal from all the abuse. Then, as soon as he stepped out from behind the wheel, he slunk back into a perfectly gentle, sensible person. It never ceased to amaze me. Much as I liked him, I preferred not to get into any car he was driving.

"Are you guys ready to go? Let's take this one," Sam said, tapping the roof of my car. We moved toward the VW.

To me, Sam said, "We'll grab a bite at Abdul's, what do you think?"

"Sounds good," I said. "I'm absolutely starving. I was too nervous for breakfast this morning."

"I thought you might be."

Sam walked to the driver's side and held out his hand with the palm facing upwards, waiting for me. I felt flustered and tried to think what he was wanted. When I realized he was asking for the car keys, I dug into my bag, and then stood holding them. *What's going on?*

"Are you driving?" I asked.

Sam nodded. I could see he considered it obvious he would take the wheel, but I was confused.

"Why?" I asked carefully.

Sam glanced at the others, who had stopped chatting with each other and were following our conversation with amused interest. Sam frowned. "Do you know the way to Abdul's? Are you familiar with the streets in that part of town? Kariobangi?"

I had never been to Kariobangi; never even heard of it. "No," I said.

"Then let me take you there."

I handed Sam the keys, my unwillingness to drive unknown streets with three guys looking critically over my shoulder winning out over the feeling that Sam should have at least asked.

I sat down in the front passenger seat. Sam took a route I did not know, and I looked out of the window.

Dennis called out from behind me, "Hey, Sara!"

"Yes?"

"Why don't you put on some music?"

Music made everything better. "What do you want to hear?"

"Ah, you are giving us options here. This is a very classy vehicle, I must say, with an entire discotheque on board," Dennis said.

"Well, I don't know about that."

I dug into the glove compartment and grabbed a random stack of cassettes, twisting behind me to hand them to Dennis and Rashid. I turned around and heard them whisper about the tapes behind my back.

"You know, Sara, this music here is not very... how to say this in a nice way? Not very *with it*," Dennis said.

I had had just about enough of these guys. "Well, I hate to remind you, but this is my car. I listen to the stuff I like."

"Such as?"

"Depends entirely on my mood." I wasn't going to go into specifics, like the Barbara Streisand tape I played endlessly, music so uncool that admitting I loved it would make me the town laughing stock for a whole week, at least.

Sam glanced at me with a smile. "I'll bet you don't have any Isley Brothers, eh? Parliament? No, I didn't think so. We're going to have to hook you up with some real music one of these fine days."

I rolled my eyes at him to let him know what I thought of his *real music* gibe and dug back into the glove compartment. I took out a Stones tape, guessing the giant lip and tongue logo on Rashid's t-shirt meant he was a fan and clicked it into the player, cranking up the volume. *BROWN SUGAR, how come you taste so good?* We sang along, all of us, and I felt myself relax.

"By the way, I looked up the meaning of your name," Sam said.

"You did?" I asked, surprised. "And what did you find?"

I rolled my finger along the volume knob on the side of the cassette player and Mick Jagger faded to the background.

"That it is official. You are a princess, exactly as I suspected." Sam grinned at me.

"Very funny. And what does yours mean?"

"Samuel means *asked of God.*"

"I'm impressed. You outrank a mere princess."

"Yes. It seems I am indeed God's Gift to Humanity," Sam said, laughing his deep belly laugh at the little joke. "On the other hand, my last name means *death* in my people's language. I suppose that balances things out."

"Draru means death?"

"Don't worry about it," Sam said, winking at me. "I'm not planning on going anywhere just yet."

We drove into a run-down part of town. Sam parked in a small, uneven lot with lines of faded paint only hinting at slots. Not that anyone paid attention to lines - cars were scattered randomly, blocking storefronts and each other. The bleached asphalt was torn in places and dark blobs of crumbled tar had bubbled to the surface. Shops were low and grimy, with fly-covered piles of garbage sagging near doorways. The smell of rotting fruit was thick in the air. Heavy metal grates were drawn tight across doors and windows - it was lunchtime and shopkeepers had left to find something to eat and maybe catch a quick nap; some were lying on the sidewalk in front of their stores.

Sam leaned over to me and said, "Hang on a minute." He hopped out of the car and loped away in a slow jog.

"Where's he going?" I asked the guys in the back.

"Just off to score a little something for the weekend."

"What? What?"

"*Banghi.* You know: grass."

Oh, shit. Here I was, sitting in my gleaming white unscratched

Volkswagen with a big round NL Netherlands bumper sticker announcing to the world that I was a foreigner in an area where for sure foreigners had no legitimate business. If some policeman walked up to the car and started asking questions, I would be up the creek in a terrible way. If my father found out I'd let someone else drive the car, and I was in this neighborhood, and we were here for the purpose of buying weed... I would be dead. My father would unleash his mouth-foaming fury on me and I would cry hysterical little-girl tears, unable to explain myself to someone who never listened to a word I said. Exactly the kind of drama I did not want to participate in ever again.

Sam jumped back into the car and handed some small bags to Dennis.

"Jesus, Sam," I said, glaring at him.

He grinned at me and drove off. I exhaled. It looked like I was going to escape without getting arrested for being an accessory in a drug deal.

Abdul's was a huge space filled with long rows of light gray formica-topped tables and backless benches, set up like a cafeteria. No one had bothered to try to create an atmosphere; there were no tablecloths or salt shakers or anything decorative. A counter stood along one wall where patrons ordered and paid for their food, and Sam went to buy lunch while the rest of us sat down to wait for him. I felt conspicuous. I scanned the place quickly, careful not to stare, and confirmed that I was the only white person here. I hoped I wouldn't embarrass myself by breaking some unknown code of behavior. Sam returned carrying a tray crowded with four plates, a stack of paper napkins and clear plastic mugs filled with water. Each plate had one oversized *samosa* on it as big as the palm of my hand, resting on a dark green lettuce leaf, with a small blob of red chutney on the side. The samosa was a perfect triangle of crispy golden-fried dough, stuffed so full it bulged in the middle, and smelled mouth-wateringly of coriander and ginger.

"Does this have pork in it?" Rashid asked.

We grinned at his question and Sam answered, "No, *bwana*. These are all vegetable. We're at Abdul's, what are you thinking? No pork allowed within a one kilometer radius of this place, at least."

Rashid was not strict about the rules of Islam in most things he did or did not do, but he refused point-blank to eat pork. Whenever anything appeared on his plate, he would not touch it without first asking intensely *does this have pork in it?* It had become a joke to those of us who knew him. But if people laughed, or weren't insistent enough in assuring him there was absolutely no pork in his food, he would simply refuse to eat. I noticed he did not have the same qualms about beer.

I sank my teeth into my samosa. It was savory with potatoes, peas, onion and thin flakes of carrot. I dipped it cautiously into the chutney before taking another bite, and felt the small drop burn my tongue with unbearable heat. Tears pooled in my eyes and I blinked quickly to stop them from rolling down my face. I took a few big gulps of water to try to quench the fire.

Sam leaned over to me and whispered, "You OK?"

I nodded and said, "This is delicious," and my voice sounded a little raspy.

Sam laughed at me.

We drove back to the motel and the boys flopped on the beds. I sat down on the chair at the dresser. Sam broke out the cards and the *banghi* and I discovered I was not in the mood for either. The thought of driving home later and having to work hard at pretending I was not high was too much. Besides, I felt uptight. I had started thinking about Sam buying the weed again, and was not fully convinced there wouldn't be consequences after all. I sat on the sidelines and watching the guys play for a while, then decided I might as well go home.

Sam walked me to my car. The whites of his eyes were bloodshot and he looked at me blearily.

"Are you OK?" he asked. I nodded yes. "I shouldn't have taken you to Abdul's, eh, maybe it was just a little too down and dirty for you."

"No, Abdul's was nice, honest. The samosa was really good." I hesitated, not wanting him to think I was that white princess he liked to tease me for. "It's just, you know, you buying the *banghi*. I'm worried because, what if someone took down the plates of my car? And found out where I live?" I stopped, realizing I sounded whinier than I meant to.

"*Mmmmmm,*" Sam growled in the back of his throat. "Right."

He opened the car door for me and I got in.

"See you."

"Yeah, see you," I answered, feeling unhappy.

My mother was waiting for me when I got home. I saw how angry she was by the way she had her fists balled up and pushed into her sides, and because she had been on the lookout for me. She was at the front door as soon as I drove through the gates.

"Where have you been? You finished your exams this morning, don't you think you ought to let me know where you're going and when you'll be home? What's the matter with you, selfish girl, I've been worried sick. I was about to call your father."

I was silent. I hoped I didn't have to tell her what I had been up to because there was no way I could tell her the truth and I was too wrung out to come up with a good story. My mother wiped her hands on her apron. "I don't have time for this. I have dinner to prepare." She turned and strode to the kitchen.

I watched her angry, stiff back as she walked away from me.

Was this the way things were going to be? Was this the freedom, the first day of the rest of my life, the post-graduation guiltless fun I had been looking forward to all year? *Shit.*

CHAPTER ELEVEN

I got up late this morning and wasn't doing much of anything. The cat rubbed her back and tail along my bare legs and I crouched down to stroke her orange fur. A purr rumbled beneath my hand.

"You have it easy," I murmured into her ear. "You don't need anyone. You run off and behave as badly as you like, you come home whenever you feel like it, and everybody loves you. What do you care what anybody thinks?"

I went to the kitchen and took a glass bottle from the refrigerator door, held it to the light, and looked through the water; clear, clean and twinkling where it caught the light; sterilized and purified. Years ago my mother attended a class on the art of being a housewife in the tropics and she came away fixated on water. It became her mission to make sure my father and I were vigilant at all times: unclean water, she assured us, was full of nasty invisible bugs that would latch onto our intestines and slowly suck the life right out of us.

I filled the kettle halfway. A cup of tea would be nice. I took a bag from the Lipton box and lifted it to my nose, inhaling the smoky smell of strong black tea. The burner under the kettle flared to life when I held a match to the gas, and I leaned against the counter to wait - it would take a while for the ice cold water to heat up. The glass slats in the windows were cranked open all the way to let the air in, and the sheer white and orange curtains floated gently into the kitchen, and then sucked back out against the bug screen. It was a beautiful day, sunny and clear, breezy and warm. Laundry hung from the clotheslines in the back yard, and white t-shirts, underwear, and my father's office shirts wove slowly back and forth.

Maybe I'd go outside to sunbathe. There was a spot behind the drying laundry, surrounded by tall hedges, where I could find privacy and lying topless wouldn't attract any attention. I liked the idea of spending a pleasant afternoon in the sun with nothing but a book, a cup of tea, and an egg timer to remind me to turn over every ten minutes.

Lisa was in the laundry room rolling socks and she called out to me without slowing her hands. Lisa had been our housegirl since we came to Kenya. She was probably only a few years older than me, but her life was so different from mine that it seemed like she was from another generation altogether. Her young son lived with family back in her home village near Mount Kenya while she worked here in the city to support him. I knew the journey to her village was far and expensive and she did not go there often. It seemed sad for a mother to be separated from her child like that, though Lisa assured me it happened a lot in Kenya where families helped each other raise children and earn a living.

Lisa brought noise and cheerful energy wherever she went, but today she spoke in a prickly tone I'd never heard her use before.

"African men are no good," she called out to me. She clicked her tongue against the roof of her mouth and shook her head angrily. "You stay away from African men, eh."

She caught me by surprise, because Lisa didn't usually start conversations about personal things with me. Did this have something to do with me spending time with Sam? I couldn't imagine why she would disapprove of him. Or maybe it had more to do with the fact that she was visibly pregnant with her second child and there was still no husband in sight. She stomped off with the folded laundry when my mother walked into the kitchen, leaving me looking after her, dumbfounded.

"Sara, good morning!" my mother said. "How nice to see you in the kitchen for once, this is not normally where I would expect to find you. Have you eaten? I cleared away the breakfast things, because you slept so long."

"I'm just making tea. I thought I'd like fried eggs, but it seemed like too much trouble."

My mother frowned. "Really, Sara. Don't you think it is time for you to learn how to prepare food? One day you will have a family of your own to look after, and you will be fully unprepared. Not that frying an egg can even be considered true cooking, you know."

"*Ugh.* I hate all cooking."

"That is not the point. It is one of those things we women do, whether we like it or not."

I doubted the truth of that statement. I imagined lots of women did not cook, and families survived.

I heard the crunch of a car driving up the driveway and stopping in front of the house. The gates were open; there was no need for security during the day. I went to find out who had arrived, and saw it was Sam. He had been coming over more often now that we were both done with school, and days floated by long and unscheduled. I had introduced him to my parents. They tried to figure out not so subtly if this was my new boyfriend, but to be honest, I wasn't sure of that myself. Lots of people came over to our house; I just left it at that.

"Hello, what a nice surprise, good to see you," I called out. I walked down to meet him and cringed when I stepped onto the driveway and sharp-edged gravel bit into my bare feet.

Sam grinned at me. "Look at you. You put that outfit on especially to turn me on, admit it."

Turn him on? My green shorts with the apple patch over the hole where the backside was worn through and the white top with billowy sleeves, thin and faded from years of washing... was he kidding?

85

"I didn't think, really," I said, which sounded like another one of my sillier replies. Why did he always make me feel so flustered?

Sam stood tall in front of me, rested his hands on my shoulders and placed his soft, full lips on mine. Gently. Warmth pulsed through my belly.

"There is something I haven't had a chance to speak to you about," Sam said. "I've been thinking about what you told me the other day after we went to pick up the *banghi*. Obviously I wasn't right in the head when I took you to that part of town, and in your car, no less."

"Nothing terrible happened in the end," I said. I was relieved my worst fantasies had not come true, and was ready to forget all about the incident. Still, it was good to realize Sam had been thinking about what I told him, and saw things from my side, too.

"In any case, I apologize. And I want you to know I don't do a lot of *banghi*, either. It's just that beer costs a lot, and sometimes I smoke a little when I'm in the mood to party."

"That's good to know."

"I don't want to get you into any kind of trouble and I don't want to piss off your father. He's an angry man and he doesn't like me already."

My father didn't like Sam? I reached into my memory, searching for something I might have missed. I couldn't come up with anything.

"What do you mean?" I asked.

"He eyeballs me bad every time. Why do you think I come by when he's at work, eh? The way he grips my hand hard like he wants to convince me he's the stronger man. You know he doesn't like me because I'm African. White people always look down on the likes of me."

"Shut up, Sam, you know it isn't true. My father is not a racist. What makes you say that?"

"He doesn't want his princess hanging around with me."

"It's not true."

Sam shrugged his shoulders. "Whatever you say."

I studied his face. It looked like he was the one who was pissed off.

"Well, do you want to come in and have some tea?" I asked.

"Are you sure it's cool?"

"Of course it's cool, what's the matter with you?"

We walked into the house and I called out, "Mama, Sam is here. We're going to have something to drink, OK?"

"Why, hello Sam, how nice to see you again." My mother came into the living room and beamed at our guest. She was always happiest when she had someone to feed and fuss over. "Will you two have tea? No, don't worry, I'll take care of it - sit, sit, sit." She waved us over to the sofa and a short time later she walked in carrying a tray with two of her best china cups and saucers, and a matching pot. She arranged everything on the polished coffee table, then hurried back to the kitchen and returned with a smaller tray with a silver cream and sugar set, a dish of lemon slices, and a plate of carefully arranged sweets. She handed us small cloth napkins with sprigs of flowers cross-stitched in the corners.

"Thank you, mama," I said, a little embarrassed by such a display, though I knew how much she was enjoying herself.

"Thank you very much, Mrs. Janssen," Sam said.

My mother looked pleased and left the room.

"I've never before met a lady as lovely as your mother." Sam looked at me, his eyes twinkling. "You know they say you can always tell what a woman is truly like by looking at her mother. Based on that, it seems clear to me that you will be one to take excellent care of her man."

"Oh, please," I said. "Wake up to the modern world. Things have changed since my mother's day, I assure you." I leaned over to the tray, picked a round chocolate with tiny red dots sprinkled on top, and popped it into my mouth. I crushed it gently between my back molars and felt the soft, creamy filling glide onto my tongue.

"So, what's your mother like? Is she anything like mine?" I asked Sam. He had never spoken of her.

"You mean my birth mother?"

"Yes."

I poured tea. Sam settled into the sofa, leaning his head back and shifting his hips forward until he was suspended in a slouch. He laced his fingers behind his head with his elbows jutting out wide and his face tilted toward the ceiling. He looked comfortable, but closed off from me, as if he had turned inward to his thoughts and they'd taken him to a place I was not a part of. I slid to the edge of my seat so I could see his face.

"Our people, the Madi, we come from the northern part of Uganda. Not much goes on up there. People grow enough food to eat and they herd their cows and goats, and chickens run all over the place... you know, just your typical African village. I was born on the floor of my mother's hut, exactly the same as the generations before me."

Sam turned to look at me with his eyebrows raised high, like he was waiting for me to challenge him. I believed him, though.

He turned back to the ceiling. "I grew up like every other snot-nosed African *toto* running around in nothing but a raggedy t-shirt with my bare ass hanging out. Us village kids went barefoot, and my mother would sit at night with a paraffin lamp and use a pin to dig the jiggers from under my toenails." He laughed. "I screamed like a newborn pig, but it was never bad enough to make me want to wear shoes."

Now I had a question: "Jiggers?"

"Sand fleas. They burrow into the skin of your foot and feed on your blood and grow fat and it is painful like crazy. You have to dig them out whole because bits that get left behind go septic."

"Disgusting," I said.

Sam took a sip of hot tea. He ignored the handle on the cup and grasped it in his hand like a bowl. He lit a cigarette and looked around for something to drop his match in. I pushed the ashtray over from my end of the table.

"It was just huts with dirt floors, back in the village. But my father, he was already making his way in the world. He built a concrete house for my mother, and Dennis was born there. Some more time passed, things got better still, and we moved south to the capital, to Kampala. We were a nice middle class family and comfortable financially, but my father never forgot where he came from. He swore he would build houses for each family in the village, and he is keeping that promise to this very day, one house at a time."

"But what about your mother?"

Sam sucked his lips against his teeth. "Sara, that is another story altogether." He shook his head slowly. "My mother is a good woman; she always looked after us children and loved us. But she could not cope when other wives and their children started appearing to become part of the family. She turned to drink to find comfort. My parents fought all the time and finally they separated. My mother went back to the village."

"Did she take you with her?"

"No. Us children stayed at our father's house."

"Wow." She lost her husband, her home and her children, all at once.

"Hey, don't look so shocked. It's just the way things work out sometimes. Here, look at this picture of her, you see?" Sam pulled his wallet from his back pocket. He took out a small, passport-sized black and white picture and held it carefully by one corner. His mother's gentle, friendly eyes gazed at me from a round face. She wore her hair brushed back from her face, smooth and airy like a windblown cloud. Her skin was very light. I looked at Sam over the edge of the photo to compare the two, but couldn't find anything of the mother in her dark, angular number one son.

"She's very beautiful," I said.

Sam nodded and carefully slid the picture back into his wallet. He kept his eyes lowered and frowned slightly, speaking slowly. "I am her favorite: her firstborn and first son. The one she relies on." He paused. "I love my mother, of course, but dealing with her many expectations can weigh heavily. When my mother calls, and cries about her situation, and wants me to fix things with my father... " He shook his head again.

I waited for him to finish the sentence, but he was lost in his thoughts. I covered his hand with my own, thinking how complicated his life was.

Sam squeezed my hand and sat up straight. He lit another cigarette, smiled at me, and said, "*Ati sasa*, let's talk about plans for this weekend, eh? Rashid's cousin is getting married. He says we're all invited - there will be a huge celebration affair. What do you think?" Sam said.

I was caught off guard by the sudden change of subject, but suspected Sam was not in the habit of discussing his mother, and I was pleased he had given me a glimpse of her. "Which cousin is getting married - do I know her?"

Rashid was famous for the endless supply of female cousins that popped up everywhere he went. We'd be sitting at the Flame Tree, or queuing for movie tickets, and a cluster of smiling girls would appear and wave bashfully at him. They looked like carbon copies of each other: petite and deer-eyed with straight, long, shiny, black hair, big dangling silver earrings, smooth skin and perfect makeup. Rashid would call them over and say to us, *please meet my cousin!* and the cousin would step forward and shyly shake hands all around. As soon as she stepped back into her group, it was impossible to tell one from the other.

"Who knows? Apparently it's going to be a huge party and he assures me everybody's welcome. We won't be going to the ceremony itself, just the reception. There won't be any booze, this being a Muslim affair, but there'll be food and music, maybe

90

some dancing. Anyway, it's in the afternoon so we can still go out later if we feel like it."

"I've never been to a Pakistani wedding."

"Me neither. You know these Asians, they keep to themselves and behave as if they never left their own countries even after they've been here for generations. Though I think Rashid's branch of the family is not as traditional as most."

"What do his people do?" I asked.

It seemed like Asians overwhelmingly owned restaurants and shops. Asian immigrants had settled in Kenya after building the railroad one hundred years ago, and the British gave them businesses to run as a reward. The British considered Asians superior to Africans.

"Chain of grocery stores. Very successful, lots of money there."

"You'd never know, looking at Rashid and his raggedy t-shirts."

Sam shrugged his shoulders. "Rashid is different that way. But most Asians have done extremely well for themselves here. They own the shops and are lawyers and professors and us poor Africans, we have somehow ended up in our own countries with nothing."

"Your family is doing OK."

Sam snorted, as if this was a joke. "I suppose. But even so, we are the exception that confirms the rule. You see why Idi Amin decided it wasn't enough to rid Uganda of the colonial dictators, but he had to chase out the Asians also, once and for all, don't you? He had to save Africa for the Africans."

I looked at him in surprise. "You're not saying Amin was right?"

The bodies of his victims were still washing up on the shores of Lake Victoria, though Amin had been banished from the country months ago and his rule of terror finally brought to an end. It was in the newspaper every day. The corpses weren't all

Asian, either. Plenty were African.

"No, I'm not. He's a sick bastard. They call him *The Butcher of Africa* for a reason."

I nodded; I knew that's what the papers called him.

"The man is certifiably insane. Not so long ago, Uganda was the most beautiful country in Africa, maybe the world. And now, after eight years of Amin, it is in ruins."

"It makes you realize how lucky we are things have been so good in Kenya since independence."

Sam nodded. "Yes. It certainly hasn't turned out that way for most new African nations. Peace and a normal life have been hard to come by."

He paused, and added, "One day, Uganda will be paradise on earth again. Then I'll take you there. What do you think?"

"I think that sounds perfect." I liked the idea of going with Sam to the place he was born.

The front door opened and slammed shut just a little too loudly. My father was home from work and he was in a bad mood. I couldn't see him through the closed hallway door, but the sounds of his anger were familiar enough. He dropped his attaché case onto the elephant chair and it hit the wooden barrier with a clunk. He stomped off to the kitchen to find my mother. We were in for some high drama.

"Wie parkeert er verdomme z'n auto zo ongelukkig dat geen mens er meer langs kan?" he bellowed. I heard my mother respond with soothing sounds.

"What's the problem?" Sam asked me in a low voice.

"Ah," I said. "Well. It seems your car is blocking his parking spot."

My father burst into the living room and I could tell by the scarlet tint of his shuddering cheeks that he was only barely keeping his temper in check.

"It is you, I see," he said to Sam. "It is your car parked out front. Would you be so kind as to put it somewhere where it is not obstructing the whole damn driveway? So the people who actually live in this house can also perhaps have some room to park their cars?"

Sam's body tightened. He sat straight and held still, his chin tucked, his eyes blazing beneath lowered eyelids. I thought he, too, would erupt. I touched my fingers to his arm and Sam seemed suddenly to remember where he was, and that I was sitting next to him. He rose slowly from the sofa, never taking his eyes off my father. Then he turned to my mother and said in a controlled voice, "Thank you for tea, Mrs. Janssen."

He looked back at my father and bowed once, slowly, almost mocking him with exaggerated politeness. He strode outside. I followed, nearly breaking into a trot to keep up with him. Sam got into his car and slammed the door. He sat with his fists clamped around the steering wheel. He turned to me and said through the open window, "He is your father. This I respect. But nobody – *nobody* - do you hear me? Nobody speaks to me that way."

Sam started the engine and drove off without looking back.

I stood still, stunned. *What just happened?* Sam was right: my father did not like him. And I knew why, too. Sam did not scuttle out of the way to let my father thunder and rage his way through a temper like my mother and I did, just because we knew from long experience that confrontation would only make things worse. Sam and my father were like two lions roaring to see who was the fiercest, and where did that put me?

CHAPTER TWELVE

I wasn't sure what to wear to Rashid's cousin's wedding and decided on my gypsy skirt only after changing my mind a hundred times. Three tiers of thin cherry red cotton, each one billowing out a little wider than the last, falling just below my knees. I'd sewn it myself. The fabric swirled around my legs and I felt girlish and pretty. My knit top sparkled gold in the light, with crocheted edging so fine it was almost lace, and a thin cord threaded along the neckline. Two round amber beads on the ends hung low between my breasts. I stroked the soft fabric. Fashion was hard to come by in Nairobi - there wasn't much clothing of any kind besides tourist t-shirts and safari gear - and being all dressed up like this for a change felt good.

Deciding on shoes was easy – I only owned sneakers and sandals. I pulled on my sandals and was happy with the way they looked, though Sam would probably complain. He called them my retreads, ugly as the shoes poor people made from tires they found in the garbage dump. I loved my sandals, though. I'd bought them at a store called *Pot of Gold* where the air shimmered with yellow light and smelled deliciously of leather and patchouli. I wore them for months on end and the leather had stretched and shaped to my feet, and wearing these sandals was as close to walking shoeless as any shoe could get.

Sam arrived to collect me. He glanced at the sandals but didn't make a comment. "You look beautiful," he said.

"Thank you," I said, smiling. Sam was critical of me as often as he had something nice to say. He was not one to throw compliments around lightly - this much I had learned about him already. I valued his honesty, but a little more sweetness every now and then would be nice.

When we arrived at the wedding reception, we spotted Rashid and Dennis and a group of friends hanging out near the entrance of the hall, and walked up the sloping lawn to greet them. Sam wrapped his arm around my waist and clasped his hand just above my hipbone, where my waist was smallest. He pulled me close. I looked at him and saw he was smiling. I kissed his cheek.

Rashid put down his paper plate stacked with food. He called out, "Good to see you two... glad you could make it!" He wiped his hands on his khaki trousers and came over to shake our hands. "Would you like to come inside and say hello to my newly married cousin?"

We followed Rashid into the building. The hall was lit by fluorescent tubes that covered the ceiling and made faces pale and clothes look like the color had been bleached out of them. A buffet with dishes piled high was set up against the wall on the far side across from the door, and the smell of garlic and curry reached us even here. A huge boombox played music that sounded like it was from one of those Bollywood song and dance films. Not that anyone was dancing. People were sitting at tables eating and standing around in small groups talking, holding tall glasses of iced tea and soft drinks.

The bride and groom sat at the table in front of the buffet. They were stiff with finery, the bride in a turquoise gown covered with sequins, her hair hidden under a veil, and the groom in a black jacket elaborately embroidered with gold thread. The chairs they sat on stood wide apart and they did not speak with each other. No one in the crowded room seemed to be paying them any attention – they looked quite lonely, as if they were not part of the festivities at all. Sam and I congratulated them on their marriage and they smiled at us and nodded. It didn't seem this situation called for small talk, so we smiled again and backed away, and followed Rashid to the food.

I hoped my own wedding one day would be a different kind of affair - I imagined I would at least have fun. I shrugged my shoulders at the thought. Maybe this bride and groom were shy, or maybe they were just behaving as was expected of them. Different cultures, different expectations.

I piled my plate high with Pakistani delicacies, spicy chicken drumsticks, rice fritters and curried vegetables with a blob of sweet mango chutney, careful to avoid the red hot kind. I sidled up to Rashid and whispered, "Does this have pork in it?"

He grinned at me, "I can answer that question today without any hesitation: absolutely not! No pork at a Muslim wedding – of that at least we can be certain."

We went outside to join our friends and stood in the shade of the building, sharing food and stories. The mood was mellow, and we wallowed shamelessly in nostalgia, remembering our friendships and the good times we shared. Who knew how few times we would have another chance like this before we scattered to colleges and jobs in Kenya and countries far away? Sam hovered close and murmured in my ear, making sure I had enough to eat and drink. He held my hand and smoothed a strand of hair that had escaped from my ponytail.

Sam nudged me and pointed at the low stone wall that stood around the yard and said, "Can you come with me to sit down over there? There's something I want to talk to you about."

I followed him to a spot just beyond the others' hearing and wondered what he had to say. Sam caught my elbow and stopped me from sitting on the wall. He sat down instead, and pulled me gently onto his lap.

"So your skirt doesn't get dirty."

I smiled at his maneuver; a little obvious, but effective. I rested my arm softly around his neck, fingers touching warm skin. I felt the width of his shoulders beneath my arm and the strength of his thighs holding me up. My heart fluttered.

"Are you comfortable?" he asked softly.

I nodded. "Are you?"

"Yes," he said, grinning at me. "I am very comfortable. In fact, there is no other place in this world I would rather be."

Dennis yelled, cupping his hands around his mouth like a megaphone, "Hey! What do you think you guys are up to, eh? Get a room if you can't resist those lovey-dovey hanky-panky uncontrollable urges of yours."

"I don't believe it," Sam muttered. He yelled back, "Dennis, can we have a little privacy, you think? I have something to discuss with my woman here."

I drew in my breath. *Sam's woman.*

His thighs relaxed beneath me and I sank into his arms a little deeper. He held me firmly. "Are we cool?" Sam whispered. "I mean, you want this, too, don't you? You and me together, like a couple."

I smiled at his stuttering.

"Yes. Yes! Yes, I want this, too." I spoke the words and felt just how much I wanted this. *Oh, man.* Heat flushed through me, like a drug, like full-on dancing, like something altogether new and unexpected.

Sam hugged me closer. He hooked a finger under the neckline of my top and pulled it taut until it bared a little patch of skin. He kissed the hollow beneath my collarbone. I bent forward and touched my lips to his forehead, pushing hard, not knowing how else to show my feelings while sitting here on a wall with our friends watching.

"It felt like this was something we had almost decided without actually talking about it," Sam said. "Like we made a choice to be together without needing words. A commitment." He hesitated. "Do you agree?"

I straightened up so I could look at him and nodded. "But the funny thing is, I didn't quite believe it until just now, when you said it out loud."

"I've been walking around with this for weeks. Part of me feared I was reading the signs wrong and you would shoot me down."

"You thought I'd reject you?" I asked, surprised.

He looked slightly embarrassed. "Maybe."

I couldn't imagine Sam, this lion, this confident man, ever hesitating to go for anything he wanted. It touched me that he preferred to avoid talking to me rather than risk hearing *no*. Apparently there was a soft side to him I hadn't seen much of yet.

Sam said, "I had to be sure, because now I have something to propose. Listen: what would you say to going away and spending some time together, just the two of us? Daniel, a friend of mine, has gone to spend time with his mother in Kapenguria. He's invited us to come up and stay on their farm a few weeks – he assures me there is plenty of room and we won't be in anyone's way." Sam grinned and winked at me. "And they won't be in our way, either."

"Kapenguria? Where's that?"

"It's a town four hundred kilometers to the west. I've been up there a few times for holidays with Daniel in the years since we were in grade school. It is mostly big farms, and the town itself is not much to speak of. Just a lot of land and space - quiet and relaxing, very beautiful."

"How do we get there?"

"By train, about twelve hours overnight. Which reminds me, I hear good stories about the effect of trains as an aphrodisiac, you know, *gaDUNKaDUNKaDUNK*. Eh? What do you think? We could make good use of such rhythms." Sam grinned. "Train sex," he whispered, jiggling his eyebrows at me, like I might have missed the point. I laughed at the expression on his face, sure he was not altogether joking. I jabbed him in the ribs with my elbow and told him to stop.

"So what do you think? About going to the farm?" Sam

asked.

"I love it. It sounds wonderful." A train ride to a farm far away from everybody, just Sam and me together for weeks? My father would never allow it.

"Good." Sam said, squeezing me. He winked, and added, "And don't pack those sandals."

I got home not too long after midnight to find the living room full of people. My parents called energetically when they saw me open the door. *"Kom binnen,"* my father bellowed, trying to drown out his rowdy guests and gesturing wildly with his raised hand. Music blared from the stereo and the room was hazy with smoke. Guests clutched half-empty glasses of whiskey and wine. What was left of a platter of hors d'oeuvres stood on the coffee table. A few broken potato chips lay scattered around my mother's signature brandied egg dip. What a mess. People called out, speaking and laughing loudly to make themselves heard over the music and each other. A woman sagged sloppily into the corner of the sofa, holding her drink at an angle.

I decided to wait out the guests, guessing most were a fair way down the road to tipsiness and the party would be winding down soon. I was anxious to get the talk with my parents about going to Kapenguria out of the way, besides, this seemed like a real opportunity for a positive outcome – my parents would be a little boozy and it looked like they were in a good mood. I sat down next to the short-haired lady who lived up the road, and she threw her arm around my shoulder as if we were friends. My mother put a glass of beer in front of me and I lit a cigarette.

It was close to 2:00 in the morning when the last couple left. The wife giggled and hung onto her husband's arm as they waddled to their car. I helped my mother collect glasses, empty ashtrays and scrape gobs of food into the trash bin, opening windows to let fresh night air chase out the smoke. My mother rinsed dishes and stacked plates and glasses neatly, but decided against washing them, admitting for once there was too much to do at such a late hour. Lisa would take care of it in the morning.

"Can I talk to you for a moment?" I asked my parents as they were getting ready to leave for bed.

"Now?" my father asked.

"Yes, please." I said.

My parents looked at each other with raised eyebrows and my father sighed deeply. They turned back into the room and sat down.

"What is so important it could not wait until the morning?" my father asked.

I hesitated, realizing I had made a miscalculation. He sounded irritated - the good mood of the party erased by his desire to sleep. But I needed to know.

"Sam has invited me to go on a trip to Kapenguria with him."

My parents were silent and looked at me suspiciously, like I had spoken to them in a foreign language.

"Why would he do that?" my father asked.

I had not expected the question and had not prepared an answer.

"Well, you know, I have never been to the western part of Kenya, it is supposed to be very beautiful, and now that I have graduated it seems like the perfect opportunity to have a look around," I said.

"That is not what I asked. What I want to know is this: why does Sam want to take you anywhere?"

I am his woman.

"Are you going to answer?" my father said. "Or have we finished this discussion and I can finally get some sleep?"

"Sam and I are dating." I chose the words carefully, presenting a watered-down version of the situation, not wanting to aggravate my parents. They were as uncomfortable with my love life as I was talking about it with them.

My father slumped in his chair and closed his eyes in defeat.

He slapped his palm impatiently on the table and mumbled *mijn God* and *here we go again* and *where in hell will this idiocy take us now.*

My mother said to no one in particular, "Well, I just knew it." At least she did not look upset.

I was quiet. I looked down at my hands, fingers tightly clasped together. I waited for what would come next.

"So? What do you suggest we do about this?"

I looked up and saw my father was asking the question of my mother.

She put a hand on his arm and told him in a calm voice, "She is eighteen years old, papa. There are things she will choose for herself, no matter what you or I think."

"And you think that is a good enough reason to let her go to this wild, unknown bush place with this arrogant African?"

This arrogant African? Sam was not an arrogant African. I bit back a protest, not wanting to make my chance of success even thinner.

"I think you should let her explain." My mother spoke softly.

My father was not a man who liked to be told what to do. He was clearly surprised by this suggestion and frowned at her before turning back to me.

"You heard your mother. Speak up."

I took a deep breath. "Sam has a friend from school named Daniel. His parents have a farm in Kapenguria and they have invited us to stay with them for a few weeks."

"Do you know this Daniel?" my father moved forward with the interrogation. My mother sat back a little in her chair, letting him take charge.

"I saw him once or twice playing rugby."

"But you do not actually know him."

"Well, not really, no."

"When can we meet him?"

"He's already up at the farm."

"Who are his parents?"

"I don't know."

"How would we stay in touch with you up there?"

"The house doesn't have a phone, because it's too remote. There is a central operator in Kapenguria where callers can leave messages."

"*Mijn God,*" my father said in disgust, as if it was my fault things were so poorly organized over there. He slapped his palm on the table again. "Does this place at least have an address?"

"There's a P.O. box for mail. The farm has a name, Something Estate."

"Something Estate? Such a strange name for a farm."

"Very funny, papa."

"How do you imagine you would get there?"

"By train to Eldoret, and Daniel will pick us up there."

"By train! Is this even safe? Have you forgotten the terrible accident some years back? Those Dutch people who got killed when the train derailed and fell off a bridge in Voi on its way to Mombasa, why, it was carnage. Bloody, bloody carnage." My father had a talent to bring drama to every discussion. Always an opportunity for a story.

"We're not going to Mombasa, but in the other direction," I said.

"Well, surely that is a completely foolish argument. What does it matter in which direction the train is going? The whole rail system and those trains, one hundred years old, *all* of them are falling apart. Any idiot who lives in this country knows it." I was sure my father was exaggerating wildly, but answering back would not help my case. I kept my mouth shut.

"That's it?" he glanced at my mother, but her eyes were fixed on the wall behind me. "You are asking me to allow you to do this thing based on a complete lack of information? Do you have any idea what kind of risks you would be taking?"

I waited in silence for what was coming, not knowing how to stop it from happening.

"No. There, you have my answer. No! You will absolutely not go anywhere with that boy."

CHAPTER THIRTEEN

There was no point in arguing. Pushing the matter would only trigger an attack of yelling, as if I understood him better when his voice was loud. *Shit.* I had only managed to make my chances much worse instead of better.

"They said no," I told Sam when he phoned the next day.

"Fuck!" he growled. "I knew it. They're the same as all the other whites in this town. Sure some kind of unspeakable danger is lurking around every corner out there in darkest Africa. And they don't trust me and my black skin either."

"Sam, please," I said. "Don't be paranoid. I'm sick of people yelling at me."

It was quiet at the other end and when Sam spoke again, his voice was calmer. "OK, don't worry about it. We'll talk about this later, make a plan. Look, you want to hang out? Maybe see a movie?"

"I want to see you," I said.

"Can you come and pick me up? I'm at a friend's place in Pangani and my rubbish car has broken down."

There was always something wrong with that car of his. It was an unusual model, far too sensitive and high-strung for the rough roads of this country. Parts were practically impossible to find and the smallest thing had to be imported from Europe. Mostly the car just sat in the parking lot like a corpse, waiting for one repair after the other. No wonder the previous owner had sold it for a handful of change.

"How do I get there?" I asked.

Sam knew finding my way was not my strong suit, and took pains to explain the route to Pangani in detail, giving me directions in plain language even I could not misinterpret. In Nairobi, street signs were not always clear and houses did not have numbers. It wasn't a problem for most things. People described where they lived using landmarks like *four houses down from the purple villa on the corner*, or *past the Shell station on your left*, but for me it was one more complication when it came to getting where I wanted to go.

The last time Sam tried to tell me how to get somewhere, I got lost. I wanted to find a newly opened bookstore that, rumor had it, carried fairly new imported magazines. Sam told me I'd get there easily by driving *up* Uhuru Highway. Of course I took that to mean *uphill*. I drove countless kilometers back and forth along the full length of Uhuru, going around and around its many overcrowded roundabouts, only to discover that Uhuru was absolutely flat. No hills, no humps, and no way *up* the road. I finally gave up and went back home, exhausted and in a filthy mood from aimlessly driving around without ever finding the store. I phoned Sam in a temper to let him know exactly what I thought of him and his stupid directions. When I stopped ranting, Sam calmly explained that when he said go *up*, he meant to just continue driving. "But I don't even know which direction is forward and which is the wrong way," I had yelled at him. We laughed about it afterward, but it seemed clear that what was obvious to him was a mystery to me.

Today, though, Sam's instructions got me to my destination without any trouble. I pulled up to the blue house with the huge frangipani in the front yard, its pink flowers in full bloom – I could smell their sweetness even before I stepped out of the car. Exactly as Sam had described. I knocked on the front door and a stout lady in a sparkling green sari opened it, politely telling me Sam was indeed at her house, and she would call him. Before she could turn around, he was already there, smiling at me from the dim hallway. He said goodbye to his friend's mother. As soon as she closed the door, he pressed me close to him and slipped his hand inside my blouse, his palm cool against the hollow of my back.

"You're sweaty," he said.

"I made it, though."

"Any unplanned tours of the city?"

"Not this time."

"You will figure this thing out, gorgeous." he murmured into my hair. "Soon you and that little white car of yours will fly around every nook and cranny of this town as if you own the place."

I handed him the keys. "Enough flying for today. You take it from here."

We drove into town and turned up three floors of tight curls in the parking garage where my father had a space in the KIKS parking area. Nobody came to work in the weekends, and family members parked their cars here when they had things to do in town. It was impossible to find a spot along busy Nairobi streets on a Saturday.

Sam and I walked down the stairs to street level and turned onto the sidewalk toward the movie theater. It was thick with people walking in both directions – the theater had only one screen, and the building emptied and filled at the same time. This was a favorite spot for beggars hoping someone would drop a coin into their cups, but right now people were too busy maneuvering the crowd to pay them much attention. I recognized a man from the sidewalk near the Flame Tree. He had two short stumps for legs and was dressed in soiled rags, sitting on a square of raw wood with small office chair wheels under each corner. He rumbled along by pushing at the sidewalk with his hands as if he was rowing a boat, his wheels making a racket on the uneven pavement. Today he was closed in by the throng. I bent down and dropped a shilling into his cup.

Sam and I slowly made our way up the wide stairs to the ticket counter and stood at the end of the line. The smell of popcorn was heavy in the air and mixed unpleasantly with the cigarette smoke hovering around us like a fog. We bought tickets and Sam went to get snacks. He returned with a bag of potato chips and small boxes of chewy mints, chocolate-covered peanuts and toffees. "I wasn't sure what you wanted, so I got a little of everything to make sure you were happy, eh? Sweet and savory for my girl," he said.

I glowed at his thoughtfulness.

"Shall we?" he said, offering me his arm while he held the goodies to his chest with both hands. I slipped my hand through his arm just above the elbow and he flexed his biceps. I squeezed back softly.

We strolled into the theater through the open double doors and I took a deep breath of clean air-conditioned air. Commercials had already started and the sound system was turned up almost unbearably loud. The place was packed. I hoped we were sitting in the pair of empty seats right near the center aisle with a good view of the screen, but Sam inclined his head and led me up the stairs to the back row. We barely had time to fall into our chairs before the lights dimmed and an image of the Kenyan flag fluttered on the screen. The national anthem boomed through the speakers. We stood up. A pair of middle-aged white ladies sitting a few rows in front of us looked around in confusion, visibly wondering whether they were supposed to stand up like the rest of us. They were new, probably. Those of us who had lived here longer were all too familiar with the story that anyone who remained seated while the anthem played would be dragged off by the police for disrespecting the flag. Not that we knew anyone this had actually happened to.

The lights dimmed and the curtains squeaked open to wide screen. People stopped talking and crunched their popcorn a little more delicately. The movie started. Sam leaned toward me and I cuddled into his side.

I took in the opening scenes and it looked like this was going to be a good movie. Also that I would have a hard time keeping my attention on the screen. Sam put his hand on my thigh halfway between my knee and hip and I stole a glace at him, but he kept his eyes facing forward. He stroked my leg and slid his fingers along the inside of my jeans, slipping higher up my leg with each back and forth motion. I wondered if the people around us could see what was going on. When I got too prickly to sit still any longer, I pounced and threaded my fingers through his wandering hand, clamping it down firmly against my leg and forcing him to stop. I covered his mouth with mine. Sam's lips were warm and moist and his tongue slipped softly along mine. I eased into the tenderness of his kiss and he caught me off-guard when he wrapped his arms tightly around me and pressed his lips so fiercely against mine that our teeth clinked and I caught the tip of my tongue on his chipped front tooth. I flinched. Sam released me and peered at me in the dark.

"I'm OK," I whispered.

I pressed my tongue against the roof of my mouth, tasting blood. The stab of pain subsided, and I settled back into my chair with Sam's arm slung around me. I leaned my head against his shoulder, ignoring the armrest barrier between us, and closed my eyes. It was too late to figure out what was going on in this movie. Not that I cared, really.

It was dark outside when we left the theater. Nairobi's daytime rush had simmered down and we strolled easily back to the car.

"What did you think? Of the flick?" Sam asked.

"I have no idea. Someone kept distracting me with some action of his own." I laughed softly, picturing us wrestling soundlessly in the dark.

"So was it, I mean, did you... have a good time?"

"The best. Absolutely." And I meant it, too.

By the time we arrived at the parking garage, it was deserted. The sound of our footsteps echoed from the walls as we climbed the cement stairwell. Most of the ceiling lights were broken and those that worked shone in blotchy patches, only lifting the gloom here and there. The VW stood alone, parked in the middle of the floor. I took the key out of my purse and settled behind the steering wheel, but when I tried to start the engine, Sam leaned over and covered my hand. I glanced at him and had no trouble imagining what was going through his mind.

I was right. Sam turned to me with a sparkle in his eye. He leaned forward and ran his fingers through my hair, cupped the back of my head and drew my face to his. We kissed, a little more gently, more carefully, this time. His hands resumed their wandering and slipped inside the front of my blouse. He caressed my breasts and tried to slide his hands into my bra, but didn't have enough maneuvering room in the small car. He fumbled with the buttons on the front of my blouse, all the while keeping his lips attached to mine. When his attempts had gone on long enough to bring me close to a fit of giggles, I drew my lips away from his and pulled back. I leaned against the car door, pulled up my leg and sat sideways, facing him, slowly undoing one button after the other until the two halves of my blouse fell open. Sam reached behind my back to unclasp my bra.

Just as it snapped loose, a bright light beamed through the windshield. Instinctively, I crossed my arms over my breasts and doubled over, hiding my face as much as my body.

"Fuck!" Sam shouted. He threw open the car door, stepped out and slammed it shut behind him. I heard him ranting in Swahili and a man's voice answering calmly. The flashlight moved away and no longer flooded the car with light. I quickly fastened my bra and closed the buttons of my blouse, my heart racing.

It took a long time for Sam to get back in the car, and when he finally fell into the passenger seat, his jaw was clenched and his face crumpled with rage. I saw a man in uniform step away from the car backwards, keeping us in his line of vision.

"Drive," Sam said.

I started the engine and drove down the spiral ramp in high gear, wanting to get away from this situation, whatever it was, as quickly as I could. I eased off the accelerator when we were back on the street.

"What happened? Who was that man?" I asked.

"That," Sam growled, "was a man who saw a business opportunity."

"What?"

Sam snorted in disgust. "An askari who happened to be doing his rounds and suddenly saw this African dude snogging this white chick, which could mean only one thing in his peasant mind, namely that there must be rape happening. Why else would Goldilocks be locking lips with the black likes of me, right? Which of course meant there was money to be made. Can you fucking believe it?"

I was horrified. Would this man find out my name somehow? Would he be back to blackmail me, or even worse, find my father in his office and approach him for more money? *Oh, please not that.* The story would go from mouth to mouth around the whole expat community in a flash, and everybody would know about me and my bare boobs. I groaned.

"Don't worry, I took care of it. The man is corrupt; all he wanted was money. He will not step to any authority now he has taken my bribe - he'd be fired on the spot. What is it we are going to be accused of, anyway? We weren't doing anything illegal. Besides, I took his name from his badge for insurance purposes, just in case he turns out to be even stupider than he looks."

I hoped Sam was right. We stopped at the motel and he got out of the car. I gave him a quick peck, but was not in the mood for anything more lingering and kept the engine running. Sam leaned in the window and said firmly, "It's all right. It's over, I swear."

I shrugged my shoulders, wanting to believe him, but not feeling so sure.

"And another thing I'll be taking care of," Sam said. "I'm stopping by your house tomorrow to talk to your father about taking you to Kapenguria."

CHAPTER FOURTEEN

Minutes ticked by painfully slowly, but I couldn't keep my eyes off the cuckoo clock on the mantelpiece. Sam was due to arrive any moment and he had made me swear not to warn my father. I did not have a good feeling about this. I wished I had told Sam not to come, that I would talk to my father again myself when I was sure the time was right. If their last encounter was anything to go by, tonight's discussion would not end well for any of us.

My parents were oblivious to my jitteriness. My father sat in his spot-lit reading chair and my mother across from him with her knitting, like they did every evening. They sipped their coffees and chatted about things that had happened in the course of the day.

"The askari from the parking garage at work got fired today," my father said.

"Really? Why is that?" my mother asked.

"It appears he has been blackmailing people, accepting bribes."

My heart pounded like a drum. I was about to be exposed.

"Why would anyone pay him a bribe?" my mother asked.

My father didn't answer immediately, as if he were mulling the matter over in his mind. "This is not entirely clear. It would appear people used the garage at night for all manner of so-called illegal activities. And the askari, rather than reporting to the authorities, extorted money from the perpetrators, which he

112

proceeded to slip into his own pocket."

I stopped breathing.

"We had quite an interesting episode this morning," he said. "A furious man stood in our office, banging his fists on the receptionist's desk and raging about how this particular askari wanted to collect one hundred shillings from him because he had not parked cleanly between the lines. Quite a creative way to cheat someone out of their money, I must say. *AHA aha ha ha ha.*"

This was not about me. If it had been, there would be no laughter in this house today or for many days to come. I exhaled with relief.

"On the other hand," my father continued. "When you listen to his story, you can't really blame the askari for overstepping his bounds. He has not received his salary from the security firm for months. With rent to pay and food to put on the table - what is the alternative?" He shrugged. "So now he has nothing. No job, no income, and nobody to blackmail. Undoubtedly he had not envisioned the potential consequences of his little scam."

A car stopped at the gate and I heard Mwaura open it. Sam had arrived.

"Are we expecting company?" my father asked with his eyebrows raised.

"Not that I know of," my mother answered.

They turned to me. I heard brakes squeal as the car stopped at the end of the driveway. He must have borrowed Rashid's car.

"I think it might be Sam," I said.

"*Verdomme,*" my father cursed. "Is it too much to ask for a little peace and quiet in my own home after a long day's work?"

I left the room quickly. Sam's knuckles rapped on the front door as I reached for the knob. I pulled open the door, and he stood beneath the porch light, wearing his black school uniform pants and an ironed white shirt, one button open at the neck. I was relieved and anxious at the sight of him.

"May I come in?" Sam asked, his deep voice steady.

I nodded. He stepped into the hallway and kissed me lightly. He smelled of soap and minty toothpaste.

Sam strode into the living room and I followed in his wake. He walked to my mother and shook her hand, then swiveled to face my father and held out his hand. My father hesitated just an instant, then gripped Sam's hand firmly.

"Would it be convenient to discuss a few matters?" Sam asked.

My father looked taken aback by the directness of this request. I saw there was really no other way for him to respond but agree to talk, and he stood up and led the way to the dining room. He switched on the mushroom lamp over the table and pink light glowed through the plastic cover. Mood lighting, my mother liked to call it: just enough to highlight our best features but not enough to emphasize our imperfections. Maybe it would work its magic on this discussion. My father took a seat at the long side of the table, and Sam sat down across from him. My mother shifted the cat from her lap and headed for the kitchen, murmuring something about brewing a fresh pot of coffee. I hesitated where I stood, in the middle of the living room, feeling a strong urge to follow my mother to the kitchen. Sam turned around and pulled back the chair next to his. I sighed, walked over and sat down.

"So, what is this all about? Speak up," my father said to Sam.

"I would like to take Sara to visit a friend of mine in Kapenguria," Sam said.

"You would, would you? Well, I believe I have already made myself perfectly clear regarding this matter in an earlier conversation with my daughter."

"Yes, she has told me about your hesitation."

I glanced at Sam. Hesitation? That was putting it mildly. My father had roared *no* so loudly my eardrums practically split.

Sam continued. "I understand you are worried about the safety of the trains but I can assure you there is no cause. The railway system to the west is excellently maintained and there has been no accident in living memory. Of course we would travel in a first class compartment. I would not leave Sara's side for an instant to guarantee her safety."

Silence greeted this remark. I kept my eyes fixed on my lap.

"You would not leave her side for an instance? Am I to take this to mean you will be on guard duty by her side both day and *night*?" my father said. I thought I heard a twinkle of amusement in his voice.

Sam corrected himself hastily. "I treat Sara with the utmost respect, always, this speaks for itself."

My mother breezed in with a tray of coffee, already poured into cups. Sam rose and took it from her so she had her hands free to serve us. She beamed at him and thanked him with a nod. She spoke cheerily: "Sugar? Cream? No, I know you drink your coffee black, papa, but Sam might have different tastes. And our daughter sometimes takes a little cream, don't you, Sara?"

The mood eased as we stirred our coffee and helped ourselves to butter cookies - homemade, not from the KIKS tin. My mother sat down next to my father, keeping her focus on making sure we had plenty to eat and drink. She didn't much like confrontations, either. Like mother, like daughter.

When my father spoke again, he sounded less hostile. Sam's manners might have impressed him. I'd often heard him complain about how Dutch kids these days were rude, unmannered scum, dressed in unwashed rags - Sam compared favorably in that department, at least. "So what about this farm... where is the place?"

"Kapenguria," Sam said. "Perhaps you have heard of it?"

My father thought for a moment. "It has a familiar ring to it."

"You may remember it from recent history. It is where President Jomo Kenyatta was arrested for encouraging the Mau Mau uprising against British colonialism. He was imprisoned for seven years and released only when independence was gained."

"Yes, Kapenguria. I remember it now."

"Of course, these days it is just a peaceful small town in the countryside. Agriculture, mostly. My friend Daniel's parents settled there and bought a dairy farm. They grow feed corn, also. Very successful."

"You have seen this farm?"

"I have been there several times. Mrs. Murgor tells me I am always welcome, and to stay as long as I like."

"You are in fact so very welcome that you can now bring your own guest."

Sam smiled. "I have told them much about Sara, and the Murgor family is eager to meet her."

"I will consider it," my father said.

Sam nodded, not pressing the issue.

It took a few days, but finally my father gave his permission, albeit grudgingly. "Go, then," he said. "Go if you must with this Sam."

"Thank you, papa," I said, hugging him tight.

"Yes, yes, now suddenly I am the popular one," he complained.

"But, Sara," he said, sounding serious, "You must take very good care of yourself. Do not take any risks. And behave yourself like the well-brought up young lady you are."

"Of course, papa. I always do."

Sam and I were on our way to Kapenguria. My mother had dropped us off at Nairobi Railway Station and kissed my cheeks, shook Sam's hand, told us to be careful, and drove away. We were alone. A flutter tickled my stomach, and I stopped a moment to soak in the astonishing fact that Sam and I were going on this safari together.

"Are you ready?" Sam asked.

"I am very ready," I answered.

Sam picked up our bags and started crossing the parking lot toward the entrance. We were early - it was 5:30 pm and the train to Eldoret wasn't scheduled to leave for another hour, but it only traveled this route three times a week and we didn't want to risk getting left behind.

The station had walls made of brown brick and a red tile roof that came up in points – it looked like a dozen small houses stuck together. We walked through the spacious main hall. One lady sat behind the ticket counter facing a long line of waiting customers while the other four positions behind the glass were unmanned. Sam had picked up our tickets earlier, and we walked straight through. I looked around the platform and admired the station, surprised at how large it was, and how spotless. A gaunt, ancient man was sweeping the floor with small swishing movements, pushing the rubbish he collected over the edge of the platform where it fell next to the rails. The bristles of his broom were thin and bent, as if he had been using it to sweep for one hundred years. Not even a plastic grocery bag or an orange peel cluttered the floor.

A green locomotive with a long row of carriages was waiting alongside the platform. I smelled diesel as we got closer and wrinkled my nose, and hoped our compartment would be farther from the engine. We wandered along the length of the train and checked our tickets against the big numbers painted on the side. Sam had booked us a sleeper for two so we would have privacy. "Look," I said, pointing at a small white card in a metal bracket on the side of the train, "it has our names written on it."

"Imagine that," Sam said. "It actually does. Very posh."

We climbed up the black metal steps and turned left. The corridor was little more than a meter wide and we walked single-file, bumping our luggage behind us. Sam pushed open the wooden sliding door to our compartment. We dropped our bags and looked around, admiring our tiny hotel room on wheels. Across from the door, a window was pulled halfway down let in

117

the cool evening breeze. Two narrow bunks were attached to the right side wall. The top bunk was folded up flat and the bottom one down so that it was a place to sit, like a sofa. I turned to the other wall and saw myself reflected in a cloudy oval mirror, too small to capture my whole face, with beneath it a miniature sink with rust stains around the drain. The paper had been removed from the tiny soap, and it looked like it might already have been used. The glory days of this train were in the distant past, that much was clear, but the compartment was all ours and I couldn't have wished for anything more.

I kneeled on the bottom bunk. It was covered in cream leather-like material, worn through and torn in places with the stuffing showing. I leaned my head through the window to watch the bustle on the platform. Passengers walked around with their tickets in hand, comparing them to carriage numbers and saying goodbye to family and friends. Baggage handlers pushed their carts along the platform and called out for people to hire them. *Totos*, young children, scuttled around with arms full of the hard, small green oranges that grew on trees alongside the roads, trying to make a sale. I cocked my head when I heard music, and it took me a moment to realize it was coming from behind me, from inside the compartment. George Benson sang *that's the time I feel like making love to you* and Sam was crooning along with him.

"Stop," I said, laughing. "How obvious are you going to get?"

Sam grinned and said, "Just trying to set the mood. Look, I brought a tape deck and a box of tapes."

"You are wonderful. Did you bring *Rumours*? You know, Fleetwood Mac?"

"No, of course not. Do you think I forgot how you and Leander never stopped playing that album? It still makes me want to tear my ears off." He glared at me, "I do not want thoughts of him intruding on us tonight."

Sore spot still, I guess.

We settled down to wait for the train to leave. The sky

darkened. Ninety minutes later, the train lurched forward and we were on our way. It picked up a little speed as it moved forward, though it crept along flat stretches and slowed to a creaking, shuddering crawl when it had to fight its way up even the slightest hill. The train stopped at every station along the way. Sometimes they were so close together that we had barely started rolling before the brakes screeched us to a halt again. Most were no larger than a bus stop in what appeared to be the middle of nowhere.

We turned our heads in surprise when we heard two loud knocks on our door. Sam called out *yes?* and a man wearing a Kenya Railways uniform opened the door. He stepped inside and said, "Jambo. I have arrived with the bedding." He held a pile of white sheets, blankets and pillows in his arms.

"OK, thank you," Sam said.

The man insisted, "I am here to make the bed."

"What... now? So early in the evening? Never mind, thanks, just leave the things here," Sam indicated the far end of the bunk. "We'll take care of it ourselves."

"No, sir, I must make up the bed."

We looked at him blankly, not sure what to make of his persistence.

"It is not an easy thing to make up that bunk up there," he said.

Probably he had a point, and we agreed he would make up the top bunk and leave us to do the lower one later, so we could use it as a sofa until we were ready to go to sleep. We squeezed past him into the corridor to give him enough room to perform his duties. A few minutes later he came out, and we went back in. The top bunk was neatly made, the bedding held in place with wide black rubber straps and pushed up against the wall so we could still sit beneath it without bumping our heads.

There was another knock on the door. A different man wearing the same uniform opened the door and said, "Jambo. Do you want soup?" He held a pencil poised over a clipboard.

It was my turn to ask, "What... now?" I wondered if he was going to insist I take a bowl on the spot.

"Hang on, let me take care of this," Sam said. He took the sheet of paper and pencil from the man and explained, "This is the dinner menu. We mark our choices here, see, and when it is time to eat, our food will be ready in the dining car. So, do you want tomato or mulligatawny soup? Chicken or beef curry? Pudding, yes or no?"

We made our selections and Sam handed the menu back to the man, who said, "Dinner is served in half an hour" and left.

"Wow," I said to Sam. "This is a luxurious train. Menus and everything."

"Yes. I know what I'm doing when I take daddy's princess on a trip."

I ignored his teasing, not planning to let him get under my skin today. Instead, I snuggled closer. Sam leaned into the corner and wrapped both arms around me, drawing me close against his chest, rubbing his cheek against my hair. I listened to the beating of his heart. "You smell good," he mumbled. "Like fruit. Sweet fruit." I turned to look at his face, and he kissed me. His lips crushed mine and stayed there, and he held me tight. But I wasn't going anywhere.

"Hey," I said, pulling away gently. "What's this?"

He didn't speak, but took my hand and held it in his own with our fingers looped. I saw what he saw. Ours were undeniably as different as two colors of skin could get.

"Cool, right?" I said, loving the way my slender light hand looked caught in his dark powerful one.

"Yes." Sam leaned over and kissed my forehead, as if I was a child.

Boom-boom-boom sounded vaguely from outside our compartment. "Well. It seems the stomach is going to win from the heart," Sam said and smiled at me. "That's the dinner gong.

Let's eat."

We made our way along the dim corridor to the restaurant car in the back of the train, diving into empty compartments or retracing our steps to let other passengers pass when we encountered them. The passage was not wide enough for two-way traffic. I was relieved when we reached the restaurant car, especially after the run-in with a short, sturdy man who refused to move either forward or backward and obliged me to slither around him with an uncomfortable amount of full body contact.

I entered the restaurant and felt as if I had stepped into the past. Rows of tables with booth seats on either side stood beneath the windows. A waiter wearing a starched white smock and matching trousers showed us to our table. We sat across from two men dressed in dark suits and ties who looked like they were at a business meeting rather than a restaurant. They spoke rapid Swahili, and did not acknowledge our presence.

The table was covered with a stiff white damask tablecloth and our places set with polished silverware and sparkling china. I picked up the knife and was surprised at how heavy it was. The plates were stamped with the golden crest of the old colonial East African Railway Corporation.

When I looked closer, I saw the tablecloth was worn and frayed along the edges, and dotted with shadows of ancient stains. The sturdy china was chipped and silverware dinged and mismatched. These trains had been running for a very long time. We were sitting in the very same seats, and probably eating from the same dishes, as elegant British folk at the turn of the century. Maybe Karen Blixen herself once rode this train while she looked out on the land she loved and prayed she'd live here forever. It was a glimpse of times gone by. Just a dozen or so years ago, Sam and I would not have been able to share a meal like this, never mind a first class compartment - and definitely not a bed.

A sliver of moon kept pace with us outside in the dark night.

The rhythm of the train chugging along the tracks soothed me like a ballad. Sam hooked his foot around mine and drew my thigh alongside his. We took our time eating and sipping our beers, talking long after every other guest had disappeared. The waiters lounged around looking bored, waiting for us to leave.

When our glasses were empty, Sam leaned over and said, "Shall we?"

I nodded. I felt pampered and content, my cheeks flushed from beer and hot curry.

We made our way back to our compartment carefully along the barely lit corridor. In the wider space between two carriages, we stopped for a cigarette and sat down on the blue canvas laundry bags stacked against the wall. We exhaled with heads tipped back to let the open window suck the smoke outside. Sam snuffed his cigarette, threw the butt out the window, and said, "Hang on for just a couple of minutes, OK? Here, have another smoke."

"Why, where are you going?"

Sam grinned at me. "Won't be long. It'll be worth the wait, trust me."

I might as well just sit there and smoke a second cigarette, like he asked – I didn't want to spoil whatever surprise he was cooking up. A waiter walked by and shot me a surprised look. Was I even supposed to be sitting on these laundry bags? Smoking? Probably not. I took another quick drag, snuffed the cigarette under the heel of my sneaker and chucked it out the window. I walked slowly to give Sam time to finish whatever he was up to.

I knocked softly on the door. Sam let me in and locked it firmly behind me. I blinked while my eyes adjusted to the dusky compartment. The ceiling lamp was switched off. A flicker of yellow light glowed from a candle stuck to a saucer by its own molten wax. The window shade was pulled down, and so was the top bunk, its clean sheets and blanket smooth, the black

122

straps removed. Barry White moaned from the cassette player: *Oooooh, can't get enough of your love, babe.*

Sam had thought of everything. He opened his arms and I stepped into his embrace. We danced slow circles in the cramped space between the sink and the bunk, the window and the door, fading almost to a stop, our bodies attached, swaying gently to the music. Sam caught my waist. He slid his hands into the pockets of my jeans and pulled me tightly to him. When he loosened his grip, I leaned back slightly so I could see his face. His eyes were soft, his full lips curved into an undecided smile. He looked happy and vulnerable at the same time. I stroked the side of his face, his skin dark next to the paleness of my hand. I brought my lips to his, touched my tongue to his, careful not to hurt myself on his chipped front tooth.

Sam pulled his shirt over his head and dropped it to the floor. He pulled off my t-shirt. He unhooked my bra and I curved my shoulders forward to let the straps slide down my arms. He stood back quietly, his eyes exploring, and I pulled in my stomach slightly. I reached up and ran my hands along his tight shoulders, his arms, feeling the sleekness of his skin, almost hairless. I pulled him against me, skin cool against skin.

The song ended. We stepped apart and climbed up the short ladder to the top bunk bed, Sam first. I giggled at our clumsy half-naked acrobatics. Sam stretched out and I crawled slowly from the foot of the bed to join him between the sheets, wedged between the ceiling, the wall and his body. This bunk was not made for two. We maneuvered until we lay on our sides facing each other and our heads shared the pillow.

I kissed him. Sam pushed his arm under mine and folded it across my back, his hand clenching the top of my shoulder, holding me steady. His free hand stroked my breast and I felt my nipples harden. I looked into his face, but his eyes were closed. I wondered what he was thinking, what he was feeling.

His hand moved smoothly down the side of my ribs and the

curve of my waist and reached my hip. He tucked his fingers inside the waistband of my jeans and searched for the button, and when he reached it, pushed it through the buttonhole. I felt my jeans loosen. His fingers found the tab of the zipper and pulled it down forcefully. I sucked in my breath, startled, and Sam stopped.

"Are you OK?" he said, his voice soft.

I tried to decide if I was. "I don't know," I said.

I hesitated. Sam waited.

I whispered, "I thought I was ready. Now suddenly I'm not sure."

"*Ahhhh, shit.*" Sam sighed deeply.

The train rattled on, Barry White sang his songs, but the compartment was silent. We did not move, and my breathing slowed to normal.

"I'm sorry," I said.

"No. There is no reason for sorry. There will be another time, another place, and then you will be ready." He spoke firmly.

He rolled me over until I faced the wall. He fit his body along the shape of mine until we both had an equal share of the narrow bunk, and removed his hand from my arm. I felt his body, but he was not holding me. I listened to the tape until it ended and the cassette deck switched off with a clack. Sam was asleep.

CHAPTER FIFTEEN

The next morning I waited for Sam to wake up, but after a while I could no longer ignore my need to use the toilet. I pulled away from him, untangled myself from the blanket and sheet, and crawled clumsily over his legs to the ladder at the foot of the bunk. I bent my arms and legs deep and tried not to hit my head on the ceiling.

Sam stirred and mumbled, "Where you going?"

"*Shhh,* don't wake up. I need to use the *choo.*"

Sam grunted. He dangled his arm overboard to point at his bag, "There's a roll of paper in there."

"Thanks."

I took the roll from his bag, retrieved my bra and t-shirt from the floor and pulled them on quickly. The restroom was down the hallway and I carefully pushed open the door, not wanting to risk barging in on someone else. The tiny cubicle was empty. I felt around for a light switch inside and outside, but couldn't find one. Finally, I opened the door wide so I could look inside by the light of the corridor windows. A squat toilet. The hole in the bottom opened to the tracks flashing below. A puddle covered most of the floor; hopefully it was overflow from the sink, though judging by the stench of urine all around, I doubted it. I sighed and stepped inside, locking the door behind me. We had hours of traveling ahead and I was not going to last until I reached a proper bathroom at the farm.

I opened the door of our compartment with my elbow, walked quickly over to the sink, and washed my hands with a lot of soap. The water was icy cold. I took off my t-shirt and cupped some in my hands in an attempt to wash more thoroughly. I tried to soap my armpits but the water splattered everywhere except where I wanted it, freezing streams running down the length of my torso and soaking into the waistband of my jeans.

"Chilly, is it?" Sam mumbled, watching me hop around through half-lidded eyes.

"Yes."

"Mornings are always cold up here. We climbed half a kilometer while we slept. It'll warm up when the sun breaks through."

I dug into my bag and grabbed a thick knitted sweater; I ignored the scratchiness of wool against my skin, feeling grateful for its warmth.

"Pull up the shade, will you? Let's see what's going on out there in the highlands."

I pulled up the shade. The landscape had changed overnight. Gone was the dry flatness of Nairobi; here the land was hilly and green. I scanned the horizon for wildlife, maybe some giraffe or zebra, but didn't see any movement. The way this train was wheezing and groaning its way uphill, it was no wonder the animals kept their distance.

"Sam."

I walked up to the bunk where he was cocooned tightly in the blanket. I stood against the bed with my face close to his.

"Sam."

He opened his eyes.

"About last night."

His eyes stayed open, but he didn't react. He was going to listen to what I had to say, but he wasn't going to make this easy for me.

"I don't want you to get the wrong idea. I don't want you to think I'm, you know, not attracted to you. Or that I'm toying with you."

Silence.

"I just, I got nervous and suddenly wasn't sure I was ready right then. It is a big step."

He didn't acknowledge what I said.

"What are you thinking?" I finally asked.

Sam rolled onto his back and faced the ceiling. He laced his fingers behind his head and dropped his elbows on the pillow.

"I am thinking about the future."

"What do you mean?"

"Are you willing to spend your life in Africa? Without the expat benefits, I mean."

"Kenya is my home now. I don't ever want to leave."

Sam glanced at me sideways, his lips pursed in a smirk.

"This is the only place I feel like I belong," I said, trying to make him believe me.

"I am just trying to discover exactly how you see this thing we have going on. If you expect a future for us. Or if being with me is just an entertaining way to spend some time, but nothing major. Nothing you are willing to commit to," Sam said.

"I am committed to you. I do see a future for us."

"You slept with Leander."

I hesitated. Then I told him the truth.

"Yes," I said.

Sam was quiet for a long time, and I waited tensely for what he was going to say.

He spoke quietly, still not looking at me. "Why him and not me?"

I wished I could explain it in a way that would not be hurtful. I wished I understood it myself. I hadn't thought things through with Leander – I was insanely in love and thought he felt the same way. I had been blind.

"It was a mistake," I said.

Sam turned his head to look at me. Tears pricked like hot peppers in my eyes. Sam climbed out of bed, wrapped the sheet

127

around his middle and took me in his arms. He rocked me gently from side to side.

"I don't ever want you to say that about me," he said.

The rest of the trip passed easily. We ate a breakfast of fried eggs, sausage, grilled tomatoes, and coffee. We hopped out of the train at one of the larger stations to stretch our legs and Sam called out his familiar *hang on* and disappeared into the crowd. By now I understood this meant he would be back whenever he finished what he had set his mind on doing. I worried he would miss the train, but he returned just as the conductor was blowing his whistle, with his arms full of loaves of sliced white bread. It seemed there was a shortage where we were heading.

The train pulled into Eldoret station. Sam took my hand and we stepped onto the narrow platform, and Daniel was there to pick us up, as promised. The boys grinned and shook hands and I stood to the side, taking the opportunity to give Daniel a quick once-over. He was African, but his skin was light: mocha-colored, or cinnamon. His nose was narrow. His lips were slender and pretty like a girl's and when he smiled, he displayed two rows of perfect white teeth. Sam introduced us, and we made our way to a battered pickup truck. We lifted our bags over the side and dropped them onto the bed next to three tall, shiny milk cans that stood lined up against the back. I climbed into the middle of the cab and leaned my legs to the left so Daniel had room to handle the long gearshift that came up straight from the floor. Daniel and Sam talked about friends from school, bantering back and forth over my head. They joked about the Irish priests who taught class in their long woolen robes, their red faces bloated and sticky with sweat and how they always looked so out of place, no matter how many years they lived in this country.

The drive from Eldoret to Kapenguria was sixty-five kilometers, and we made good time. The asphalt was in reasonable condition, though Daniel kept his eyes stuck to the road in front of us. Some of the potholes were deep enough to force him to sweep around them - luckily there wasn't much traffic in either direction. We drove away from town and were soon flanked by farmland, long fields planted mostly with maize. Small herds of cows and goats grazed alongside the road, each animal tethered to a stump of wood by a rope that looped around its back leg. We turned onto a dirt road. Daniel put the pickup into first gear and we hobbled along slowly, bouncing wildly in our seats at a speed barely faster than walking.

"Luckily it's been dry for a few days. It's a real pain to get through this stuff when it rains," Daniel said. "Black cotton soil. Like glue when it mixes with water. You have to keep the car moving. If you stall, you're stuck." The earth was baked solid now.

I was a little disappointed to find the farmhouse looked pretty much like any of the older homes around Nairobi. No thatched roof or black wooden beams crisscrossing the walls. No clouds of rose bushes creeping up white trellises. No flock of chickens clucking around, scratching for bugs. Apparently I'd been looking forward to the storybook version of farming. Still, I liked what I saw. Cement-floored patios were attached to either side of the house – Daniel explained that when one was in the sun, the other was in the shade, so there was always a comfortable place to sit. Green lawns the size of rugby pitches rolled out on all sides, merging into maize fields that stretched to the horizon. The crop stood tall and ripe with golden tassels rising up like crowns, nodding in the breeze.

We went inside and Daniel took us on a quick tour of the house. The front door opened right into a spacious living room, furnished with a mishmash of fat furniture and low tables. The kitchen was a large square room with walls of whitewashed brick. For one this size, the place was quite bare; there were few cabinets and even fewer appliances. An oblong sink in the middle of the counter looked large enough to wash a small farm animal in. An ancient white stove with a two square doors in the front stood against the wall. I thought it was a cupboard until I noticed the burners on top. After Daniel concluded the tour with the bedroom that Sam and I would share, he said, "Come and meet my mum."

We went outside. A woman stepped from the path that ran straight as a ruler between the fields and walked steadily toward us across the grass. She was white. This explained the soft color of Daniel's skin and his thin nose: he was *nusu-nusu*. Half-half. Her light blue dress was patterned with small yellow flowers and it looked faded, as if it had been washed many times and dried in the sun. It had a flat collar and buttons down the front, a slim belt around the waist, and a wide skirt. On her feet she wore green rubber boots that reached up to her knees. She came closer and I saw her brown hair was set in a style that hadn't been fashionable for many years: parted on the side with big curls flipping up from her shoulders. Her arms were strong in the sleeveless dress.

She smiled shyly, and spoke in a mild voice, "Hello. Nice to meet you, Sara. Wonderful to have you back, Sam."

"It's good to be back, Mrs. Murgor. Thank you for having us," Sam spoke for us both.

I shook her hand, her grip not as firm as I had expected.

Daniel said, "My little sister is probably running around somewhere, I'm sure we'll bump into her soon enough. I'll show you around the grounds first."

The sun was past its peak and shadows were lengthening. We walked along a dirt path wide enough for farm equipment. Here the view into the distance wasn't blocked by maize plants, and we could see just how much land there was. It was impossible to tell where the fields ended. A pair of galloping yellow dogs ran by us and suddenly braked almost to a stop, then adjusted their pace to ours and loped easily alongside us. Nobody paid them any attention and they didn't expect any - they walked in the same direction as we were as though it was just a coincidence.

130

Daniel said, "Do you know how to ride?"

"Ride what?" Sam said.

"A horse."

"A horse? Me?" Sam laughed. "Look at me, *bwana*. Do I look like the kind of person who would have a horse at their disposal to ride around on?"

"How about you, Sara?"

"No, actually. I've never even seen one from up close before. I really am a clueless city girl."

We continued down the road and gradually approached a long rectangular building made from rough dark wooden boards. Daniel went inside first and we followed; the dogs stayed outdoors and settled against the wall, in the shade of the building. It was a stable. The air inside was stuffy and smelled of hay and damp. Most of the boxes were empty, but at the far end, two horses' heads stuck into the wide passageway. They kept an eye on us without turning to face us. The far one was silvery black. He threw his nose into the air and harrumphed angrily, stomping his foot. The nearer brown horse was smaller, but once we reached her I was surprised to find how huge she was, too. Daniel stroked her nose and scratched behind her ears; she seemed to like that. At least she didn't stomp her feet.

"Hello, there, beautiful. Such a good horse you are," Daniel crooned. To us he said, "Don't get too close to Midnight over there. He doesn't take kindly to amateurs. If he senses you don't know what you're doing, he'll take a hoof to your leg, given half a chance."

Daniel opened the box door and stepped inside with the brown horse, putting a saddle on her back and various straps and things on her head. Finally, when everything was in place, he led her out. She followed meekly like a pet on a leash.

"Who wants to ride first?"

I looked at Sam. I didn't want to be rude, but I was really not feeling very enthusiastic about this plan. Sam didn't look much happier than I did.

"Come on, you two sad urban dwellers. Here, let me show you how it's done. You just stick your foot in the stirrup like this and, *hup!*" Daniel swung into the saddle. He pushed his heels into the horse's belly, gave her a noisy smack on the rump with the flat of his hand, and off she went. Not in a hurry. "This one never breaks a sweat if she can help it," Daniel said, grinning down at us.

We walked along the road like a parade, with a horse and dogs and two guys and me. I felt the quiet in the air around me and the space that went on forever - we were going to have a good time here.

After a while, Daniel stopped and hopped down from the horse. It was Sam's turn. Clearly Daniel had made things look easier than they were, and it took Sam several attempts to claw himself upright in the saddle. Once he was sitting firmly, he pulled his back up straight and instantly looked the part of a rider. But nothing he did or said got the horse moving. Finally Daniel smacked her rump again and she put one foot in front of the other, ambling along the path. Sam relaxed a little and glanced down at me with a grin, "Pay attention, now. Watch closely to see how it's done."

I rolled my eyes at him but he had already returned his gaze back to the path in front of him. I heard him mutter *fuck!* as the horse lurched forward for a few fast steps, then took an abrupt turn to the right, apparently deciding it was time to stop for a snack. Her head drooped to nibble on some tall grass. Sam took this to be the perfect moment to pass the reigns to me.

I had watched Sam's struggles to land in the saddle and tried to do a better job of it, but I made even more of a hash of it than he had. By the time I finally found my seat and pushed my feet into the stirrups, the horse decided enough was enough. She felt my weight land on her back and stopped eating, threw up her head, turned around, and trotted back to where we'd just come from. I had no idea what to do. I tried to sit up straight like the boys, but could not adjust to the strange rhythms of the horse. I bounced up and down like a rubber ball on a string. Racing to my downfall with glasses jiggling off my nose suddenly seemed like such a ludicrous way to go that I dissolved into weak giggles. The boys ran after me, yelling things, and then I left them behind altogether. The last thing I heard was Daniel shout: *duck when you reach the stables!* and I was on my own. *Duck?* Was he joking? It was all I could do to hang on to the saddle and not end up a pile of broken bones on the ground. I giggled some more. The horse was indeed heading for the stables, and once home was in sight, she slowed to a walk and I stopped bouncing. I ducked easily as she entered through the door. She strolled into her box and stuck her nose into the trough. I slid from her back and sprawled onto the straw beside her, and lay there trying to regain my senses.

It took minutes for the guys to arrive. I was fine, except maybe for the insides of my thighs which felt like they had been worked over with an electric sander - I wondered what I would find when I peeled off my jeans tonight. Daniel tore around the corner first, yelling "Sara?"

"I'm here!" I called, and stood up gingerly.

"Are you alright?" He stepped close to me, looking me over to make sure I was still whole. He looked concerned.

"Yes, I'm OK. I think."

"You scared me shitless when you took off like that."

"Me, too, let me tell you."

Sam jogged into the stable and slowed to a stop when he saw me. He doubled over and rested his hands on his knees. "*Wah!* Am I ever out of shape. When the hell did this sneak up on me?" he said, waiting for his heaving breath to quiet down. He raised his head. "Sara, damn! Do you like having men chase after you? Is that why you took off on the horse like you had another train to catch today?" He laughed.

"Very funny, Sam."

"Don't look at me angry, woman, I'm only kidding. From where I was standing, you looked like you knew exactly what you were doing. How did you manage to get that animal to go back to the stable?"

"Are you joking? I had absolutely no idea what I was doing. The horse decided to go back to the stable all by itself, which is lucky for me, otherwise I might be bouncing around in the saddle until we carried on clear into Uganda or wherever the hell else it felt like heading off to."

I glared at him, hardly believing he was being such an asshole.

"Relax," Sam said. "Nothing happened in the end, did it?"

Sam reached out to put his arm around my shoulder, but I shrugged him off and shot up my hands to stop him from getting closer. He knew how much I hated to be told to relax when I was pissed off.

"Well." Daniel said. "Enough adventure on the farm for one day, I think. You two up for a beer?"

CHAPTER SIXTEEN

Tempers cooled, Sam and I smoothed over our argument, and we settled in to enjoy life on the farm. We spent our days exploring the area and sometimes tagged along with Daniel on his trips to the milk collection center or the petrol station mini-mart. There was not much excitement to be had around Kapenguria, but soon our craving for city entertainment dwindled and we found quieter ways to pass the time. We adjusted to the rhythms of the farm: early nights, early mornings. Not in a hurry to get out of bed, followed by long, lazy breakfasts at the kitchen table.

I found out why the white stove looked odd – it burned wood. That is to say, it would have burned wood if that had been available, but it actually burned maize cobs. Cobs were not the best cooking fuel, Mrs. Murgor explained to me, because the heat they generated was uneven and gave off a sticky smoke that caked the inside of the oven and the exhaust pipe, which had to be scraped clean every few days. It didn't stop her from baking the lightest, fluffiest cakes and casseroles full of vegetables straight from the garden. She was probably used to the stove's peculiar ways after all these years.

Daniel had left to deliver the day's milk, and Sam and I were alone, sitting on the patio in the early morning sun, sharing a thermos of coffee and chatting.

"Is Daniel's father from this area?" I asked Sam, curious about our friend's African side, about which I had heard nothing, and his parents' mixed marriage.

"He is. Although he works in Mombasa."

"He works all the way down at the coast?" I asked in surprise. "How does he get home?"

"I don't think this is his home so much. He owns the farm, sure. But Mrs. Murgor has run it for the past twenty years or more. He's a doctor and his practice is on the other side of the country."

I mulled this over. No matter how nice this place was to visit, it was hard to imagine Mrs. Murgor would choose to live here all alone with little else to do but work, and no company except the people she employed. Not even a telephone. A husband who lived a full day's travel from home. Her children away at boarding schools since they were seven years old, and who only visited during the long holidays when there was enough time to make the long journey back.

"It is said he has another woman there. Although technically she is only his second wife, or maybe technically not even a wife at all, she has all the advantages of being number one, just because she's always with him."

I was hurt on Mrs. Murgor's behalf. How could such an arrangement stand for twenty years? "That's terrible," I said.

Sam shrugged his shoulders.

I couldn't believe he was being so callous. "What do you mean, shrugging your shoulders - don't you think that's shocking? Mrs. Murgor is so nice, and she works really hard to keep the family farm running all by herself... just so her husband can run off to a cushy job a thousand kilometers away, and take a new woman to keep him company? It's completely unfair," I said angrily.

Sam grinned at me. "Touchy, touchy! Does the subject hit a little too close to home?"

He threw his arm around me and I wriggled out from under him. "Don't you think for one second I would stay quietly on the farm while you went gallivanting off with some hot chick on the

136

beach."

Sam threw back his head and roared with laughter. When he was done, he whispered in my ear, "No worries, my lovely white princess. I plan not to let you out of my sight, ever."

"Good."

I pulled his arm around me and leaned against his shoulder. I knew I was being ridiculous, having a fit of jealousy about an imaginary rival, but still. I'd been hurt before. I breathed until I felt calmer and said, "Do you know how Daniel's parents met?"

"She was studying to be a nurse back in the UK, in London, and he was there for a few years to complete his studies in medicine. They fell in love and married, you know how these things go, and she came with him when he returned to Kenya."

I couldn't imagine how Daniel's mother coped. It was one thing for Sam to call himself a traditional African man, used to growing up with many stepmothers and half-siblings. It was another thing altogether for a woman born and raised in England to step into a life like this.

"I wonder if this is what she was hoping for when she got married."

"It's a hard life, no question. She is alone a lot. She has no family here."

Shhh... Sam turned to me with a finger to his lips. I dropped the subject when I saw Daniel's little sister skipping toward us. She was nine years old and small for her age, all knobby knees, sagging shorts and crooked ponytails. She was quiet and wary around Sam and me, but openly worshiped her big brother, and usually hovered somewhere nearby. We got accustomed to having her around without being quite aware of her. Now she stood a few steps away, looking at us, waiting, like she might have something to say.

"What's up, Scooby Doo?" Sam said. It was the name of the brown sausage-shaped puppy that ran around the farm, but because child and dog were inseparable, calling one was the same as calling the other, and eventually both answered to the dog's name.

The girl didn't speak. She pulled a sheet of white paper from behind her back and handed it shyly to Sam. I peered over his shoulder and saw it was covered in pencil drawings. At first it looked like an unconnected jumble of images, but then I realized these were all things to do with Daniel: a pickup truck, a rugby ball, his favorite breakfast cereal, a pack of cigarettes. I felt a twinge of regret for this girl who loved her big brother so generously while being mostly ignored in return. Daniel was a nice guy, good to his mother, but barely seemed to know his kid sister was alive.

"What's this, eh? A drawing, I see. Did you make it yourself?" Sam said.

"Yes."

"What are you going to do with it?"

She shrugged and looked embarrassed, her eyes on her wriggling toes.

"You should give it to your brother, don't you think? He will be pleased to have it. I know I would be pleased if my little sister drew me something as clever as this," Sam said. He handed the paper back to the girl.

Scooby Doo nodded, as if this confirmed what she had hoped, and skipped away with the puppy close on her heels.

"Hey, wait!" Sam called. "Could you do me a favor?"

The child stopped and turned around, waiting for instructions.

"Can you bring me a pair of scissors?"

She nodded and tore off toward the house.

"And don't run with those scissors!" Sam hollered after her.

He turned to me and said, "So, Sara, will you do me a favor also? You have noticed, I'm sure, how long this hair of mine has been growing. I want you to trim off a few centimeters, OK?"

"Sam, really, I have no idea how to cut hair, especially not hair like yours with all the tiny curls." The only experience I had with cutting any kind of hair was when I snipped off a few of my own split ends when they caught my eye.

"Where else am I going to get a haircut here? There doesn't appear to be a barber between this farm and Nairobi. Besides, it's easy. Anybody can do it."

Scooby Doo came around the corner carefully carrying an enormous pair of metal sewing scissors.

"You can't be serious," I said.

"No, no, these will do fine. These scissors are fine, thank you very much, Scooby Doo."

The child crouched down a short distance away to watch the entertainment while the puppy galloped back and forth between us.

Sam took his wooden afro pick from his back pocket. "Let me just comb it out first," he said and slid the wide teeth deep into his hair, then yanked the comb from roots to ends, dragging it through with effort. It looked painful. He worked his way around his scalp and tiny black circles of hair broke off and sprang from his head in all directions. I brushed a few from my arms and t-shirt. When he was done, his hair stood around his head like a halo.

"Does that hurt?" I asked.

"Yes. It will be much easier to comb when it's shorter."

"I see."

Sam dragged his chair onto the lawn and I stood behind him. I poked the long blades of the scissors into his afro at various angles, but hesitated to make a cut. *Well.* Thinking about this wasn't going to make doing it any easier, so I finally slapped the blades together and made a few shallow snips. A layer of hair came off linked like fleece. I got it. This hair was going to stay in place while I shore off the top layer. I snipped away, following the contour of Sam's scalp. Sheets of hair floated on the air and landed lightly on the grass. When I was done, Sam ran both his hands over his hair and nodded in approval. It did look good, a perfectly smooth half-dome. I handed Scooby Doo the scissors, and she carried them back to the house.

Daniel returned from his chores and poured himself the last cup of coffee from the thermos. "And what have you children been up to while I was out doing an honest day's work?" he asked.

Sam looked at me and winked. "This coming from the guy who had to plant three alarm clocks strategically around his bedroom to force his eyes open this morning."

"True, true, I can't deny it. The early hours these farmers keep are the absolute pits. Here's to future nine-to-fives spent comfortably behind a desk. Cheers!" Daniel raised his coffee in a toast. "As for today, what would you say to a trip down to the Country Club? It is the one place around here people go for entertainment. You really can't have been here and not visited."

Sam and I were both game, and we left as soon as Daniel finished his coffee. We got to the Club after a slow half hour's drive and soon discovered the name was more impressive than the place itself. It was deserted, for one. The few staff members on duty slouched around, making no effort to hide their boredom and lack of interest in us. The man attending the reception appeared to be in a vile mood.

"Your name?" he demanded of Daniel.

"Murgor."

"Member?"

"Yes, we have a family membership."

"And them?" He snapped his hand at Sam and me, like he was flicking away a fly.

"These are my guests."

"Day passes?"

"Pardon me?"

The man sighed deeply. "If a member wants to bring a guest,

there must first be an application for day passes. It is clearly stated in the bylaws."

"I see," Daniel said. "Well, I am sorry to admit that I have forgotten to do so. Can you please sign them in as guests on the spot?"

The man stared angrily at Daniel. Daniel stared back until the man looked away. After another deep sigh, he reached beneath the counter and pulled up a large ledger. A few minutes later our names had been entered and we wandered inside.

The building was one of those odd structures that appeared to be stuck between two eras; not fully hanging on to its old colonial past, but not taking on a new African identity, either. Dark wood and dull lighting shut out the sunny day and left the place in gloom.

We walked into the games room where a massive pool table stood in the middle. Cues leaned against the nearby wall. We each picked one. Sam racked the balls and we tried to play a game, but it soon became clear there wasn't enough light to see by. He jiggled a switch and tried screwing the bulbs of the overhead lamps tighter and looser, but they would not turn on. We put the cues back and moved to the dartboard; it had better lighting, but couldn't find any darts. When we went to ask, the cranky receptionist said the Club did not provide darts for common use – guests were required to bring their own.

We gave up on the games room and wandered into the lounge where clusters of red chairs stood around small metal tables. We were the only customers, but nobody came to take our order. Daniel finally stood up and pushed through the swing doors into the kitchen, and asked for someone to bring us a drink. He returned and we sat in silence. Just as we were beginning to give up hope of ever being served, a waiter plunked down three bottles in front of us. Lukewarm orange soda. We sipped sleepily through straws stuck into the bottles, feeling groggy in the midday heat.

"Who's up for a game of squash?" Daniel said, trying to bring some life back to the party.

Sam sat up. "Man, are you asking for me to kick your ass again?"

"Again? What do you mean, *again?*"

Sam and Daniel cheerfully threw insults back and forth as we made our way to the squash court. It was a separate building, just a few minutes' walk from the clubhouse. The boys ignored the flagstone path and cut straight across the field while I trailed behind, enjoying sunshine warm on my face and admiring the thick green grass. Nearby, a pond was surrounded by a cluster of trees. Enormous blue and green dragonflies hovered over the water with rays of light bouncing like sequins from their wings.

"Hey, Sara," Daniel called over his shoulder, "careful where you step." He hung back, waiting for me to catch up.

I glanced around, but couldn't see anything potentially hazardous.

"This is a golf course, see, and they imported this special grass for the greens, which apparently is soft and tasty and hippos cannot resist its delicious flavor. They come up for a snack at night and plow up the grounds altogether. It's quite dangerous to walk here because you can turn your ankle badly in the giant hippo footprints - they can be half a meter deep, easy – and you can't see them because of the grass cover. Never mind what it does to your game!" Daniel looked serious. "They're known to be really aggressive, hippos are. Recently the club has started sending guards out at night armed with pointed sticks to chase them off by poking them in the behind, which is a risky business, let me tell you."

I looked at Daniel suspiciously. Was he pulling my leg?

"It's true," he said, winking at me. "Hey, are you joining us for a game of squash?"

"I don't know. I've never played before."

"Nah, don't worry, you'll get the hang of it in no time. Just watch closely as I slaughter your man Sam here, and you'll learn all the tricks in the book."

"Hey!" Sam called loudly from where he was standing near the door of the building. "Are we playing or chatting, eh?" He wrapped his irritation in a joke, but I heard it anyway.

We entered the low building, which was surprisingly cool inside - it had no windows and the sun's heat was blocked out. Daniel flipped a switch and the overhead fluorescent lights buzzed on. I walked up to the glass that spanned the full width of the building and looked down on the squash court. It was nothing more than a rectangular box: white walls and a polished wood floor with red and blue lines painted on both. Sam and Daniel grabbed rackets and walked down the stairs and onto the court. They closed the door firmly behind them and took up positions. *Bam!* Sam launched the small rock-hard rubber ball against the wall. It exploded back and up from the floor and Daniel tore after it. He stretched to reach the ball and whacked it against one of the side walls. I couldn't figure out the rules, but smacking the ball around like that looked like fun. This was more to my taste than riding a horse - all those years of tennis lessons my father insisted I needed might actually be put to good use today.

The boys climbed back up the stairs, dripping with sweat. Daniel had won and Sam needed a few minutes to pull himself together - he was not a good loser and we all knew it. They took turns drinking deeply from the water fountain and waited for their panting breath to slow. Daniel stood across from me, flashed his superstar grin, and challenged me with a quick nod of his head toward the court, "You and me, babe."

I took Sam's racket from him and followed Daniel downstairs. He explained the rules but confusion must have shown on my face, because he stopped and shrugged, and told me I would learn on the job. I smacked the ball. *Damn!* Just like tennis, only a hundred times faster. No annoying net, either. I caught Daniel by surprise, and actually scored a point. He opened his eyes wide and lifted his arms in a show of astonishment.

"Right, clearly this is my punishment for taking it easy on the new girl. No more! Take cover, because now I start playing for real," Daniel bellowed.

I glanced up and saw Sam's shadow against the glass window. I hope he hadn't missed my move.

I picked up the ball and hit it again, but my beginner's luck didn't last. Neither did my energy. Fifteen minutes into the game I was completely exhausted and missed a ball in the far corner despite my desperate attempt at a sprint. It was all over, and Daniel had beaten me easily. I stood hunched over, leaning on my knees, heaving breaths in and out.

Daniel sauntered over, smiling widely, and wrapped me in a sweaty hug, clapping my back while I hung in his arms like a dishrag. "You are a natural," he roared, "I've never had such a good game with a beginner, and a girl at that!"

"Oh, stop," I protested weakly, grinning at him. I was secretly flattered by his words, whether they were true or not. We took turns at a few more rounds but soon all anyone wanted was a shower and something cool to drink. Sam was quiet in the car on the way home.

CHAPTER SEVENTEEN

Later that evening, Sam and I lounged on the sofa, taking up the whole length of it, legs entangled. He leaned into the corner and I leaned against him, my just-washed hair soaking a damp circle into his clean t-shirt. When it became too dark to see, Daniel went out back to start the generator - we would hear the engine chug in the background until it was switched off at 10:00 to keep petrol costs down. It was the farm's only source of electricity and not normally used during the day when the place could manage without. Switching on the generator meant we could use the record player.

Daniel stood over the turntable, carefully placing a little stack of coins on the label of the spinning record. The generator's power was never exactly the same from day to day. Nothing could be done if the music was slow, but if it was fast, the weight of the coins brought the speed down. Once the needle was lowered into the groove, it took a good ear to hear whether a song needed a shilling more or less, but we'd keep experimenting until everybody was happy.

Sweet, wonderful you-ou-ou... I sat upright. *Rumours*, the album Sam hated because it reminded him of my past with Leander. Still my favorite, though. Familiar tunes burst from the speakers and Daniel cranked up the volume. I couldn't resist opening my mouth and singing along with words I knew by heart and soon I couldn't sit still, either. I hopped off the sofa and started to dance, feeling good. The music flowed through my body and I rolled my shoulders in lazy loops, sank low with knees bent deep, pushed up slowly. Bare feet slid along the cool tile floor. I closed my eyes, lifted the damp hair from my neck with both hands, eased my head back, murmured *and I don't have to tell you you're the only one.* The song ended. I was brought back by the boys' applause and Daniel's shrill wolf whistle. For a moment I had forgotten I had an audience. I felt flustered and bounced back onto the sofa.

"Scrabble, anyone?" I said.

After the generator fell silent, we opted for bed instead of stretching our waking hours by candlelight like we usually did. Squash had tired us out. My muscles were already complaining, and I would be stiff tomorrow, no doubt about it. I stripped down to my t-shirt and undies, slid between the sheets and cuddled up to Sam's warm body. He pulled away from me.

"Hey, is something wrong?" I said, feeling rejected.

"No."

I tried to remember if anything had happened, a problem, an unresolved argument. I drew a blank.

"So you think I can't tell what's going on, eh?" Sam growled.

"What?"

"Do... you... think... I'm... blind?" His voice rose, as if speaking louder would make me understand.

"What?" I said, feeling panicky.

Sam sat up in the bed, smashed his fists into the mattress and roared: *"FUCK!* Will you stop already with the idiotic *whats?"*

I jumped.

Sam closed his eyes in frustration and continued with slightly less volume, "Don't pretend you don't know what I'm talking about. I can see it happening with my own eyes, that asshole Daniel hitting on you and you loving every minute of it. All that flirting and me, I'm *right there...* what does that say, eh? What does that say about how you feel about me? It says you have no respect whatsoever. It says you treat me like rubbish."

I sat up, mystified by his accusations. He wouldn't look at me.

"Sam, how can you say such a thing? I don't know what you're talking about."

"Then let me explain to you precisely." He turned to face me, his eyes blazing. "What is up with all the snickering and hugs at the squash place? What is up with the solo dancing in front of him like you're putting on some kind of peep show? What is up back with that runaway horse and he goes tearing after you like it's his own damn girlfriend who is in trouble? Well?"

I swallowed the next *what?* when I realized Sam was jealous of Daniel. How about that.

"Stop yelling, Sam, please."

He frowned at me, but he didn't say anything. I guessed his case had been made.

I felt my way hesitantly, not sure how to make Sam believe me. "There's nothing going on between me and Daniel, honest. Because I know his type: he flirts with every girl he meets. He's the exact opposite of you."

"So?"

"It means I would never be interested in him."

"It certainly looked like there was something going on between you."

I shook my head. "There wasn't, though."

Sam turned to me. "Nothing going on, you swear?"

"I swear."

"You don't have feelings for him?"

"No! Sam... come on now, you know there's only you."

He looked at me intently for a moment, as if to bore deep into my thoughts. Then he grinned and the anger washed off his face. He placed his hands around my waist and I felt his strong palms push into my skin. He let his hands slide down my hips, pressing gently, on behind my back, and all the way down, low around my ass. "Man, the way you move when the music plays," he whispered, pulling me to him, leaning his chin on my shoulder. "The things you make your body do. It ought to be illegal."

I smiled and kissed his short tight curls.

We sat quietly for a moment. I relaxed, relieved we weren't fighting. Sam mumbled into my hair how he needed a good long night's sleep, because I had worn him out altogether with my mischief. But I wasn't ready for sleep. I was hungry now to feel his naked skin against my own. I pulled my t-shirt over my head and dropped it to the floor. I pulled off his.

Sam looked at me questioningly. I smiled.

"Are you sure?" he asked.

"I am sure. Unless you're too tired, of course," I said, teasingly.

"Too tired for you? Never."

He took a deep breath, or was it a sigh? He looked at me closely again, his eyes searching mine. I nodded slightly, encouraging him.

He kissed me, slowly. He let his lips wander down my neck, his face so close I felt his eyelashes flutter against my skin. When he pulled his lips away, he lowered me softly onto the bed and kneeled beside me. His eyes lingered on me, his hands tender - feeling, touching, stroking like butterflies.

I reached to switch off the lamp, but Sam clasped my hand and murmured, "No. Leave it on."

I closed my eyes.

He slipped a finger under either side of my panties and slid them down my legs. Thank goodness I was wearing my nicest pair, shimmering satin with tiny hearts.

I lay uncovered. He eased down beside me. I opened my eyes to look at him, to find his face, but the lamp was like a floodlight. I felt exposed and clamped my hands over my eyes.

"Too bright," I moaned.

Sam laughed softly. "You are a prudish thing, aren't you?"

I nodded, feeling slightly ridiculous. *I guess I am, once my clothes are off.*

Sam switched off the lamp and I dropped my hands. After a

few blinks my eyes adjusted to the darkness.

"I see you," I whispered.

"Yes." I could tell he was smiling. "I see you, too."

I felt his mouth warm on my breast and his lips close gently around the skin. He breathed a flurry of kisses down my belly, soft like a breeze, and my body shimmered deliciously. I ran the flat of my hand along his skin and felt the tautness of his muscles just below the surface. I tasted the saltiness of him.

He rolled on top of me and locked his body onto mine. His hips moved slowly, with the pulse of a drumbeat, and I followed with mine. I clung to him and knew there would be nothing to regret in the morning.

I woke with my naked body curved around Sam's and no idea what time it was, but felt rested, and brightly awake. Sam was asleep. With my mind, I touched the memory of his body. I pulled the blanket up to cover his bare side, laid my arm carefully around his chest, and pulled myself a little closer. We made love.

We couldn't bear to be separated and held each other in the shower. Our elbows touched while we ate breakfast and I could hardly let go of him long enough to tie my shoes. We clasped hands and went for a walk. The crisp air tingled my cheeks and the sky was a sharp uncluttered blue without even the wisp of a cloud. The tassels on the maize plants stood stiffly upright; not the slightest breeze stirred the air. We took a new path, curious to see where it would take us. It stretched ahead in a straight line to the horizon and split the maize field in two. The yellow farm dogs sensed we were going off on our own and seemed to consider it their duty to escort us. They caught up, sniffed our hands and circled our legs, then settled beside us as we continued on our way.

"So, Sara."

"*Hmn?*"

"After we get back to Nairobi next week, I am heading home to Uganda for a few days."

"You are?"

"There is some business I have to take care of."

"Is something wrong?"

"Sara, listen to me." We stopped walking and Sam turned to me, his eyes serious, a frown creasing the space between his eyebrows. "My father is not at the family house in Kampala. He's been detained, locked up in prison."

I looked at Sam in shock. He continued, "He is innocent, of course, the charges against him are entirely bogus. He was open to such an attack, simply because he is an honest customs official, maybe the only one in all of Uganda." Sam snorted in disgust. "He intercepted smuggled goods from fat cats in government who were moving ivory and coffee illegally, making themselves piles cash on the side. You can see how this would cause anger right up to the highest levels. So they found a way to get rid of him. They accused him of being in league with Idi Amin."

"In league? What do you mean?"

"It's a load of bullshit. Tribal politics. Amin is a Kakwa and we are Madi, which is like a cousin tribe. Closely related. Ugandans hate Amin, and then they hated all of the Kakwa, and now they hate Madi also."

"This is the reason your father's in prison?"

"This is the excuse to put my father in prison. And it is the reason he will stay there for some time. Amin got rid of everybody in the country who was educated and now the legal system is a joke. It will be a struggle for my father to prove his innocence."

I knew he was referring to Idi Amin's hatred of anybody who made him feel stupid – he had barely attended any school at all and was even rumored to be illiterate. So now Uganda had no teachers, no doctors, no lawyers, no judges – only friends appointed by Amin. The real ones got deported, or they disappeared, or left the country themselves if they were smart and lucky.

"How long has your father been in prison?"

"It will be two and a half years next month."

Two and a half years. What had Sam had been coping with since he was sixteen, just a kid himself? I couldn't begin to imagine. This is what he tried to make me understand when he told me he was number one son, and responsible for his family in his father's absence. It wasn't just a theory, but real life. Sam was in charge of a family of six wives and eighteen children.

"What are you going to do?"

"It is time for me to go home to look in on the family and make sure everybody is well." He scowled. "There has been some trouble lately, particularly with this woman Matilda. The middle wife. In Nairobi she called me every day, several times a day, with wild accusations against the rest of the family. She's neurotic, imagines everybody is out to cheat her and her child both." He muttered something that sounded like *crazy bitch*. "Also, I have to pick up my traveling papers and money. And get my flight booked."

I blinked, trying to remember whether Sam had mentioned a flight to anywhere.

"I have been accepted to the University of London," he said with a wide smile. "Classes start in September, but they've told me to get there a week or so early. Apparently they need time to explain how the modern world works to a traditional African man." He laughed lightly.

Sam was leaving? My stomach lurched. What would this mean for us, for me?

"University of London?" I asked.

Sam nodded. "Yes. Admitted on scholarship, special for downtrodden African sods like myself. So you see how this works out well for us, eh?"

"Not really, no."

"Look," Sam stopped walking and pulled me around to face him. "You can't stay here in Kenya, this much is clear, isn't it? You have taken your education as far as it will go and have no work papers." He took a deep breath and continued, talking fast as if he was making his case. "Why don't you come to England with me? You've told me how your folks are willing to send you to Holland for your studies - England is really close, basically just around the corner, and it won't cost more to send you there instead. There's bound to be plenty of secretarial colleges, and you can get your degree just as easily, maybe find a job after. We can take a small place together. After I've completed my studies, we'll come back home and build a good life right here in Kenya. Or even Uganda, God willing."

I looked at Sam in amazement. "Go with you to England?"

"I know, there is an irony there. Newly liberated African turns to land of oppressor to get a proper education."

I lowered my head, trying to grasp plans that seemed too big to take in so suddenly. Sam was right. Much as I hated the idea and wanted to avoid dealing with it, I knew I would be forced to leave Kenya soon. My only alternative was to go to Holland, this country where I hardly knew a soul and my thick accent marked me as an outsider as soon as I opened my mouth to speak the language. At least in London, people spoke English. And I'd be with Sam, and he wanted to be with me, and we would be coming home to Kenya, together, in a few years. He was right, why would it make any difference to my parents where in Europe I went to school, as long as I got the education they wanted for me? On the other hand, London might as well be Timbuktu, for all I knew about the place.

"I hate the idea of not having you with me," Sam said. "It will be hard for me to go if it means leaving you behind."

I didn't want to get left behind, either. "Sam? When is all this happening?"

"I was thinking to go to Uganda pretty much immediately

after our return to Nairobi, so I can start getting matters sorted out. With things the way they are back home, it will take some doing for me to leave for Europe with a clear conscience. I may be gone for a week or two."

"And then? When do you leave for London?"

"By the end of August. Five weeks from today. Give or take."

I was surprised to feel a sudden sadness come over me. It felt like loss, or loneliness.

"What do you think, eh? Do you want to come to England with me?"

What *did* I want? I tried to think my options through calmly, but couldn't get my racing thoughts to simmer down.

Sam suddenly reached into his back pocket, as if he had remembered something important. "Look here, maybe these will help. Give you some idea what I'm talking about."

He handed me three glossy postcards, bent and ragged around the edges where he had jammed them into the too-snug pocket of his jeans. "Look, this is the main campus, one of the original buildings - been around forever, just see how huge it is. Like a Greek temple, with a dome, eh? Can you picture having a lecture in there?"

The building stood blinking white in the sunshine, with wide stairs leading to a dozen engraved stone pillars, easily three stories tall. In the shadows I could just make out a wooden double door, opened slightly, not revealing what was inside. It was the most beautiful building I had ever seen.

Sam pulled up the second card. "And here, the quad out front. The kids are probably all students, hanging out between classes."

A thick mat of grass surrounded by wooden benches, with bicycles parked here and there, haphazardly leaning against each other. People my age chatted with each other and lounged on the benches, reading, jotting things in notebooks. One couple was kissing. They all looked so happy.

"And look at this one. London, just some random place downtown, I guess."

A night scene of a narrow street, with small shops and eateries lit by neon signs in every color. The street was paved with bricks, or cobblestones. The sidewalk teemed with people strolling arm in arm, stepping out of one of the little shops, sitting at small outdoor tables, smiling, sipping from glasses of wine.

"Isn't this cool?"

I nodded; it did look like a place to have a great time.

"No, I mean this here. Look carefully."

I drew the postcard closer and examined it again.

"Fish and chips!" Sam said triumphantly, turning to me with a wide grin. He poked his finger at the postcard. "A real London fish and chips shop. See that? They've wrapped the food in sheets of newspaper. I heard that's how it's done, but never quite believed it. It seems like such an African solution."

I smiled at him, enjoying his excitement.

Sam took the cards from me, and put them back in his pocket. "Well?" he said. "What do you think?"

I stood with empty hands, contemplating the world Sam had just shown me. Would this turn out to be that first day of the rest of my life I had been waiting for? I wished I could go to London, to attend its grand university. Would they accept me? What would I study? There were many unanswered questions, but one thing was clear: this plan would keep Sam and me together. And it would bring us back to Africa, eventually. I took Sam's face in both my hands and gazed into his eyes. Happy and vulnerable; I knew that look. I stood on my toes to kiss his lips and said, "Yes."

Sam held me close and laughed happily. "It'll be so good, you'll see. Just some few little things to take care of, and then we'll be free. Free! Only ourselves and a future together to look out for." He threw his arm around my shoulders. "Come on. Let's walk back to the house. I'll fix you coffee."

I looked around for the dogs, but they had deserted us.

CHAPTER EIGHTEEN

I could not let go of thoughts of Sam leaving for Uganda, and of both of us moving to London. I became too restless to enjoy the stillness of the farm. I could not reach my parents, and was anxious about how they would react when I talked to them. It was always hard to predict what my father would think of an idea, but once he roared *no, never!* that was pretty much the end of it. No doubt there would be a lot of roaring when I told him about London, and Sam wouldn't be with me to help change his mind, either.

Sam and Daniel were off to the petrol station to buy cigarettes, and the Scooby Doos had tagged along. Mrs. Murgor was away, tending to farm business, and I wandered around the house alone. A dozen or so photographs in mismatched frames stood on a small table in a corner of the living room. I went to look at them more closely and picked up a snapshot of Daniel's little sister sitting on the patio steps, holding the puppy in her arms, two pairs of brown eyes scrunched up against the sunlight. Behind it stood a smaller, plain plastic frame and I saw it was a picture of Mrs. Murgor standing on the lawn, shading her eyes and laughing at the camera, her feet slightly apart, bearing her weight evenly. She wore a faded pair of overalls and her shirt sleeves were rolled up above her elbows. Her hair was pulled back, and a few loose strands danced around her face. I recognized the green rubber boots. It seemed a much more practical outfit for running a farm than the dress and curls she'd been wearing while we were here.

155

The car pulled up and a wave of noise entered the house along with the boys. Scooby Doo tugged at her brother's shirt, trying to attract his attention, but Daniel was caught up in a heated discussion with Sam about the state of rugby in Kenya and was too busy making his point to pay her any mind. The little girl finally gave up and left the room. She returned a few minutes later with a sheet of paper in her hand. I recognized the drawing she had shown Sam and me earlier. She stood close to Daniel, looked up at him and waited to be seen, but this was a half-hearted attempt; she did not seem to expect to be noticed, and Daniel never did. I watched her leave the room. She looked a little beaten down.

Sam and Daniel called a truce and as soon as they stopped arguing, we heard a strange noise from somewhere outside the room. We stood still, listening, and it took me a moment to recognize the distorted voice and high-pitched screaming.

Daniel spoke first, "My sister."

He and Sam raced for the kitchen where the noise seemed to be coming from, with me a few steps behind. They stopped in the doorway. I peered over their shoulders. The child was tearing the drawing into shreds, and Mrs. Murgor was trying to stop her by placing her hands softly on her thin shoulders. She threw them off and lunged at her mother, banging small fists into her hips, crying and howling words I could not understand.

Sam stepped into the kitchen and reached the child in two long strides. "Hey!" he hollered. The screaming stopped and the girl turned to him, tears and rage covering her face. Sam drew back his hand and slapped her with an open palm. The *crack* echoed in the silent kitchen. Sam hit the small girl hard.

"Don't you ever treat your mother with disrespect, you hear me?" The child froze, raised her hand to her cheek, dipped her head, and ran from the room. My eyes locked with Mrs. Murgor's for a stunned instance. She looked as shocked as I felt. Neither of us spoke.

I followed Sam to the bedroom and sat down on the edge of the bed next to him. He was seething. "It shouldn't have been me. It was Daniel's place to set the kid straight. You saw how he wasn't going to face up to his responsibilities, eh? I had no choice."

My heart ached for the little girl. I spoke slowly, feeling my way, not sure what to say or think. "Sam, she just seemed really upset. Because Daniel doesn't pay her any attention, you know? Her feelings were hurt when he ignored her. Besides... she's only a child."

"No. It is unacceptable. The father is not around. Who will teach this girl how to behave, how to respect her elders properly? Daniel, he is the man in this house and should have put a stop to this bullshit."

People did not hit their children where I came from. On the other hand, I knew nothing about being responsible for raising kids as Sam had been ever since stepping into his father's shoes years ago. Was this how African families raised their children? Or had Sam taken things too far, slapping a child he was not even related to?

He was still looking at the floor when he growled that it would be better if we went home.

"Now?"

"Yes. We should go. We've been here long enough and affairs going on are not our business. A train leaves at 7:00 tonight - we can make it if we hurry. I'll let Mrs. Murgor know. You pack up our things."

"Sam, wait. Don't you think it's kind of sudden, rude, to pick up and leave like this? Especially with the... you know, the thing that just happened. Don't you think you should say something?"

He turned to me. "Do you expect me to apologize?"

I hesitated, then nodded briefly.

His eyes locked mine in a glare, his voice low. "You think I was wrong?"

"Maybe you shouldn't have hit her."

"You are mistaken to think so. Children must have discipline and learn their place, especially the girls."

I was quiet, feeling Sam's anger radiate from him, knowing we were inching closer to a huge argument for which I had no taste. It bothered me that he thought girls shouldn't be allowed to scream out their frustrations; that they should know their place. What place was that? I shook my head. No. Sam always treated me exactly like his brother and guy friends. Better, actually.

Sam left to look for Mrs. Murgor. It would have been awkward to stay on, I could see that now.

I unzipped my small suitcase, a present from my mother for my first sleepover when I was a little girl. How proud and grown up I had felt, packing my suitcase all by myself. I used up every centimeter of space, putting in things I really didn't need, like my Barbie and all her clothes, even though I didn't even like playing with dolls much. I insisted on carrying the suitcase myself and became discouraged when I discovered my arms were too short, and I wasn't strong enough to keep it from dragging along beside me. My mother finally took the suitcase from me, scolding me that I had damaged the bottom. Since then, I had packed and unpacked this suitcase countless times until it became an ordinary thing to do. I ran my fingers along the familiar rough red and black tartan fabric, now worn thin in places. I collected my dirty laundry from around the room and put it on top of clean clothes I hadn't bothered to unpack, and stuffed Sam's things into his bag. It wasn't much, just a few t-shirts and some socks. I almost forgot his shampoo and toothbrush and threw them on top of the rest.

Sam came back into the bedroom. "Are you ready?" he asked. He gave the room a quick once over to see if anything had been forgotten, but nothing had.

"Yes."

"Alright, let's go, then. Daniel will drive us to the station."

I shook Mrs. Murgor's hand and thanked her for her hospitality. So did Sam. She was polite in the way the British always are, but her eyes had lost their warmth.

The train was waiting when we got to the station. We said goodbye to Daniel, bought our tickets, and got on board.

"At least Daniel now understands you and I are serious," Sam said as we settled in our compartment. "That we are a couple. We stick together. He can't just move in with his pretty face and try to make a claim."

I suppressed a sigh. If only Sam could sometimes just relax a little and not make every situation more complicated than it needed to be.

My parents were surprised when I came home a few days earlier than planned, and clearly relieved to see me in one piece. Probably they had worried far too much while I was away.

I missed Sam immediately – I had gotten used to having him around all the time. When he called the next day to say he was on his way to pick me up, I was eager to see him. He parked his car in the driveway, leaving plenty of room for any other cars that might be coming or going, and walked into the house to find my mother. He shook her hand, which always delighted her because it seemed so formal – and talked to her about taking me out to lunch. My mother looked happy to be included in the plans.

"Should I put on something more dressy, Sam?" I asked him, not knowing where we were going.

"No need, you look fine."

Sam took me to a little place far from the busy city center. It was a small building made from weathered wooden boards, with enormous windows that had no glass in them. Shutters were open to let fresh outdoor air float through. Wide eaves sloped down from the roof to prevent rain from dripping inside. Square tables were scattered throughout the room, and it looked like all of them were taken.

When we got close to the entrance, Sam said, "Hang on just a second, will you?" He walked over to speak to one of the waiters. I turned and looked out over the garden. It was lush with tropical plants – bright red and purple flowers and thick waxy green leaves. Two mimosa trees leaned in from the back corners and their branches reached out to each other, knitting an airy roof over the grass. Most of the fluffy neon balls had fallen from the branches and coated the ground in a yellow layer so bright, it seemed like the grass was glowing.

I rubbed my arms, grateful for the long sleeves of Sam's old blue and white striped rugby shirt. Today was going to be nippy all the way through with the sky overcast, looking like there might be rain later on.

I felt Sam step up against my back. He slipped his arms around my stomach and I covered his hands with mine. He leaned close to my ear and whispered, "Ready for luncheon, milady?"

"Yes," I said, smiling up at him. "Hanging around in the garden waiting for you to finish whatever mysterious thing you are up to this time, has made me hungry."

"Please follow me."

I turned to face the restaurant and Sam dramatically stretched out his arm. His hand pointed at a small table that hadn't been there earlier, standing by itself on the secluded right side of the veranda. The wooden deck was only barely wide enough for the table and a pair of chairs, tucked under the eaves, so private it was a hideaway for just the two of us.

"Eh?" Sam said. "What do you think?"

"I love it... how did you arrange this?"

"Knowing the right people in the right places, as always." Sam said, grinning and clearly feeling pleased with the success of his plan. "Actually, the waiter is an old school mate and he

160

helped me out. Are you sure you won't be chilly?"

"I'm sure. This is perfect."

We pulled up our chairs and Sam ordered soup to start, followed by baked tilapia with boiled potatoes and peas. I enjoyed the food, and enjoyed sitting quietly with Sam.

After we finished eating and were served coffee, Sam took my hand.

"Sara, I leave for Uganda tonight."

"Tonight?"

"This fellow I know offered me a lift - it's an opportunity too good to miss. He's driving through the night and it means I'll get to Uganda tomorrow morning. You know the border is still closed to most traffic; I'll be crossing on foot. It'll be easier to find my ride on the other side during the day. Someone from the house in Kampala will come to collect me."

I looked down at the cup that sat warm in my hands and blew at the steam.

"OK," I said.

"Now, listen to me. I'll try to call you whenever I can, but the phone lines are unreliable. I don't want you to worry if you don't hear from me for a while."

"Alright."

"And I don't know exactly when I'll be back. Two weeks tops. I'll get word to you somehow."

I looked him straight in the eye, so he could see I was going to be fine and he didn't have to worry about me. "I know you will," I answered.

"Have you spoken to your parents about London?"

I had been procrastinating, not looking forward to the conversation. I had not figured out a backup plan if they refused to help me.

"Not yet. I will, though. Soon."

Sam looked at me seriously. "You're not having doubts, are you?"

"No." I smiled at him. "I am more certain with every minute that passes, which is why it's hard to talk to my parents. I'm afraid they'll kill my dreams."

"Look, don't worry about it too much. If your parents won't help, we'll figure out another way."

I wondered what that might be.

"Here, keep these with you. It will remind you of what we have to look forward to." Sam handed me the three postcards of London.

I leafed through them again, briefly, knowing I would have plenty of time to enjoy them at home, in the privacy of my bedroom. The pictures always worked their magic to cheer me up. I tucked them in my purse.

We finished our coffee, and Sam dropped me off at home. He told me he had many things to take care of before he could leave tonight with a clear conscience, like arrange affairs for Dennis at the motel, and buy supplies for his people in Uganda where there were shortages of just about everything. It was awkward saying goodbye in my own front yard with my mother and Lisa unseen in the house behind me. Still, I hugged him close to me one last time and planted a brief kiss on his lips. "Come back soon," I whispered. "Don't get into trouble."

He nodded seriously, kissed me again, and I knew a promise had been made.

Raindrops started to fall. One or two hit my head, cold and wet on my scalp. Sam got into his car, and after one last wave, he was gone.

I dragged my feet and walked slowly back to the house. I heard the phone ringing and hoped it would stop; I was in no mood to chat. No such luck - my mother heard me enter through the front door and called out: "Sara, is that you? Could you please pick up the phone?"

I sighed and lifted the receiver to my ear. "This is Sara."

"Hi Sara, this is Chloe. How are things?" I heard the smile in her voice.

I sat down on the elephant chair and took a deep breath. Chloe. It would be good to talk to her. I pushed the yellow phone directories to the floor and settled down.

"It feels like we haven't talked in forever," I said.

"I knoOow."

"I just got back from Kapenguria yesterday."

"How was your trip? Did you have fun?"

"We had a wonderful time. I love the farm and Daniel's mother was really good to us. And I got to be close with Sam. Very close. In the end there were some small *shauries*, you know, and we came back a few days early."

"What happened?"

I was tempted to tell her everything that had gone on at the farm, but there were too many loose ends, and I wasn't quite clear yet what to make of it all, myself. I wasn't ready to hear what she might have to say.

"Nothing, really. Never mind," I said. "Hey, what about you? What have you been up to?"

"Yes." I heard a rasping noise, like she was clearing her throat. Then silence.

"Chloe?"

"We're leaving Kenya."

"Leaving Kenya? What do you mean, like on a holiday?"

"No, leaving for good."

"What?"

"My parents have been talking about it for years, you know? Always worrying one day things would go badly for us here as white non-citizens. And now my sister Fiona has picked up her family and moved to Canada."

"She has?"

"She left months ago. Their family wanted a fresh start, especially for the kids. They got tired of the corruption, and of worrying that this stability won't last much longer. Look at the mess in Uganda; they think it's only a matter of time before some crazy dictator takes over here, too. Anyway, Fiona has been sending such glowing letters that my parents decided the time has come for all of us to go. My other sisters, too."

"But Chloe, you can't be serious. Why would Kenya go the way of Uganda? Dictators aren't contagious like some virus. Besides, you were born here. This is your home - what are you going to do in Canada?"

Chloe spoke gently. "My heart is broken, what can I tell you? But my family sees things differently from me and I can't stay here alone. They're all leaving."

I understood the logic of what she was saying, but it was hard to stay reasonable in the face of another unwanted surprise. I suddenly realized the last time I had seen her was on the morning of our exam, when I ditched her to be with Sam. I had neglected my best friend shamefully, and now she was deserting me.

"I can't imagine this place without you. Shit, Chloe, this is terrible. If you leave now, will we ever see each other again?"

"Of course we will," she said. But we both knew there was no way we could be sure.

CHAPTER NINETEEN

I spoke with Sam briefly on the phone late on the day he arrived in Kampala. It was a terrible connection with crackles and strange echoes, but at least I knew he was safe. And that he missed me.

Now that Sam was away, days were longer and I found time to spend on things I had been neglecting. I dug up the pieces of a blouse I had cut and planned to sew months ago, and lifted the fabric against the light to admire its design: big golden tropical flowers with various shades of green leaves fanned out in the background. I lifted the dust cover from my sewing machine and rummaged through my box of materials. *Damn.* No matching thread. Maybe I should go downtown, to Biashara Street? It was one of my favorite places to spend time, an ancient street lined with narrow stores stacked floor to ceiling with rainbows of fabric: modern imported prints, silks from the Far East, traditional African *kanga* and *kitenge,* and glittery fabrics for saris. Local cottons were so cheap I couldn't imagine how they were made for the price, though the quality was not very good, and they shrank and faded terribly no matter how carefully washed.

The phone rang. It was probably Dennis. Since Sam left, he had taken to calling me every day around this time.

"Sara! How is my favorite sister, eh? What are you up to?"

"Hi, Dennis. *Habari?* Not much, just sitting down to do a little sewing, actually."

"You know how to sew? What kind of things?"

"All kinds of things, really. As long as I have a pattern to help me cut the pieces."

"This is good news, very good news indeed. An idea has occurred to me just now – do you think you could maybe sew me a pair of trousers? I need some black pants for this church choir performance and I can't find any that are long enough. You know it is not an easy thing to shop for a man as tall as myself. Also I want the bottoms wide-wide-wide, to cover my shoes completely. Can you do this?"

"I'm not sure. I guess so. When do you need them?"

"Two weeks from right now. This gives you plenty of time, yes?"

"I suppose. It will probably give me enough time to figure out how to make you some pants. Things are pretty quiet around here right now."

"Sara, you have made my day, I swear. I was worried I'd be standing there up on the podium in one of those ugly *mzee* old man trousers, too short with my socks uncovered entirely for the world to see. I will speak with my Kenyan mother today. Susan. I'll ask if she can go out and get me just the right fabric. In fact, I have something in mind right now."

"Sounds good. Don't wait too long, OK?" Dennis was famous for letting things slide until the very last minute, or until it was too late altogether. He would tell endless, complicated stories to cover up his dawdling and was so entertaining in the process, you would almost forget that he had simply created his own problems. Or, if something had gotten completely out of hand, he would flatter and cajole big brother Sam into taking care of it. Sam would lift a critical eyebrow and make Dennis suffer a while. Then he would fix the mess.

"Now, Sara, you have not heard from my brother for some days, I think."

"No, I haven't. Sam called the day he arrived, but that's the only time I spoke to him."

"I want to let you know things are alright, we hear some

news here and there from the family and such. He is well. You should not worry."

"OK. I won't."

"So, do you want me to pick you up tonight?"

"What?"

"It's Friday today, have you forgotten? That particular night of the week for you to be shaking your big blue-jeansed backside all over the dance floor and for me to have one or two or as many beers as you will sponsor me, eh? No, no, no, I'm only joking. You know you don't have to buy me beer."

"I wasn't really planning on going out."

"You cannot be sitting there in your parents' house only talking with your sewing machine, eh? I'll pick you up at 9:00. Don't wear those sandals."

I grinned. It would be fun. "OK, see you then."

I hung up. I couldn't remember ever talking on the phone to Dennis before Sam left, never mind going out with him. It was a little weird. No Biashara Street today; I would just take it easy and get ready to go to the disco, though Dennis would no doubt be late.

My father came home from work with the mail, bringing with him a surprise: a letter from Sam. It was a small white envelope, bulging with paper. I took it from him and went into my bedroom and closed the door behind me. Sam had not told me he would write, and I hadn't expected him to. I stepped out of my shoes and sat down on the bed with my back against the wall, drew a quilt over my bare legs, shook a cigarette from the box and lit it. Exhaling through the window and balancing the cigarette carefully through the hole in the screen, I picked up a nail file and sliced open the top of the envelope. I looked in amazement at the sheets of paper, two of them, closely covered with writing, front and back.

Sam wrote about the ongoing squabbles between the mothers

at the house, especially the middle one, Matilda, for whom he seemed to have a particular dislike. He wrote about the children, the ones who behaved and the ones who in his opinion were spoiled beyond saving. He wrote that things were slowly becoming more peaceful in Kampala, though you could still hear random gunshots in the neighborhood and it was not safe to be out on the streets at night. He was hopeful for the future of his country, but grateful he had an opportunity to study abroad at a university where the degree he earned would mean something in the world.

He thrilled me by writing that he loved me, words he had never spoken. He startled me by writing other things I never realized about him:

I know I am not a handsome man. I fear in my heart you will one day leave me for someone whose front tooth is not chipped, who does not have these thick lips, or skin so dark. My mother is a beautiful woman, soft brown like a gazelle. Yet here I am, the spitting image of my black-as-night father. He had wished better for his children, he knew life would be easier for us if we were light. It was not to be, haha. The joke is on me.

I walked over to my desk and pushed aside the clutter that had piled up since I no longer used it for school. I dug into my drawer, looking for an old stationery set I knew was in there somewhere. It was a birthday present from years ago; light pink envelopes and matching paper edged with sprinklings of daisies and tiny butterflies. Sam would get the joke, receiving such an unmanly letter. I spent the next few hours writing. I promised him the color of his skin mattered nothing to me one way or another, and I knew mine didn't matter to him, either.

Dennis picked me up, almost on time. He was too young to drive and his friend Ethan sat behind the wheel of a small dingy

Datsun already crammed full of people. I quickly scanned the car to confirm my first impression - there was not a single girl among them.

I was not going to squeeze into the back seat with all those guys, no matter how enthusiastically they were calling for me to hop onto their laps. Dennis finally announced he had the solution, and folded his long, skinny frame onto the rear shelf behind the back seat. Now there was a sight. His butt and shoulders jammed against the sloping glass of the rear window, his knees and arms jutted out, poking the backseat passengers, and his head pressed against the roof. "Sara, get in quickly!" Dennis called over the racket. I hesitated, but supposed this was as good as it was going to get. I slid onto the back seat and firmly pushed Dennis' feet away so they were not resting on my shoulder. I leaned into the car, lifted my hips partway and managed to slam the door shut. And locked it, just to be sure it didn't pop open and drop me onto the road somewhere without anybody in this chaotic car even noticing. The pushing and shoving for space and moaning and groaning about the lack of it continued as we turned onto the highway. I was beginning to think this might not have been such a great idea.

We turned onto Langata Road and traffic thinned to a trickle as we left Nairobi behind us. The cars on the road with us were probably all heading toward the Drive Range; maybe one or two were on their way to Karen - there was only wilderness beyond. The Datsun made some coughing sounds, and Ethan shushed the passengers. We fell silent, and so did the car. It cruised along a few dozen meters without sound and slowed as it rolled forward. Ethan managed to bring it to a stop on the shoulder of the road, the wheels just grazing the deep ditch beyond.

Dennis was the first to speak, raising his voice to yell over everybody's heads, "Ethan! What the hell? What's the matter with this piece of shit tin can now, eh?"

Ethan turned the ignition a few times, but the engine refused

169

to start. He jiggled the little light in the ceiling, but couldn't get it to work. He brought his face all the way to the steering wheel and got close enough to peer at the dark dials and numbers on the dash. Finally, he sighed and sat back.

"What is it?"

"It seems we are out of petrol."

"My God, bloody idiot, how could you allow this thing to happen?" Dennis yelled. A wave of insults landed on Ethan's head, though nobody seemed actually upset. I opened the door and stepped out of the car that was becoming fuggy with the breath of too many people. It was dark outside. No streetlights, no headlights, no lit windows alongside the road. Only the tiny dots of stars in the clear sky above, so many of them, you would expect the world to be bathed in light. Instead, it was impossible to see anything just a few steps away.

"Sara, where are you? Are you alright?" a voice called out.

"I'm fine, Dennis."

"Now, don't you worry," he yelled. "I will take care of all of this, OK?"

"Yeah, yeah, I'm sure."

The boys stood around and warmed to a discussion about the best possible course of action. Maybe we should just leave the car and walk to the Drive Range? That idea was quickly abandoned - it was probably more than fifteen kilometers along an unlit road with a deep ditch running beside it. Who knew what slithered and crawled down there in the dark? Someone suggested walking back to town for a canister of petrol, but no one was exactly sure how far the nearest petrol station was, and then, who was going to volunteer for the long hike? This caused Dennis to suddenly remember he had contributed several shillings of his own beer money for petrol: now where had all his money disappeared to, could someone please explain? And who was going to donate even more shillings to this petrol-guzzling machine? Or perhaps Ethan had not quite been honest about which shillings were contributions for petrol, and which belonged in his own pocket? Accusations became more outrageous, and we weren't any closer to actually getting to the Drive Range.

A pickup truck pulled up and stopped in front of us. The door on the driver's side opened, and an elderly white man stepped out, his fists pushed deep into his khaki pants, a baseball cap low over his eyes. He walked right past me to the group of guys. He had the same slow, determined walk I remembered from the farmers up in Kapenguria, and seemed far from home - there was no place for farmers in our big city.

"Car trouble?" he said.

"Yes, it seems we are out of petrol." Ethan stepped forward as our representative, being the owner of the car.

"Where you heading?"

"We're on our way to the Drive Range there down the road, do you know it?"

"I'll tow you." It sounded like his decision was final. I wondered for an instant if it wouldn't have been smarter to ask this man to take us to pick up petrol somewhere, but this was clearly not somebody who was going to stand around *palavering* about how to proceed, and we didn't have alternatives.

"Some of you get in back of the pickup. Less load in the car," he said.

"Right, thank you. Thanks for helping us out."

The man shrugged. He was one of an older breed of locals, the kind who still lived by certain rules, like never leaving anyone stranded by the side of the road because it could be him next time. He walked over to his pickup and returned with a coil of thick rope. He leaned underneath the front of our car and tied it to some hidden part behind the front bumper. He tied the other end to his pickup truck's tow hook, put down two knots close together, and waved that we were ready to go. I got into the Datsun with Ethan and Dennis. The four others sat in the back of the pickup.

The pickup started its engine and Ethan switched on the headlights of the Datsun. We took off suddenly when the rope yanked taut, and were slammed back against our seats. Our small car was swept along like it was weightless, almost as if it was going to take off any minute like a kite. Ethan cursed and fought with the steering wheel, trying to keep the car steady on the road, but it was impossible to anticipate what was ahead with the much larger pickup blocking the view. I peered through the windshield and saw the guys in the back of the pickup hanging tightly onto the sides. It looked like they were getting thrown around pretty badly. My heart skipped a beat when the pickup leaned into a bend and we were launched like a pebble from a slingshot, wheels slipping off the road onto the narrow unpaved shoulder, sliding dangerously close to the ditch. I closed my eyes and didn't open them again until we slowed down and turned onto the Drive Range driveway.

Our ordeal wasn't over until we had been dragged through every pothole and across every bump between the road and the parking lot. It was hard to believe we were all still in one piece when we finally stopped. Ethan said shakily, "I didn't dare touch the brakes. The rope would have snapped."

The driver stepped out of his pickup and raised his hand in a kind of salute and came over to untie the rope. Ethan got out to thank the man, and shook his hand. He drove off the same way he had come, like someone who never doubted his ways. There was a subdued silence as people rubbed bruised limbs, and I for one considered how much worse things could have ended. But this group could not be serious for long.

"Ethan, where did you manage to get your driving license, eh? Perhaps you earned it by putting a small present of money into the right hands, just admit it. I have never in my life been abused so badly sitting in a car," Dennis said. We laughed at his little joke, and the tension eased.

172

Dennis and Ethan announced they would find someone to drive them to the petrol station, but first they needed a beer or two to steady their nerves, and we headed into the Drive Range together. Waves of music surged from the building and raised my spirits. I walked up to the window to buy a ticket and saw a familiar face near the door, and called out, "Rashid! Long time no see... I thought you weren't much of a disco fan? What are you doing here?" I was relieved to see someone besides Dennis and his nutty friends. Those boys spent more time giggling than most girls I knew.

Rashid rolled his eyes extravagantly. "It's because of my cousins, you see those two there?" I looked over to see two pretty Asian girls standing close together, pinkies linked, wearing shimmering lip gloss and bright embroidered silk tunics over their jeans, their long black hair falling sleekly around their faces. I waved at them, and they smiled back, their eyes sparkling. Rashid continued, "They convinced my uncle to let them go out, please don't ask me how. You know how strict our Asian families are about their girls. Of course I was the one assigned to be their chaperon."

"You're all heart," I said, smiling at him.

"Where's Sam?" Rashid asked, but he was distracted before I could answer. He suddenly sprang toward his cousins, "Girls, hello, what the bloody hell is this?" He lowered his voice and hissed at them, "Don't tell me you are smoking a cigarette, is it? If I bring you home and you're smelling like tobacco, your father will take my head off. Put that out, right now!"

The girls opened their round brown eyes wide and pouted their bottom lips slightly. I watched Rashid melt and rush to comfort them, "Don't worry, it's alright, *sasa*, my lips are sealed. But don't do it again, OK? Otherwise this will be the last time you ever see the inside of a discotheque, I have no doubt whatsoever."

Dennis waved me over to join him in the dance hall and I

walked through the double doors, leaving Rashid to sort out his wayward cousins. I stepped onto the dance floor with one of Dennis' friends, and though he was more high energy and good intention than skill, I found myself having fun.

Hours passed pleasantly. I danced a little, but mostly just sat and chatted. Dennis talked to me in his usual flamboyant way about the fabric he was going to buy for his trousers. He went into long-winded detail about where the belt loops were to be placed, and what kind of pockets he wanted, and the matching buttons he had in mind. He told me to be prepared to sew by tomorrow, because by then he was sure to have convinced Susan about the necessity of these trousers.

"And," Dennis said, leaning close, "I have good news. I spoke to Sam this afternoon and he says he will be back in time to see these particular trousers perform at the choir event. For certain."

"You spoke to Sam?"

"He tried to call you first, Sara, only your line was busy."

I shrank back in my seat in disappointment. I had missed Sam's call just because someone was on the phone.

"He'll call again. You can count on it."

"I know."

Ethan wandered over and told Dennis they should hurry if they were going to buy petrol for the car. Some guy over there was driving them, but the station was closing soon. It took some convincing to get Dennis up and moving, and he continued to loudly protest the inconvenience of it all as he left the building. Dennis. He had lots of silly bark to him, but no bite at all.

Someone plopped down next to me, and I looked up to see Rashid.

"Where are your cousins?" I asked him.

"Over there. They found some girlfriends from school and they're spending all their time talking about boys but not doing anything about it, thank goodness. I can keep an eye on them from here, and safely take a break from up-close watch-dogging.

Tell me, how are you? What have you and Sam been up to these past weeks? You have been spending far too much time together and ignoring your friends."

"Do you think so?"

"I do, absolutely."

I filled Rashid in on the latest developments in the lives of Sam and Sara – our trip to Kapenguria, and how Sam was now with his family in Kampala. It was all news to Rashid. We leaned our heads close together to talk without having to yell over the thump-thump of the music. In the middle of my description of Sam's plans to attend university in London and my hopes of joining him there, Rashid put a hand on my shoulder and said, "Hold that thought! I must visit the *choo* right this instant, or there will be unpleasant consequences. Do not run off to the dance floor just yet, I want to hear the rest of it. Back in a jiffy."

Rashid was back soon enough, but not because he wanted to continue where we left off. He didn't sit down and barely looked me in the eye when he said in a few short phrases he would not be talking to me again, he was sorry, but he had not understood how things were. I was confused and it must have shown on my face. Rashid lowered his voice as far as he could, and explained. Dennis had approached him in the restroom and told him he would kill him if he did not back off from trying to hit on his brother Sam's girlfriend. *Kill him.*

I tried to understand. Dennis was off with Ethan to buy petrol. Was he back already? Surely he would never seriously say such a thing to Rashid, of all people. Rashid was Sam and Dennis' friend, my friend, we were all friends. But there was no mistaking Rashid's strained face. He rounded up his cousins without standing for argument and left without looking back. I turned and saw Dennis standing against the far wall, watching, his arms crossed in front of his chest. Not a shadow of his normal joking self.

175

CHAPTER TWENTY

I was cocooned in my bedroom, rereading the last letter I got from Sam while I waited for my father to come home from work with today's mail. I looked forward to this moment every day, though there wasn't always a letter - it was impossible to predict how long mail would take between Kampala and Nairobi. There was one memorable day when four envelopes arrived at once and plenty when there were none.

This letter had ended with a promise: *Dennis will look out for you. Tell him if there is anything you need.* I wondered whether Sam would approve of his brother's interpretation of these instructions. I was tempted to write him about the incident with Rashid, but worried that I would unleash his jealous streak and the matter might blow even more ridiculously out of proportion. Or that he'd be furious with Dennis; I didn't want to cause trouble between them. Instead, I wrote Sam to ask when he was coming back. He had already been gone more than two weeks. I dug into the back of my nightstand drawer and drew out the postcards of London, hidden behind a box of cigarettes. Sam and I were going to have a perfect life there, once we disentangled ourselves from the complications of our families.

I heard the front door close and ran out to meet my father, home from work. "Anything for me today, papa?" I asked.

He placed his attaché case on the dining room table, stretched back his neck, reached for his collar button and undid it. He worked his fingers underneath his tie and pulled it loose, then shook off his jacket and hung it neatly across the back of the nearest chair.

"What is this?" he said. "Is this any way to greet your father when he arrives home after a long day's work? Quite a disappointment, I must say." He was going to make me work for my letter - if there was one.

I rolled my eyes at him, but with a smile so he wouldn't take offense. "I'm sorry, papa the breadwinner. How was your day? Were the cookies buttery and crisp? Have the good people of Kenya been convinced to eat nothing but KIKS three times a day?"

"Well, you may mock our KIKS all you like, but the truth is they *are* indeed buttery and delicious, and people would be delighted to eat them all day long, given half the chance."

"You're right. I love our biscuits, too. I'm just joking."

"*Hmmn,*" my father harrumphed.

"So?" I prodded him.

"Yes?"

"Is there a letter?"

"I do not recall. Let me see," he clicked open the two combination locks on his attaché case and lifted the lid. He made a big show of peering into every pocket and inspecting each piece of paper. Finally he grabbed the corner of an envelope and swooped it high over his head, like the checkered flag at the end of a race. "My, my, what a surprise... there is a letter for you, after all."

I reached for it. My father lowered the letter as if he was going to hand it to me, then changed his mind and pulled it away again.

"Before I give you this, there is something we should talk about."

I grimaced.

"Sara, you must make a decision concerning your future. You have graduated secondary school and it is all fine and good that you have taken some well-deserved time off to celebrate, but life is not one big party. You should prepare to continue your education."

My father was right. I could no longer avoid the subject.

I cleared my throat. "I have given it a good deal of thought, actually. And I've made up my mind, too. I've made a decision."

"Excellent. This is not a matter to be taken lightly. It is important step in your life, and you are right to think your options through conclusively."

When I remained silent, he added, "Well? What have you decided?"

I took a deep breath. "Sam and I want to go to London together. I thought I might apply to university."

My father looked at me with complete lack of comprehension, for once at a loss for words. We each waited for the other to speak. I kept my mouth shut and he leaned his face closer to mine, his eyes intense.

"What do you mean?"

"London. It's in England," I said carefully.

"I know this. Do you think I am an idiot?"

"Oh. I see." I swallowed. "Sam has been accepted to the University of London. It seems like a good idea for me to join him, to attend school there. People speak English, I'll fit in better."

"Really? It seems like good idea? More preferable to you than returning to your home country where you have loving aunties to welcome you with open arms, and your parents have offered you an apartment to stay as long as you like, free of rent? Where you can earn a solid secretarial degree that will guarantee employment for the duration of your life?"

"I hardly know my aunties, papa. I hate being in Holland and feeling like an outsider when I speak Dutch, and people laugh at my accent. And the aunties have stupid ideas about Africa, that we live in huts and sleep in trees like Tarzan, and eat roots. They don't believe me when I tell them we have supermarkets and nice houses and live ordinary lives just like theirs. I hate that. And I don't want to be anybody's secretary, anyway." I realized I was rambling and snapped my mouth shut.

"You would rather go to an alien city where you know nothing and nobody and you have no plan. Somehow this seems to you like a more intelligent solution."

"I'll have Sam."

"Why, how could I forget? You will have Sam. *AHA aha ha ha ha.*" My father threw back his head and laughed sarcastically. "The boy you picked up in desperation after you were thrown aside like rubbish by the boyfriend before him. This so-called *traditional African man...* which, believe me, is nothing more than a flimsy excuse to take a dozen wives and have dozens more women on the side. They are all the same, these Africans. Not adjusted to modern civilized society."

"That's ridiculous, Africans are just as civilized as anybody else. And all Africans are not the same. Sam isn't like that."

"Really? And you are sure of this how?"

"He loves me."

My father snorted. "Words are cheap, and you are a gullible fool. You have no idea what goes on in the real Africa outside of the pampered life you lead."

It was a slap in the face to understand my father saw me as a foolish little girl incapable of deciding her own future. It hurt to hear him speak badly of Sam, and to discover he had never taken the two of us seriously. I was shocked that he turned out to be just as full of prejudice as any other expat – I'd thought my father was better than that.

"Let me be perfectly clear," my father spoke each word slowly and loudly. "So there can be no misunderstanding. You will receive no support, not a cent, from us for your harebrained plan. Do not think to come weeping to your parents when your life falls to pieces and you are forced to face the disastrous consequences of your decision. If you choose to do this... you stand alone." He tossed the letter at me and strode out of the room.

It was official. I was leaving home to start a new life in London without my parents' blessing. I had to speak to Sam. I would phone him and face my parents' wrath later, when they found the expensive international call on their bill. I ran into my bedroom and rummaged through the desk drawer, looking for the number Sam had given me to call in case of emergency.

I found it and ran to the hallway, making sure the door was closed behind me, and dialed a long string of numbers to place my call to Uganda. I heard the busy signal and slapped the receiver onto the cradle to break the connection, waited for the tone, and dialed the numbers again. Nothing. Absolute silence. Had I skipped a number? I hung up and dialed again, more slowly this time, making sure I got it right. I held my breath when I heard the garbled sound of a phone ringing somewhere, as if it was underwater.

"Hello?" I heard a distorted man's voice, muffled and far away.

"Sam? Sam, is that you?" I didn't dare speak too loudly, not wanting to alert my parents.

"Hello? Who is this? Speak up, please, I cannot hear you," the voice yelled.

Shit. I pulled the receiver closer to my mouth and spoke as loudly as I dared. "Is this Sam?"

"Sam? You want to speak to Sam? Who are you?"

"This is Sara, calling from Nairobi."

"Who? Speak up!"

I groaned in frustration, and tried again. "Sara, S-A-R-A. Sara calling for Sam. Please. It's urgent."

"*Ehhhhhhhhh,*" the voice said, and fell silent.

"Hello? Are you there?" I hissed.

"OK. I will see if he can be found."

I heard the thud of the receiver at the other end dropping on something hard. Then I heard nothing but static. Minutes passed. I felt close to despair, when I heard a deep voice from a great distance saying, "Sara, is that you?" I recognized his voice instantly despite the faulty connection.

"Sam! Thank goodness. Yes, it's me."

"Are you alright? Is something the matter?" I heard his concern through the telephone cable. Sam did love me.

"No, I'm fine. It's just, I spoke to my father about going to London and he's furious. He has pretty much disowned me, you know? I don't know what to do, because I don't have money to pay for a plane ticket or tuition or what. Sam, I do really want to go to London with you, but now I have no idea how to make it happen." I was rambling again. I stopped, and hoped Sam had understood.

"Sara? What did you say about London?"

He hadn't heard me. I tried again, speaking slower and louder, "Yes. Yes, I am coming to London. But my father will not pay."

"Ah. Well, it was to be expected, wasn't it? Don't worry, I'll take care of everything."

"How, Sam?"

The connection crackled and I did not hear his answer.

"Sam?"

I heard him yell, "Home in one week. Hang in there!" and the connection was lost.

CHAPTER TWENTY-ONE

By the time Dennis came over in the evening to get me started on his trousers, my hands had stopped trembling. He handed me a flat package wrapped in brown paper and I opened it carefully. I admired the fabric inside - plain matte black, no sheen at all, and a nice thick quality. I ran it between my fingers and felt its smoothness. Dennis' Kenyan mother had included the zipper, buttons and thread in a separate little parcel, or maybe Dennis had taken care of it himself. It wouldn't surprise me - he seemed to have very particular ideas about these pants. But there was something I had to know before we carried on with everyday things.

I looked him in the eye and said, "Dennis, what happened at the disco? With Rashid?"

"Sara, listen to me." Dennis had recovered his flashy manners. "Pay attention, now. The last words my brother Samuel spoke to me before he went off on this trip of his, was to take care of you in his absence. To look out for you on his behalf, you understand? So while you may not have supposed anything was going on, I could see this guy Rashid who you consider to be just a friend, was in fact getting to be a little *too* friendly with you."

"You don't trust me? Sam doesn't trust me?"

"Of course Sam trusts you, come on now... that's not what this is all about, Sara, please! But Rashid is a different matter altogether. I could see what his intentions were, even if you apparently could not."

I alternated between wondering whether I was blind to a

friend's ulterior motives and being pissed off at Dennis, who I suspected had wildly overreacted. I wasn't thrilled with either scenario.

"I can take care of myself," I muttered, annoyed with Dennis' interference, no matter what Rashid's motives might have been.

"Also, there is Sam's honor to protect," he continued, as if I hadn't spoken. "You understand it would not do to raise the impression that you were disrespecting him in his absence."

"But I wasn't doing anything wrong!"

Dennis shrugged. "Sometimes it is enough for a thing only to look a certain way."

Dennis didn't stay, and I put the fabric aside. I felt suffocated by what he told me. With Sam gone, was I expected to worry what any stranger might be thinking of me? Was I supposed to see myself as *Sam's woman* at all times and behave in his best interests, whatever they might be? Should I be suspicious of my friends?

Sam wrote to confirm that he would be home in time for the choir performance, on what would be the day after Chloe left for Canada. The week passed by slowly. I worked on Dennis' trousers and worried for a full day about taking scissors to fabric that looked far too expensive to ruin. Luckily he wanted the legs flared as wide as I could make them, so only the hips and waist had to fit properly. By the time Dennis came to try them on, I was relieved to see these pants might actually work.

"Sara?" Dennis asked with a touch of hesitation as he swirled around to look closely at the side seams. "These are the best trousers in the world, to be sure, *kweli*. I am pleased very much with how the tightness here," he slapped his hips, "and the wideness here," he lifted his foot, "are just exactly right. I can see how these will be the most beautiful trousers on stage and everybody will be staring at me with envy, wishing they, too, could look this good. Now, I do not want you to be offended."

"What's wrong?"

"Sara, I have noticed when I bend over like this," he demonstrated, "I can see the stitches showing from the inside. Also, they are not the same color as the fabric, and it doesn't match very well." He looked pained.

"Dennis, you dork, these aren't the permanent stitches. I just put these in quickly so you could try the pants on and it'll be easy to change if something is wrong. You see? I'll finish sewing with the machine - in matching thread, obviously - and then I'll take all these colored ones out." I giggled, imagining Dennis wearing trousers tacked together with big green and red basting stitches and a pin or two, standing on stage with the rest of the choir thinking this was the way his pants were supposed to look.

"Yes, yes, I understand now," Dennis said haughtily. "How am I supposed to know these things, eh? This is not my territory of expertise, I think. Anyway," he recovered his sunny temper, "*Asante sana.* Thank you. I am lucky to have such a big sister as you." He shook my hand, changed his mind, and clamped me in a hug.

Today was the last day Chloe's family would be at their house, and I was going over to visit and see if I could help with packing. Almost all of their belongings were already boxed up, ready to be shipped to a new home on the other side of the world. Chloe and her family were leaving as soon as the house was empty, and the front door of their home in Karen would close behind them forever.

The house looked the same as it always did as I drove up the driveway and parked the VW, but inside little was left of the home I had visited so often. Nothing was in its familiar place. The huge dark wooden table in the dining room where Chloe and I had spent so many slow, lazy hours was gone. The table where weekend breakfasts turned into lunch and we had nothing better to do but fritter away the day without a plan. Where we drank pot after pot of tea and ate cold slices of toast that had been standing in a bent silver rack for hours. We covered the toast with a thin layer of soft butter and an even thinner layer of salty black Marmite, slowly swiping the knife back and forth until the bread became crumbly and flimsy. Sometimes Chloe's mother baked a yellow sponge cake and tell us to help ourselves to as many squares as we liked. Sometimes Gabriel the cook would prepare mangoes. He'd cut two halves by slicing closely around the great flat pip in the middle, then carve the syrupy orange flesh into cubes, careful not to pierce the skin. He bent the peel inside-out so the little blocks of fruit stood up like a fat-spined porcupine. We took the mango in our hands and clipped each cube with our teeth, or if the fruit was really ripe, pushed them off with our tongues. We leaned over the plates, careful not to let the sticky juices drip down our chins and onto our clothes. We ate and talked and laughed about the things happening in our lives. We smoked cigarettes and pressed the butts into discarded mango peels. Not a care in the world.

Now the table was gone and boxes were stacked in every room with traces of packing everywhere. Rolls of brown paper lay in a pile on the floor, flat cardboard boxes leaned against the wall, and open cabinet doors had things inside them waiting to be put away. I tried to set the sadness aside, so I could make the most of these last few hours with my friend.

"Chloe!" I called into the house. My voice sounded hollow in the bare room.

"Sara, are you there? Just a sec, I'm on my way." She came down the wide wooden stairs in shorts and a faded yellow t-shirt and her bare feet, no beads or bangles today. "Hi, how are you? It's so good to see you again; it's been too long."

"The house looks strange."

"I knoOow."

"How are you holding up?"

"I'm OK, really. Feeling lucky to have so many happy times

to look back on, and trying to remember to look forward to what's ahead."

Just like Chloe. Always focused on the positive.

Because there was nothing to be done about the way things had turned out, we set about making the most of our last day together. I helped Chloe sort through the mess in her closet and we got everything packed in boxes. I carefully folded the slinky green and gold number that was really a nightdress but looked just like an evening gown. She had worn it to the disco once on a whim and looked glamorous all night. We shared memories of good times and imagined our futures, hopeful that everything would work out for the best but unable to shake altogether our worries that things might not be easy, at least not at first. We planned on staying friends despite the oceans between us, and promised we would one day meet again. Finally, we took a long walk along nearby paths and fields like we had so many times before. The sun started to set and I got ready to leave.

"You have the flight information?" Chloe asked.

"Yes. The day after tomorrow. I'll meet you in the departure hall."

We didn't say goodbye. We would see each other one last time at the airport. I hugged Chloe, stepped into the car and reversed away from the house, waving at my friend as I turned onto the main road.

Chloe's flight departed at noon. The airport was not hard to find - Airport Road ran straight out of town with only the one destination. Still, I hadn't driven the route before, I knew I could get lost where others said it was impossible, so I left home in plenty of time. I wanted to say goodbye to Chloe without having to rush. It was an uneventful drive and there was nothing much of interest to see along the road, just one or two blinding white industrial parks with cement parking lots that bounced sunlight into my eyes, and shanty towns and slums further back. I turned off at the big green sign with the little airplane and drove the car onto the parking lot.

Chloe's flight was departing from the new Jomo Kenyatta terminal. The sliding doors opened as I approached and I stepped inside, picking up instantly on that typical restless airport energy. People carried too much luggage, uncomfortably dressed in their best travel finery. Overtired babies cried and complained. Travelers seemed anxious and walked quickly as if they were afraid to miss their flight, or peered at the small letters on their tickets, trying to figure out where they were supposed to be. Airports always gave me mixed feelings – they brought back sad memories of leaving behind places and people I loved as much as the excitement of heading for new adventures.

I walked through the spacious building with its clean, polished floors and modern, unchipped plastic chairs. It was sparkling new – sterile, almost. It inspired confidence, like nothing could ever go wrong in a place so efficient. I saw Chloe and her parents surrounded by people who had come to see them off. A small stack of neatly folded gift wrap balanced on the chair next to Chloe. I waved hello at her and went to greet her parents and shake hands with people I knew and introduce myself to those I didn't. Finally, I pushed aside the pile of colorful paper and sat down beside my friend. Chloe was herself, all smiles and peace, but her eyes - bright and shiny and stretched open too wide - betrayed tears. I slung my arm around her shoulder and handed her my present. It was a brand new copy of *Out of Africa*.

"So you won't forget," I said.

"I won't forget."

"I know."

We sat quietly for a few more moments, then I released her. We turned our attention to a man in his twenties who was trying to banish the melancholy by telling funny stories in a big voice, with large gestures to increase comic effects. He was in the middle of something about a wedding or a funeral; I hadn't picked up enough of the joke to make sense of it. Like the rest of his audience, I was happy to laugh a little louder than I normally would have, relieved to forget for a moment why we were here. I smiled at Chloe's mother walking toward me and sat up to hear what she had to say.

"Sara, I believe your name was just announced on the intercom."

My name? At the airport? Who even knew I was here?

I stopped breathing and leaned my body forward, listening to the crackling microphone which meant an announcement was about to be made. "Paging Miss Sara Janssen. Sara Janssen, please go to the nearest information counter at your earliest convenience."

My breath wheezed as I exhaled sharply. I squeezed Chloe's arm and saw in her eyes she also knew this could only mean something bad. Racing through the options, I could think of a million tragedies that would result in such a call, and not a single good thing.

"Go," she said gently. "Go find out what this is.

CHAPTER TWENTY-TWO

I rose from the airport chair and realized I had no idea how to find the nearest information counter. I glanced left and right, then went in the direction of the most activity. I walked in a beeline to an airline desk, quickly, not wasting steps meandering. I told the uniformed stewardess an announcement had been made with my name in it and I had to find the information counter. She looked up from her paperwork and pointed a long red fingernail in the direction of a booth marked *Information* in large black letters.

My feet hurried to the counter. The man in charge was dealing with an angry middle-aged couple – tourists, by the look of their red fried skins. I tried to attract his attention, but he refused to acknowledge me. I stood to the side of the couple, keeping him in my line of vision, making sure he could not forget me. Finally the tourists picked up their bags and moved on, complaining loudly about the horrible African experience they would never repeat. *Go back to where you came from,* I cursed them in my mind.

"Yes?" the man behind the counter said. I explained that I was the one named in the announcement. He nodded his head and picked up a telephone from his side of the counter, lifted it up to me, told me I was to call a gentleman named Dennis Dragu, and gave me the number where he could be reached.

I dialed the number. Dennis picked up after the first ring. He told me to come to his stepmother's house in Langata and gave me instructions. He told me to come now, immediately. I walked out of the terminal and stepped into the taxi at the head of the

189

waiting row. I would never find this address by myself. I handed the driver a scrap of paper on which I had jotted the directions. *"Haraka,"* I said. Drive fast.

The taxi pulled up to the side of a bungalow. Dennis was sitting slumped in a chair in the corner of the patio from where he could see the car arriving. I flew out of the taxi. Dennis rose, then fell onto me with his arms around my shoulders; I teetered as I tried to keep him from falling to the ground. He wailed and thumped my back with the flat of his hands.

"No, Dennis. No... stop. What is it? What?" If I could get him to behave normally I might somehow change this thing he was about to tell me.

"Sam is dead."

My head reared back as if from a slap. I felt the blood rush from my face.

"Sam is dead," Dennis repeated when I remained silent.

"No."

"Yes, yes, yes, it is what happened! It cannot be denied."

"No."

Dennis stared at me. He drew himself up straight and blinked his eyes, took hold of my arms, placed me in the chair. I sat down. I looked at Dennis's face, trying to understand what he was saying to me, his voice quieter now.

"Sam was feeling sick some few days."

Sick? He never wrote about feeling sick.

"He did not want to upset you, he did not want you to know, he forbade me to tell you."

He was sick badly enough to have worried me, if I had known. What could possibly have made him suddenly so sick?

"He had pains in his stomach, very bad pains. They took him to hospital, the doctor did not know what was wrong and before he could determine it, already Sam was dead."

"Sam had stomach pains?" There must be some mistake, this was just ridiculous. Sam was strong and healthy, an athlete, he never even caught a cold - how were stomach pains going to kill him?

"It was so bad near the end, he could not stand on his own two feet. He crawled along the floor crying, crying for someone to take him to the doctor and they had to carry him to the car and lift him onto the hospital bed. There was no medication to help him. There was no treatment. He died right there."

Just like that, I stopped struggling. I saw Sam crawl along the floor before my eyes, Sam cry from pain so savage he could not bear it, Sam suffer without relief and without understanding until death took him. I accepted this as the truth. It became very hard to breathe, like something had been jammed down my throat. I tried to clear it away, but could not swallow. A hacking sound escaped me.

When Dennis took my hand, I stood. When he walked into the house, I followed. Many people stood inside along the four walls with somber faces, speaking in low voices. We went past them into the hallway. Dennis opened the door of a small room and sat me down on the bed. He talked to me softly; I did not hear enough of his words to make sense of them. He pushed me to lie down and I did. He shut off the light and closed the door behind him.

I was alone. Now maybe I could figure this out. There was probably some mistake, really. After all, Sam was far away in Uganda and we all knew communication was nearly impossible what with the crackling phone lines and letters that sometimes took a week to get here. *Sam, I think there's been some mistake. What's going on?* Sam crawling along the floor, howling. Clutching his stomach. He suffered terribly. My tears dropped into two round damp spots where I clamped the pillow to my face. I rolled onto my side and pulled the blanket over my legs and all the way up to my chin.

I caught my breath with a gasp as I broke back into

consciousness. Dennis was sitting next to me on the edge of the bed with his hand on my shoulder. I believed for one bright moment that everything was fine. Then I saw his face, and his eyes swollen and red. It was a bad idea to sleep, a moment of foolish waking happiness followed by the vicious slap of reality, hitting hard as though death was new. I would not survive this every time I woke up.

"Sara, we must talk."

I nodded.

"Sam must be buried at home, in the village where he was born. We will travel to Kampala to collect his body and travel north for the funeral."

I understood.

"Sara, we are leaving for Uganda tonight."

"I'm coming with you."

"Yes. I will take you. There are things then you should arrange quickly before we go. You should bring clothes and such."

"I have to call my parents."

I followed Dennis into the living room where people still stood. The phone was on a shelf in a tall bookcase, and Dennis dragged over a low stool for me to sit on. My finger trembled as I aimed for the holes in the dial. I had no idea what my number was. I frowned, trying to focus. Dennis handed me his address book and I read the numbers, turned the dial. The phone rang. My mother answered.

"Mrs. Janssen speaking."

"Mama."

"Sara, is that you? Where are you?"

"*Mama, er is iets vreselijks gebeurd.* Something terrible has happened." I spoke Dutch for privacy.

"What do you mean, are you alright?"

"Yes, mama, I'm fine. It's Sam." My voice wouldn't make more words.

"Sam? What's the matter with Sam?"

"He's dead."

"*Ach,* child, surely that's not possible. Sam is dead? How could such a thing be... Why, just today papa brought home another letter. I was saying how it is a good thing he writes so often. I am impressed, and I think even your father agrees, though you know he would never admit it. Sam is almost on his way to come back to Nairobi in time for his brother's choir performance, didn't you say so?"

I squeezed my eyes tight: *please, mama, just listen to me. Don't make me have a long conversation about this.* "He got sick, something with his stomach. They took him to the hospital but he couldn't be treated and he died. That's all I know."

"Dead? I can't believe it, dreadful, horrible... such a young life, such a bright future."

"Mama, I need your help."

"Yes, of course, tell me what I can do."

I explained to my mother that Sam was being buried in the village where he was born in Uganda and I was leaving with Dennis tonight to attend the funeral. I needed her to pack me a bag and bring it to the house in Langata because my car was sitting in the airport parking lot. My mother was silent. Then she said, "I am fetching your father. You will speak to him."

My father came on the phone with the booming theatrical voice he used when he was uncomfortable. "So, daughter, I understand you have had some very bad news, shocking news. We are sorry for your loss, very sorry indeed. Please express our condolences to the family."

My eyes filled with tears.

"Now," my father continued, "What is this about going to Uganda? It is not that we don't appreciate your desire to attend the funeral, of course we do, it is only natural you would feel this way. But you must understand it is absolutely impossible. Uganda at this time is a country in a state of complete lawlessness. All whites have been evacuated. Even the consulate has been closed and only one Dutch person remains in the entire country, a priest out in the bush somewhere - there is a strong suspicion he is somewhat mentally deranged. It is a guaranteed death sentence for you to go into that country at this time."

I suppressed my despair; there was no time for it. "Papa, I have to do this. I am going to Uganda to bury Sam."

"I forbid it," my father roared, "I forbid it, do you hear me?"

I took a deep breath. "Papa, do you have a pencil? I am going to tell you the names of the people I am traveling with, and the address of the house I will be staying at."

CHAPTER TWENTY-THREE

I carefully replaced the phone. I shook my head at Dennis. "They won't bring my stuff. They don't want me to go."

"It's OK, Sara. We can find someone to drive you over to your place, no big deal."

"No. I can't face seeing them now. I'll just wear this, it doesn't matter."

"You can borrow things from my sisters when we get to Kampala."

Dennis led me to the sofa in the room and someone got up to make room for me. I sat down while he went off to do things. He told me they were important but I couldn't remember why. A toddler waddled over. She came right up to me with bowlegged, thick steps and placed her tiny hand on my knee, leaning into me for balance. I placed her warm coffee-colored hand on my open palm and patted the cushion on the back of her hand. Her round face lit up with open-mouthed laughter. She had four small white teeth on top and four on the bottom. I touched her soft curly hair, caught in a headband with a glittery flower over one ear. It matched her princess dress, pink and shiny with a wide skirt standing out on layers of stiff petticoats. She bounced, bending her fat little knees, up and down, up and down, up and down. Then she wandered off.

A man leaned toward me until his face was at my level. He was holding a plate of food. It was a mound of brown meat cubes with sauce and something in it, maybe onions or the leaves of some vegetable, and a scoop of rice. The man was trying to hand me the plate, telling me I should eat. I wondered where the food came from. I looked around and saw the kitchen door. Women were walking in and out, carrying platters and bowls and the smell of cooking with them. I looked back down at the plate and took it, put it on my lap.

"You must eat," the man said again.

I picked up the fork and he seemed satisfied and walked away. I put down the fork. The warm spot where the plate sat on my lap gradually cooled.

People came and went. Crying broke out, then faded away again. *Let's stay together, loving you, whether times are good or bad, happy or sad...* the song looped endlessly and hopelessly through my mind.

A man came close and tried to tell me something. Was it the same one who brought the plate of food? Maybe he wanted me to eat again. I frowned. He touched my arm, "Someone is at the door for you."

I walked to the entrance. There, just inside the screen door with the harsh hallway light blanching her face, stood my mother. She looked tired, her mouth and eyes sagging. She had forgotten to put on a shade of lipstick that matched her outfit and her pink lips clashed with the bright orange circles on her dress. My mother kept dozens of lipsticks neatly arranged in the top drawer of her vanity: she always wore pink with pink, orange with orange, red with red.

She held my small plaid suitcase in her hand, and carefully put it down on the floor beside her when she saw me.

"Mama."

She held me. I cried like I might never stop. Finally my mother took me by the shoulders and gently pushed me away. She waited for me to pull myself together.

"Your father is very upset."

"I'm sorry."

"We wish you would not do this."

"I have to go."

My mother blinked her eyes a few times. "Yes, I understand how you would make that choice. I don't suppose it will make any difference to ask you to be careful, especially careful. I know you think we worry too much, but this is a truly dangerous thing you are doing. You will be a target, being a white person in Uganda at this time."

"A target for what, mama? I won't be alone. Dennis will be with me and so will the rest of the family."

"Just be careful, please." She kissed me and left.

"Thank you." I called after her through the screen door. She turned and waved, the corners of her lips pushed up in a smile that did not reach her eyes.

I watched her car pull away and leaned my forehead against the screen until the evening breeze dried my cheeks. I squatted down next to the suitcase and pulled open the zipper. My mother had packed a black blouse with the little pearl buttons. It was slightly sheer but probably the most suitable thing I owned for a funeral. There were two pairs of jeans and some t-shirts. Also the sandals Sam hated so much. He would be sure to appreciate the joke. My mother had stuffed chocolate bars, a tin of KIKS, and little bags of potato chips in every nook and cranny. Right at the bottom of the suitcase, I found a white envelope with my name on it. I opened it and discovered a few hundred shilling notes and my passport. I hadn't thought to bring those. I put everything back and closed the zipper.

Dennis walked into the hallway. "Someone dropped off your case?"

"My mother."

Dennis nodded. "Can you be ready to go in half an hour?"

"I am ready."

It was time to leave. Susan, Sam's stepmother, led Dennis and me to her car. Dennis explained, "We are traveling now, ahead of the rest, because of the many preparations I must assist in. Those people you saw at the house will start following soon, and we must be ready for them, as well as for others already in Uganda."

I glanced at him. "So many? For Sam?"

Dennis nodded. "African funerals are big events, people with the slightest connection to the deceased must come and demonstrate their grief; pay their respects. Sometimes they stay for days, even weeks. In this particular situation, with my father an important man in the village, and Sam his number one son..." His weary face briefly took on an anxious look. "There is no telling how many people will show up. And they must all be fed and housed. It is a lot for the family to bear."

Susan drove us into the city. The streets were dark and deserted with few cars on the road and none of the crowds of pedestrians that swarmed the sidewalks by day. Here and there a beggar lay curled on a flattened cardboard box, covered by a piece of plastic sheeting or newspaper for warmth. Storefronts were hidden behind steel gates and closed tight with big, solid padlocks. Most of the neon signs advertising bars and restaurants were switched off. We drove in silence.

When Susan parked the car, I looked around, not knowing where I was. Dennis stepped onto the sidewalk and took his bag and mine, and I went to stand next to him. Susan and Dennis had a rapid conversation in Swahili. She handed him a wad of bills.

"Come with me, Sara," Dennis said, and I followed him to a somber brick building. As we got closer, we were met by the stench of urine. I exhaled sharply and clamped my hand to my nose. Inside the air was not quite as bad, though the dimly-lit hall we stepped into was dirty and shabby, with overflowing trash bins in the corner and fat black flies hovering over the mess. Backless wooden benches with missing slats leaned against the walls. People sat or stood, surrounded by their belongings packed in cloth and tied together with a piece of string, or in cardboard boxes. Most of the women were dressed traditionally in a top and *kanga* folded around their hips and tucked tightly at the waist like a skirt, not in Nairobi city clothes. Dennis walked up to the man sitting behind sliding glass windows at the counter and bought two tickets, and I realized we were at a station of some kind.

"The bus will start boarding in ten minutes," Dennis said.

"I forgot to say goodbye to Susan."

"Don't worry, you will see her again soon enough in Kampala."

"Are all of these people going in one bus?"

"It seems that way."

I didn't think so many people would fit, but when the man behind the glass stood up and shouted that it was time to board, everybody gathered their things and moved toward the exit. I followed Dennis and stayed close by him, taking my place in a sloppy queue as he waited to hand our bags to the attendant who stood by the side of the bus. The attendant took the baggage from each passenger and threw it up to a man standing on the roof of the bus. The roof man never missed and easily caught even odd items like a round woven basket full of live chickens, and a stalk of big green bananas more than a meter long that looked like it weighed a ton. He quickly and cleverly stacked each item, and soon my case was hidden inside a mound of baggage. He tied everything down with ropes, then spread a net and tied it down, too. Most passengers stood on the sidewalk watching, some calling out instructions to make sure their belongings were not left behind or at risk of dropping off along the way. People boarded the bus and looked for a place to sit. Dennis led me all the way to the back, put me in a corner, and sat down next to me. He held my hand. The driver started the engine with a roar. I smelled exhaust seeping in through the windows.

I looked outside and watched the empty city fall behind me until we turned onto the highway. Soon there was nothing left to see but my own pale reflection in the window. My first trip to

Uganda was not supposed to be like this.

I leaned my head back against the padded seat. The bus was packed with people squeezed into every bit of sitting space. Bodies were glued to bodies and heads bobbed back and forth in a shared rhythm as we jerked along the road. A conversation started up between the passengers. I recognized the language as Swahili, understood a word here and there. It made no difference. I was a stranger. Talk grew louder and more people joined in – laughter rushed through the bus. Dennis jumped up from his seat and yelled at them. His speech was met by another burst of laughter. A fat lady halfway up the bus pointed her many chins in my direction and made another comment, apparently also very funny. I got it. Everybody was laughing at me.

"What are they saying?"

"Don't worry about it, Sara, these here are primitive, illiterate, stupid Africans. Only just come down out of the trees to join civilization," he sucked his lips against his teeth in disgust. "Ignore them."

The bus quieted down as minutes, then hours, passed by. Bodies sagged against each other as people fell asleep. I may have dozed off now and again, short snatches of sleep that left me feeling disoriented, not rested. The night was long. It was a relief when the first rays of morning light broke through the darkness, and a thin strip along the horizon turned green and then shades of blue. There were no clouds to block the view of the big orange sun as it rose. How odd, such a beautiful sunrise. I pressed the heels of my hands against my burning eyes.

The bus shuddered to a halt and the driver cut the engine. He turned to face us and called out something. People roused themselves and started jostling toward the open door in the front. Dennis and I sat quietly. When we were the last ones left in the bus, Dennis looked at me and said, "Shall we?" and I nodded. I sidled through the aisle behind him and stepped outside. The air smelled good, fresh. The hairs on my arms rose against the cool morning, and it was not an unpleasant feeling. I walked in a slow circle and felt the circulation return to my cramped legs. I rolled my arms and shoulders to unlock them.

The road that brought us here was not much more than a ridged dirt track ending in this wide open area, though I could see asphalt back farther down the hills. The bus was parked haphazardly as if it had been dropped from the sky. This place did not look like any kind of official station, or even a parking lot. A few cars were scattered here and there, but no other buses. The red earth was packed hard and dry, and dust swirled up with every step. A thin scattering of trees had a leaf or two of green and some thin clumps of grass stood wherever there was a bit of shade, but otherwise the land was bare.

We stood near the bus - hardly recognizable as the one we started out in, now covered in a thick coat of red dust - and waited for our bags to be unloaded. This time the roof man threw the baggage down in a gentle arch to the ground man, who handily caught each item and put it on the dust undamaged. Our cases stood on the ground next to the other bags and parcels. We went to pick them up.

"We will eat first, then we can clean up a little before we continue to Kampala."

"Dennis, where are we?"

"We are at the border. The bus cannot go any further because no traffic may cross in either direction, you know the border is still officially closed because of the recent war in Uganda. When Amin was thrown out. This here is not an official border post – it is some kind of no man's land. We are not in either Kenya or Uganda. We'll walk across to the other side and someone from the family will collect us and take us to the house."

A lady sat on her haunches in the shade of a tree, waving a square of cardboard back and forth to keep the coals in her brazier glowing. Some ears of maize were roasting on the grate.

The ones that were ready to eat stuck upright in a basket like a bunch of stiff blackened flowers. Dennis bought one for each of us. "You must eat," he said to me. I tried, but the kernels were tough and I lacked the strength to chew them. My mouth was dry and I could not work the food down my throat.

"Can we get something to drink?" I asked.

"Yes. Come with me. I will buy you a soft drink, eh? There is a public standpipe with water over there, do you see it? You cannot drink the water from it, it is not what you are used to and will make you sick, really sick. Only drink water if you can be sure it was filtered and boiled."

The pumped water looked cool and clear and my dry mouth longed for a swallow. Instead, we walked to a vendor who produced two bottles of orange drink. The warm sugary beverage went down easily and soothed my throat, but didn't do much to ease my thirst. I felt better anyway. Following Dennis' lead, I opened my suitcase to find my toothbrush. I discovered the dust had not only attached itself to the outside, but had also crept in through the zipper – everything inside was pink. I blew away the fine layer, but the dust swirled up in a cloud and flew into my face, then floated back down into the suitcase.

Dennis produced a short green plastic cup, and filled it for me at the pump. "Do not swallow the water," he said again.

"OK."

I walked to the edge of the parking lot and squeezed a little toothpaste onto my brush, cleaned my teeth, and brushed the dryness from my mouth. Fellow passengers stood on both sides of me, a dozen meters or so between us, all of us doing our best to tidy up and wipe off the travel grit. I spit toothpaste onto the ground, and carefully trickled a little water onto my toothbrush to rinse it, then crouched down to pour water into my cupped hands and splash it on my face. Water dripped onto the ground and sat on top of it in round bubbles next to gobs of white toothpaste and spit; this earth was too dry and hard to absorb any moisture. I ran my fingers through my hair and felt it was thick with dust. I would have liked to relieve myself, but didn't want to squat among the sparse bushes like I saw others do. I'd just have to hang on until we reached the house in Kampala, where there would be bathrooms and toilets.

"Are you ready?" Dennis asked as I walked back toward where he was standing.

"Yes."

"Do you have your passport with you?"

"In my suitcase."

"You should carry it on your person. Always. Many times in Uganda you will be asked to identify yourself at roadblocks and maybe just like that in town, even for no apparent reason. Be prepared to do so quickly whenever the soldiers ask you, eh? The government has not put itself together since Amin. Uganda is still under control of the military."

I did as he told me, stuck my passport in the back pocket of my jeans, and as an afterthought, also the envelope with money. We walked into Uganda on the other side of the open space. A small yellow car stood parked off to the side of a road. A man stood stiffly beside it with his arms crossed. Dennis went straight to him. They shook hands and spoke in low voices. I stood and waited. Dennis waved me over and introduced me to his uncle.

"Welcome to Uganda," the man said grimly.

CHAPTER TWENTY-FOUR

I got into the back seat of the car and fastened the seat belt across my lap. I had promised my mother to keep safe and this seemed like one thing I had control over. It was a long drive to Kampala. The color of the land shifted from red to green, and fields of tall grass stretched into the distance on both sides of the road. Small one-room square houses built from gray cinder block stood scattered beside the road. There was no glass in the windows now, but maybe there never had been. Roofs were partially or completely torn off. Doors hung lopsided from a single hinge and walls were only half standing. The small dings of bullet holes peppered every brick, door and sheet of roofing - not one building was undamaged. Violence had come close to home along this road. People seemed to be living in the houses, even though they were barely standing. Sticks of furniture were visible through the broken walls and small naked children played in the grass.

Our car pulled over and stopped. We had reached a roadblock controlled by four men in uniform. One slouched on a rusted metal folding chair and two stood in the road flagging down traffic. The fourth - a big man, his camouflage jacket stretched tightly across his fat belly, huge pistols strapped to either side of his hips - walked over to the driver's side and peered into the car. He barked a question, and Dennis told me to hand the man my passport. The soldier examined it closely. He took it to show the man standing in the road, who shrugged his shoulders. I suspected they didn't see a lot of Dutch passports here. He walked back at a leisurely pace and handed it to me, reaching deep into the car with his massive arm, and took Dennis's ID from him, as well as the small stack of bills discreetly attached to the back of it. The soldier slid the bills into his pocket, returned the ID without looking at it and waved our car through. When we were back on the road, I gave Dennis my envelope with money, so I could contribute at least something.

"Who are they, Dennis?" I whispered, as if the soldiers might hear me as we drove along the road.

His uncle answered. "UNLA. Uganda National Liberation Army. An army made up of those exiles who lived across the border in our neighboring country of Tanzania for years, preparing and waiting for the right moment to come home and liberate us from Amin. Also probably some soldiers remaining from the Tanzanian army, the ones who spearheaded the campaign. And anyone else who found themselves a uniform to wear." He shook his head. "They finally cast Amin out, and now they are here on the streets to keep the peace, and fill their pockets in the process. We have suffered enough, all of us. We can only hope the soldiers will be gone entirely, soon, and life will start returning to normal."

A few kilometers further down the road we stopped at a similar setup. This time we were all ordered out of the car and it was thoroughly searched. My suitcase was opened and a soldier dug through my things, holding a bra over his head by the strap for his colleagues to admire, yelling out things that were met with snorts of laughter. Dennis placed his hand lightly on my shoulder, maybe to warn me to stay quiet. I needed no warning. I felt confused and exhausted, and could barely make sense of the things that were happening to me one after the other. Sam was dead. I was powerless in the face of it all, and whatever would take place right now depended on the whims of these armed men. The bra was thrown back in the suitcase and all the food removed before we were allowed to pass.

In one of his letters, Sam wrote about traveling down this same road. He had quickly run out of cash because there were so many more roadblocks than the last time he had been here, and he found himself unprepared for the many payments he was forced to make. When there was no money left to collect, a soldier took his shoes and socks. At the next roadblock, Sam showed his bare feet and empty wallet to prove there was nothing left to take, but it turned out there was something: the small picture of me Sam kept in his wallet. I remembered the one, nothing special, just a black and white passport picture. The soldier wanted it. Sam resisted, telling him this was a picture of his wife and it would be dishonorable for another man to carry it. The soldier took it anyway. Sam was furious. I wrote back asking him if he had lost his mind – it seemed like such a little thing to give to a soldier as a fee. Maybe I should send over a stack of pictures he could use instead of cash? Think of the money he'd save! I was just kidding, but Sam did not like my joke. He wrote back that now all he could think of was this animal, this ape, wanking off to my picture, telling his beer buddies all kinds of filthy lies about the things he did to me on his stinking, maggot-infested mattress.

Your wife, Sam?

By the time we passed by a sign announcing Jinja Town, I had lost count of the roadblocks. We were flagged down at every one, and so was every other car. Jinja sounded familiar, and I remembered this was where the cheap cottons were woven that I bought back home on Biashara Street. Smoke rose from the factories in the distance. Textile mills were humming. Life went on as usual for some.

At last we pulled up to tall, black iron gates at the end of a short cement driveway. We had arrived at the Dragu home in Kampala, and Dennis' uncle beeped the horn. People streamed from the house and children raced to see who could get to the gates first to open them. Behind them, women walked slowly in clusters, wrapped in bright yellows, reds and blues. They wailed and beat their breasts in anguish. A woman broke out in high-pitched ululating, keening in the African way. It was too much to bear. Dennis was engulfed by arms that reached out to clutch him and I watched him bend under the weight of it. I stood apart and tried not to let the loneliness of this moment be the final straw to break the fragile grip I had on myself.

"Sara?"

I turned toward the small voice to see a young girl looking up at me, her eyes wide and friendly and her head tipped sideways in a question. Two girls of similar age, maybe ten or twelve years old, stood close behind her. They waited expectantly, like a flock of birds - curious, but ready to fly off in a heartbeat if the situation turned sour.

"You are Sara?"

I smiled at them. How funny to hear these girls I didn't know call me by my name.

"Yes, I am."

"Oh," the first girl said with obvious excitement, "We are so happy to meet you. Sam told us many things about you, Dennis also, and we always hoped to meet you only it never seemed likely. And now here you are with us, imagine!" The girl beamed, seeming oddly oblivious to the disaster that had brought me to her doorstep. It was strange, but something of a relief, too - this cheerful child piercing through the grief that hovered so thickly around us.

The girl, perhaps picking up on my confusion, set about making introductions. "Sorry, now, I am being rude. Let me introduce you to us girls. This here is Anna, she is the eldest, and this is Abigail, she is the youngest, and me, I am Adela, right in the middle."

"You are Sam's sisters."

"Yes, we are... how did you know? Did Sam talk to you about us?"

I nodded. I was happy to be with Sam's sisters. I looked them over for a glimpse of something familiar, but found little to remind me of Sam, just the strong bones of their faces and the way they wore their hair trimmed short. I thought I saw Sam in Anna's serious expression, but she did not have that reserve he used to keep people at a distance. The girls had nothing like Sam's tight muscles or Dennis' stringy leanness. They were rounder, more cuddly versions of their brothers, and shorter - pretty as pictures.

"Will you come inside?" Anna spoke shyly.

"My suitcase is in the car."

"Don't worry about that just now, please, we will collect it for you later. We will look after you," the girls said.

They took me by the hand, and I followed them into Sam's home.

CHAPTER TWENTY-FIVE

The house was huge - an imposing cube of brick. The sisters and I went inside through the wide open double doors and stepped into an entry hall, grand like the foyer of a hotel. There was a lull in the bustle of people moving in and out of the house, and the girls and I stood alone. The floor was light marble and walls and doors were painted white. The ceiling reached up two stories. To the right, a wide staircase curved up to a hallway on the first floor with a black railing running from the bottom of the stairs along the length of the upstairs hallway. The railing was beautifully crafted from wrought metal turned in swirls and diamonds, a frilly touch in otherwise plain surroundings, and I could not understand why I felt a spasm of dread as I looked at it.

"I saw him, you know," Adela said.

"What do you mean?"

"Sam. Just before they went to take him to hospital. I saw him."

"Here?" I turned to look at the upstairs hallway, following her eyes.

Adela pointed at one of the doors on the upper floor. "Over there is Sam's bedroom. On the day he got so bad, he came out of his room, crying. He could not stand and there in the hallway he fell down to his hands and knees and dragged himself forward holding on to the railing, calling for someone to help him, help him, the pain was too terrible and he could not take it any longer."

I stared at the railing in horror.

"I was standing here where we are now, looking up at him. I saw his eyes, the fear so huge inside them. For a moment I was too stupid to think. Then I screamed and everybody came. They carried him down the stairs, holding him by his arms and legs, the women who were home, and put him in the back seat of a car. He cried the whole time, and fought when they lifted him. When they finally put him down he curled up like a little baby."

No, Sam. No, no, no.

Adela looked at me, her eyes stretched wide and moist. "I'd never seen a man cry." She covered her eyes tightly with her hands to block out what she was remembering. She leaned against me and pressed her face into my side, her eyes still covered.

"He is an angel with God now," the sisters murmured, patting her gently.

Adela's sisters peeled her from me and we stood another moment, waiting until it became possible to walk. They took me by the hand again, by both hands, and we turned toward the stairs. They held on to me tightly and we climbed each step together. I heard the sound of many voices talking and smatterings of laughter from behind one of the doors. The girls pushed it open and stood aside to let me step through first: it was a large bedroom. Heavy drapes were partly drawn to keep the afternoon heat out, but let in enough daylight to see by. Two beds covered with matching bedspreads stood side by side with the headboards against the wall, separated by a nightstand.

The room was full of women – seated on the beds, leaning against the walls, squatting or sitting on the floor with their legs stretched out straight in front of them, body against body. The talking stopped when I stepped into the room and every face turned to look at me. It started up again as the women called out words of consolation and shuffled to made room for me and the girls. We stepped carefully over legs and made our way toward the farthest bed. Gestures made it clear I was to sit down at the

210

top end, and a pillow was eased behind my back as I leaned against the headboard. I pulled my knees up close, feet flat on the mattress, so I wouldn't take up too much space. The women nearest to me leaned over to touch my legs and arms and whisper condolences. Soon attention turned away from me and conversations started up again, and the women slipped into languages I did not understand.

The door opened and a girl leaned in through the opening with a saucer of food. The person closest by reached and took it, and it was passed overhead from hand to hand until it came to me. A single layer of fried chicken livers was arranged carefully on the plate. The one food in the world I hated more than anything. I tried to pass the plate to the next person, but it was pushed back to me. The liver was for me. I hesitated, but saw no alternative - I took the smallest piece between forefinger and thumb and dropped it into my mouth. Around me women cooed approvingly. I chewed warily on the rubbery meat, its bitter taste flooding my mouth. Quickly I worked it down my throat, but the taste stayed. It was all I could do to stop myself from gagging.

Dennis stepped through the door. A friendly howl rose from the women - it was clear a man was quite out of place here. It sounded like they were teasing him and he responded by grinning and throwing remarks back at them. It was good to see Dennis behave like his old self, and I watched with fondness as he joked and flirted with the older ladies. He clambered as near to me as he could get, then bent toward me when he could get no closer and supported himself with one straight arm on the mattress. He handed me a set of flatware: an ordinary spoon, fork and knife.

"Sara, this is your own personal cutlery. Do you know what I mean?" It seemed he was trying to have a private conversation with me in this crowded room, but we were really too far apart for intimacy. I edged as near to him as I could.

"Yes," I said with some hesitation. I knew what cutlery was, obviously, though I wasn't quite sure what the implication of personal cutlery could be.

"What I mean is, you must keep this with you always, not give it to anyone else, wash it by your own hand, and eat only using this."

"Why?"

"I'm going to tell you why, but I don't want you to get too worried, you understand? Everything is going to be fine. I am looking out for you."

"OK."

"There is some reason to believe perhaps Sam was poisoned. And for whatever reason he was poisoned, it could be that person also would have put you on the list."

"Sam was poisoned?"

"Now, this is just speculation at this point. Just a theory. We are only being careful. Don't eat any food I didn't give you myself."

I thought of the piece of liver I had swallowed earlier, but immediately discarded the notion that someone had poisoned me. It was too outlandish to be taken seriously. Someone poisoned Sam? Who would do such a thing? This sounded just like the old Dennis, all crazy overreaction and wild stories. I put the flatware aside on the nightstand.

The rest of the day passed slowly and I was relieved when the sky turned dark. My limbs were heavy from the distance I had traveled and from sitting still for hours on the bed. One by one the women left the room, and finally only the girls and I remained. I asked whether there was anything I could do to help – I presumed they were off to cook or take care of other chores - but I was told to rest. The sisters stayed with me and chattered among themselves, trying to decide who was to sleep where, taking it for granted that one of the beds was reserved for me. I felt embarrassed. I was one of the youngest ones here, and I tried to explain that I could sleep anywhere and didn't want preferential treatment. There was no budging them. I suspected they thought a white girl could not sleep without a comfortable bed but I was so tired I could have slept on gravel. A lively discussion followed to decide who would spend the night next to me on the bed, and who on the floor beside me. I didn't get involved again, because I didn't mind one way or another.

"Do you want to go outside for a little, Sara? You've been cooped up inside all day," Anna said.

"Yes, I'd like that."

We walked down the stairs and past the large kitchen. Half a dozen women were chopping piles of vegetables and meat and stirring huge aluminum pots, talking all the while in their big voices. Movement and words were calm and deliberate; here in Africa even the most stressful situations never seemed to cause much urgency or anxiety. People did not get flustered easily. We passed the open door and walked through a humid fog fueled by boiling water and gas burners turned up high. The smell of cooked onions hung thick in the air. The girls bunched closely around me and talked softly with each other as we continued on our way to the back door.

"Sara," Anna said, "are you going to wash?"

"What do you mean?" I asked.

"Yourself. Will you be bathing?"

"Now?"

"No, wait, let me explain." Her voice and face were serious. "Here among our people it is traditional for members of the family close to the deceased not to wash their body, or even their hair, from when the death occurs until after the funeral. It is a sign of respect, and proper mourning."

Adela added, "Sometimes relatives, the women, also shave their heads. Mostly in the villages, I think. You don't see people grieve much that way in the city." She thought about it for a moment, then went on, sounding a little ashamed, "I don't want to shave my head."

"Well, I might," said Anna. "I am thinking about it. What about you, Sara? Will you take part in our traditions?"

I was silent, thinking I wanted more than anything to be accepted as a member of Sam's family. His *almost* wife, or his *might-have-been* wife. I did not want to be alone or different. I yearned to feel like I belonged, and honor the customs in the same way as everybody else.

"I won't wash," I said. I would shave my head if it came to that.

We stepped outside, into the back yard. Considering the size of the house, it was not a very large area. A bonfire roared in the middle and the heat pushed all activity to the outer edges along the tall cement walls surrounding the yard. This was where the men had gathered. Most of them held a bottle of beer and a plate of food and sat on the many different pieces of furniture that had been dragged outside – even a bulky velvet-covered sofa, its tassels sagging onto the grass. The fire washed everything with a soft reddish glow. It looked like a party, except faces were sad and there was no music or laughter.

"These men here will take care of the fire. They will tend it and keep it alight for three nights, until we leave for the village, for the burial. People will wake throughout the night, and gather about this fire. It is a mourning tradition."

"When do we leave?"

"A day or two, maybe three. It depends. There are things to be arranged."

I heard some popping sounds on the other side of the wall. A smattering of single pops, then a few strung together, *pop-pop-pop*, followed by silence. I dug into my brain, trying to place the sounds. Finally, I asked and Anna, the eldest sister, who answered matter-of-factly: "Those are gunshots."

"Gunshots?"

"Yes, just random shots. Not an attack or anything, no intention to hit any person. Maybe whoever is on guard is scaring people off. But probably some guys are just fooling around, shooting in the air, making sure everybody knows they are carrying weapons."

I believed her and did not feel threatened, convinced she knew what was going on outside these walls. We stood awhile. My eyes felt scratchy and irritated. I yawned so widely, it hurt my jaws. I followed the girls back to the bedroom and they put me on the bed, covered me with a sheet, fussed over me as if I were a doll. Gratefully, I felt sleep take me quickly.

I woke the next morning to a delicious feeling of normalcy before I remembered where I was, and why. Grief heavy as an elephant roused in me. Watery light poured in where the curtains did not close completely. I did not move.

Others started stirring and I saw how many had spent the night in this room. At my feet, with her head facing the foot end of the bed, Abigail, the youngest sister, was still curled in deep sleep. I hoped she would stay asleep and we could lie here, not participating in this day at all. But soon the waking sounds around us disturbed her and she sat up, looking very young with tousled hair and blurry eyes.

The morning passed slowly. I wasn't encouraged to take part in chores, but not left to be alone, either. I sat with Abigail as she washed the breakfast dishes under an outdoor tap in front of the house - there was not enough room in the overburdened kitchen. I watched as she placed a blue plastic tub beneath the tap and filled it with cold water. She sprinkled laundry soap into the water; the default detergent of Africa, used to clean anything from babies to cars. Little white grains floated on top of the surface in a thin crust. She stirred the water with her hand, her fingers spread wide, until they dissolved and bubbles appeared. Each plate and piece of cutlery was carefully washed with her hands moving firmly along the surface, and then rinsed under the tap and left to dry in the sun on a striped towel. She was a quiet girl, Abigail, and her comfortable silence set me free to be with my own thoughts. I tried to imagine how Sam would have spent his days here, but couldn't. I saw only women doing the things women were expected to do.

After she was done and went back inside, I sat on the cement driveway next to a circle of women sitting cross-legged around a large pot filled with water, preparing *matoke* for dinner. It was a lot of work - the unripe green plantains, twice the size of an eating banana and hard as stone, were difficult to peel. A sharp knife and steady hands were needed to separate the skin from the slippery fruit, and the big stalk of bananas waiting to be peeled only gradually shrank in size. Most of the women laughed and seemed to be enjoying themselves, but a few grumbled about how many they were expected to feed every day, and voiced suspicions that some people's grief touched their stomachs rather than their hearts, and they attended this funeral only for the free food. I sat watching until an old lady, her wrinkled skin hanging loosely from the bones of her face, took pity on me sitting there alone, empty-handed, and gave me a big green banana and a knife. I felt like a poorly adjusted child who was given something to amuse herself with. I cut off the stub and white fruit was exposed under the clean slice. I worked the blade underneath the peel and pushed downward, but could not get it to separate smoothly from the fruit. I made nicks and dents in the banana and left behind bits of peel. I tried yanking off the green strip with my hands, like an ordinary banana, but it disintegrated into sticky shards. My *matoke* went into the pot with the others. I was not given a second one.

My hands were covered with black streaks from the slimy inside of the peel. I wondered why it was so difficult to wipe off. I rubbed my hands together until the black stickiness rolled into little pills and dropped to the ground. I wandered inside the house.

Anna was ironing clothes. She had installed herself at a

corner of the dinner table with a blanket spread out to create a makeshift ironing board. She wept as she carefully pressed a khaki-colored safari suit and ironed the same ten centimeters of pant leg over and over again until the fabric was as wrinkle-free as a new sheet of paper, and the crease sharp as a razor blade. It did not seem strange to me that she was crying, but soon her sisters came up and threw their arms around her shoulder.

"It will be alright, Anna."

"Look," Anna whimpered, pointing at a crease she had accidentally ironed into the fabric near to the cuff of the pants. "He will be so angry with me. You know he won't stand for sloppiness. Especially on this particular occasion. How could I be so careless?"

"It will be alright, don't worry." Adela, always upbeat, patted her back comfortingly.

"I can't believe he will be here, only to bury his first son. His heart will be broken. And us, we will see him so shortly and he will be taken from us again."

"Your father?" I guessed, because their demeanor and voices had taken on that hushed quality it always did when they talked about him.

"Yes. We have just been told our father is on his way to be released from prison for the few days it will take to attend the funeral. Apparently we must wait for the officials to organize guards who will escort him the whole way up north, and find money to pay them. We are very relieved, of course, that our father will be with us, but it is hard to accept he must return to prison after the funeral. It may be a very long time before we see him again. He will be gone and Sam will be gone and there will be nobody to look after us. Now it is up to Dennis and he is still too much of a boy. Who can rely on him?"

Dennis, the prankster. But I had seen another side of him in the last few days. I knew he would do right by his family.

After chores were done, people settled down to rest and nap, or sat in small groups to chat. I found myself a spot near the front door, sitting on the edge of the enormous stone planter with one tall aloe plant, careful not to prick myself on its spines. Soon the three sisters approached and stood before me, looking serious. They were tidily dressed, as always, wearing shirts and blouses that weren't school uniforms but similar in neatness and simplicity. Anna, the eldest, stood in the middle holding a shoe box. She hesitated, choosing her words carefully before speaking.

"Sara, we here in the family have been dividing the things Sam left behind so we may each have something to remember him by. There is not much, just some clothes and such. Maybe other belongings will appear when his things are returned from Nairobi. But we are in agreement that this belongs to you, and you should be the one to keep it."

I took the heavy box from her with both hands and rested it on my lap. Sweat bubbled on my lip. I gripped the box, unable to imagine what the contents might be.

The girls watched and waited. No one spoke. I lifted the lid. On top lay an airplane ticket. I brought it closer to my eyes, but could not decipher the jumble of letters and numbers that danced in front of my eyes. I glanced back and forth without knowing what I was looking for, then settled on the name of the passenger: Sara Janssen. Destination: Heathrow Airport, London. Date: August 23, 1979. Beneath it lay a second identical ticket made out to Samuel Dragu. We hadn't even had a chance to dream about this trip together, and now it would never happen.

My breath hissed between my teeth when I saw what else was in the box: my own letters to Sam. A stack of pink envelopes with flowered borders, tied together in neat bundles with rubber bands. Sam cared enough about my chatter to save them, maybe to read them again and again, maybe to keep them forever.

I was not ready to revisit the past. I took another shaky breath, and replaced the lid on the box.

CHAPTER TWENTY-SIX

"Wake up, Sara. It is time to prepare to leave." Foggy with sleep, I slowly followed young Abigail's orders.

This morning women were bustling with more purpose than usual. Not knowing what was going on, I moved aside and returned to my spot on the planter. More people seemed to be arriving, though I couldn't be certain – there was so much coming and going all the time. But when a dark sedan with tinted windows pulled up to the house, it was immediately clear something was different. A uniformed man stepped from the back seat of the car, and a second one on the other side. The person who had been sitting between them – an imposing man, squat and sturdy, very dark skinned – also got out and stood beside them. He was dressed like any business man in a navy blue suit and white shirt. Ululating flared up here and there and women worked their way toward him in heavy jogging steps, grief suddenly overwhelmingly present in the air once more. This was Sam's father, the man who had lost his firstborn son. He was a prisoner, though the only evidence of it was the two armed men who stood somewhat to the side, not obviously on guard duty, but not participating in the commotion, either.

When the crowd around the man thinned and people went about their business again, Dennis came for me. I had not seen much of him since arriving at the house; he was no doubt busy with his new duties as a responsible man and had left the women to look after me. I knew I would be expected to meet Mr. Dragu and the prospect made me jittery. Would he blame me for what had happened to his son? I was afraid there would be some justification in it, because if it wasn't for me, Sam might never have decided to go to London or return to Kampala when he did to get his traveling papers in order. He might still be alive. I knew from the stories that Sam's father was a formidable man, and I was anxious what he might say to me.

Dennis asked me to come with him. He showed none of the attentiveness I had grown used to; it seemed his mind was busy with other things, and not concerned with how I was feeling. I followed a step or two behind him, and we crossed the driveway to where Mr. Dragu was still standing by the car. We waited to be acknowledged. He glanced at Dennis, who took this as his cue to speak. They exchanged words I did not recognize the sounds of - maybe Madi, the language of their tribe.

Dennis stopped talking and turned toward me. Mr. Dragu did not say anything in response to Dennis' introduction, but took a moment to look me over carefully. His eyes traveled from my face to my feet, and I was unhappily aware of being unkempt and dusty; unfit to be evaluated. He did not appear to think much of me. Without changing the rigid expression on his face, he twisted his torso to extend his arm to me, and we shook hands briefly. Dennis took my elbow and walked me back to my planter.

"How are you, Sara?"

I nodded. I wasn't sure how I was. *OK, I guess.* Relieved Mr. Dragu was not going to take a special interest in me, relieved to be outside the focus of his attention.

"Today we depart up north, to the village. Do you have your things ready to go?"

"Yes."

"You will ride in the lorry. In front, in the cab. There will not be enough room for everybody, others will follow in cars. I am leaving now in advance to warn the people in the village of what has happened. They will not have heard of Sam's death, there is no telephone, and will otherwise be unprepared." He hesitated. "Especially *mama Samuel*, our birth mother."

"She doesn't know?"

Dennis ran his hand across the tired lines in his forehead, and shook his head slowly from side to side. "She will be devastated. You know Sam was not only her eldest, but also her favorite. Our mother is the sweetest, kindest, gentlest of women, but not strong. I do not know how she will cope with this tragedy."

I put my hand on his arm. He pulled himself together, stood straighter, and smiled grimly.

"I will see you in a few days. You will be alright," he said.

It sounded more like an order than a question, but I nodded anyway.

Dennis drove off and I raised a hand in farewell, and he flapped his hand back at me distractedly. Poor Dennis, what a terrible task laid ahead of him. To think Sam's mother had been living her everyday life as if nothing significant was happening in the world, when everything had actually changed forever. Only she hadn't known.

The gunning of a large engine intruded on my thoughts and I looked up to see a lorry pull in through the gates. The driver leaned his head out of the window and called down for instructions, gesturing with his hands, wanting to know where to park. It was a sizable lorry and this driveway could not accommodate it. The driver sawed clumsily back and forth in and endless three-point-turn until it was parked sideways across the driveway, in the middle of the courtyard. It was a flatbed, with wooden benches along the length of both sides. A skeleton of metal hoops held up a cover of light canvas that formed a shady roof over the bed. The tarp looked new, not tattered and wind-torn like most on the road.

A coffin stood in the middle of the floor of the flatbed, in between the benches. I stared at it. It was a plain box, made from a light wood, and undeniable in its purpose. The sides flared out to make room for the body's shoulders. Copper handles were mounted on both sides. I clung to the hope that the coffin was empty, but something had changed in the air around me. Voices were hushed, and the movement of people going about their business had slowed. Sam was in that box. I was transported back to the terrible moment when he was taken from me, when Dennis made sure I understood his death. His body, with no breath in it, no life, was here in front of me. I could walk right up to him and touch him, but there would be no point.

The waiting became harder to bear. If we were going to leave on this journey, I wished we would do so quickly. The day heated up and the shadow attached to my feet shrank. I lifted my hand to touch my head and was surprised at how hot my hair felt. Almost hot enough to hurt my fingers. I wanted to go inside the house to find some shade, but I was moving up against the stream – everybody else was purposefully on their way out. I turned again and went with the flow. Men, women and children headed for the lorry and stood around it, touching it with some part of their body if they could reach it, standing as close as they could if not. Finally, it was encircled by people standing two or three thick. The silence was complete. The waiting continued, but now with a sense of anticipation. I used my height to look over the heads of those clustered near me to see if I could find familiar faces, but they were huddled outside my reach, captured by their own thoughts.

A scrawny man appeared from nowhere and stood a few meters from us. I thought he might have stepped out of the hedge, but how could he have been inside the hedge? He was very thin and dressed in an old, torn shirt and dirty shorts many sizes too big, tied to the waist by a piece of rope. He wore retreads on his chapped feet. His skin was dusted with white powder, clumped in patches, giving him a moldy look. His hair sat on his head in wild uncombed heaps. I thought he might be a madman, but nobody seemed to feel threatened. Softly he began to chant, his voice high and reedy. Slowly he moved to accompany his words, lifting a knee, stomping a foot down onto the ground, leaning forward, swaying to the sound of his own voice. He called out suddenly to the crowd in a strong voice, and they answered in a single syllable, exhaled like a sigh: *aaaaaahhhhh*. The beat of his chant surged, louder and faster, his movements kept pace, and now it looked like he was going into a trance, his eyes rolled back in his head and his face toward the heavens in a grimace, arms raised imploringly. I felt frightened. I kept my fingertips attached to the side of the lorry and my eyes locked to the ground, trying to be inconspicuous. A piercing squawk cut through the chanting and I jerked my eyes up to see the man holding a chicken upside-down by its feet, head chopped off, blood dripping from its neck. The man muttered as he carried the chicken wide-armed in a circle around the people clustered to the lorry, dripping blood in a dotted line that enclosed us. We stepped aside to make room for him to climb into the cab and the coffin and the bed of the lorry, trailing blood there, too. Finally, he drew the chicken over his head and brought his arm forward violently as if he was beating suds out of a piece of laundry, and a mist of blood sprayed over the lorry and the people. After he had repeated this in four directions, he shrank back into the mangy man he first had been and stepped down to the ground with the chicken under his arm. It seemed this was the end of the ceremony. Relieved chatter broke out around me.

I breathed the cloying smell of blood. There was a smear of it on my arm, and a spot on my t-shirt. I hesitated between leaving it on like everyone else, or rubbing it off because it was disgusting. The lady next to me, freckled by spatters on her hair and face, must have noticed my confusion. She explained, "We are good Christians, you know. But we also honor our heritage, our ancient beliefs. We will depart now. This journey is protected."

CHAPTER TWENTY-SEVEN

After our personal belongings and enough food to last several days on the road had been packed in car trunks and on top of their roofs, the only thing left to do was decide where travelers were to sit. There was lot of talking and weighing of options, and it became clear that Dennis had left instructions for me to travel in the cab of the lorry. I politely refused. Some pressure was applied. I was told this was going to be a long journey and I would be much happier sitting on the padded seat inside, rather than the hard wooden benches outside. I balked at being singled out. I climbed onto the back and sat near the middle of one of the benches, trying to find a comfortable position. My scalp was itchy and I scratched at it through the cotton of the bandanna I had tied over my greasy, dirty mop of hair. I fidgeted, trying to position my feet on the floor in the least cramped way, but it was hard to do without touching the coffin. I sat stiffly, looking down at the box, and fought the urge to inch my toes forward and make contact with Sam. He was dead.

The driver started the lorry and lumbered it back and forth until finally its nose faced the gates and we drove out into the street. The tarp overhead did not reach all the way down and it was like having open windows all around. A string of cars popped out of the gates behind us and followed us down the street. Not many sat in the lorry, maybe a dozen or so men, and I shifted my hips so that I took up more space and stretched my legs out diagonally. A breeze floated in. I relaxed. We were on our way.

The lorry shuddered as it ground through its many gears and picked up a little speed. Vibrations ran through the bench and I imagined my cheeks trembling and my teeth chattering visibly. I peered out at the streets of Kampala. This was the first time I was seeing the neighborhood in which I had been living and I found things looked similar to Nairobi, except that it was conspicuously quiet. In Nairobi, anyone who had some peanuts or newspapers or a carton of cigarettes to sell, or who knew how to repair shoes or braid hair, would set up shop in a shady spot on a convenient sidewalk corner. Here, neighbors did not stand around chatting about the day's news. Instead, there were soldiers. They lounged in small groups with heavy rifles slung casually over their shoulders, or patrolled the neighborhoods in jeeps. Some threw our convoy a curious glance, but no attempts were made to stop us.

As soon as we left the city, what was left of the road disintegrated completely and the ride quickly became agonizing for those of us sitting in the back. The lorry lurched and was thrown off balance by every little stone and hollow in the road. There were no soft landings from the really big bounces, and we smacked down hard onto the wooden benches again and again. Where the road wasn't paved, my nose was filled with the smell of smoky swirling red dust, so familiar to me, and I felt somehow comforted. The checkpoints started up again, fewer along this road, and we seemed to have little trouble passing through them. Probably our uniformed escort made a difference, or maybe the fact that we were carrying a coffin.

As the white hot afternoon cooled and dusk started to fall, we pulled into a large dirt parking lot, followed by the cars still on our tail. I climbed out of the lorry and shifted my weight from one leg to another, rubbing my bruised behind.

I looked around. A row of low buildings stood at the far end of the parking lot, shaped like a horseshoe with the open ends facing away from the cars. I was surprised to see two women dressed in full nun's habits, complete with black and white head covers, talking to some men in our party. They stood quietly, listening, only giving short replies. Finally, the nuns bowed their heads and stepped aside, and the men waved us in. I followed the crowd, and was happy to see Sam's sisters walking toward me. They seemed none the worse for wear, having been considered too young to ride in the lorry and seated comfortably in one of the bigger cars.

"Sara, how are you?" they chirped, hugging me and fluttering in a circle around my legs.

"Fine. A little banged up," I said. "Where are we?"

"This here is a convent. Mother Superior has given us permission to stay overnight, and so we will find protection within the walls of the compound. Like safe haven, you know?"

"We are so many, can they put us all up?" I said, glancing around at our group, which might easily be one hundred people, maybe more.

"I don't think so, not like people will be assigned a bed or a room. Most will sleep in the lorry or just on the ground. Do you see there is a cement walkway all around the buildings in the courtyard? I'm sure it will be good enough for sleeping with blankets or coverings of some sort." The girls sounded thrilled, as if we were on a camping trip.

A plain church stood at the open end of the horseshoe - a cube with a tented roof and a simple cross reaching up from its short steeple. Its silhouette looked peaceful against the evening sky. Soon fires were built and the women started to prepare meals. The flickering light of candles indoor illuminated some of the windows in the buildings around us. The night here was blacker than in Kampala. Instead of jeeps and gunfire, the darkness sounded of chirping crickets, the occasional swoop of a low-flying bat, and something whooping outside the walls, maybe a monkey.

I took off my shoes and sat on the edge of the walkway. I

dropped my bare feet to the ground and the short, dry grass tickled my soles as I wriggled my toes and rubbed the red indentations on top of my foot with my thumbs - marks made by the thongs of my sandals, where they had pressed into my skin all day. A glint of firelight bounced off a shiny black beetle scurrying around my feet in the shadows, trying to make its escape. I curled my big toe under and tried to flick it away, but it was too fast and just hurried along, changing course around tufts of grass whenever my foot blocked its path. Finally I lost sight of it altogether. I lifted my head and saw a nun step out of one of candle-lit doorways and glide unhurriedly toward me. When she reached me, she asked for my attention by placing her fingertips on my shoulder. I stood to face her. I could tell she wanted me to come with her, though she had no English. There didn't seem to be a reason for her request, and I glanced around to see if there was someone I could discuss this with, but there wasn't. I followed her to the lit door and stepped inside a large room. It was sparsely furnished - the only decoration a dark wooden cross on one of the whitewashed walls.

Chairs stood around a long table made from uneven wooden planks, shiny with age, and at its head, a single place was set for a meal. The nun took me to it. I looked at her uncertainly, but she indicated firmly that I was to sit down. I did, feeling like I had walked onto a stage without knowing my lines. In the clean, plain room, I was painfully conscious of how filthy I was. I grimaced to think how my hair must look, unflatteringly tied back in a bandanna. My face probably shone with grease. I wondered if I stank – most likely I did. I turned my eyes down in embarrassment. The bottom of my t-shirt was coming undone and I pulled on the thin thread dangling from it and tried to break it off, but instead the stitches bunched up and the ratty hem looked even worse. I restored the damage as best I could and looked away, trying to ignore the thread.

My escort had left the room. She returned carrying a large

bowl, filled halfway with water. She rested it on the table long enough to hand me a sliver of soap and a small towel, then picked it up again and held it close by, over the floor. She nodded at me in encouragement. I didn't know if cleaning my hands would break the no-washing mourning rule, but it looked like the nun thought it was OK for me to do so. I dipped my hands inside the bowl and watched as swirls of red dust detached themselves from my skin and clouded the water. I soaped my hands and when I was done, the nun rinsed them by pouring clean water from a pitcher. I dried my hands with the towel, and was surprised at how much better I felt.

People had entered the room, and I turned to see who they were. Four nuns joined me at the table, though their places were not set for food. To my left sat a nun with white skin, a teenager like me.

I stared at her longer than was polite and it took me a while to realize she was looking back with equal fascination. Her smile was timid as she leaned in to talk to me. She spoke softly and I tried to decipher her words, but could not understand what she was saying. I thought for a moment she might be speaking French; I knew enough of it to ask her about her life, how she came to be here, was she happy at the convent? But she wasn't speaking French. I tried a few words of English, but she shook her head. My disappointment was reflected in her eyes. Maybe she was new to Uganda, and maybe this was why I had been brought to the table, to talk to her, but we were as foreign to each other as we were to everybody else.

Food was brought for me. The nuns bowed their heads and spoke a short prayer and crossed themselves at the end of it. One said to me in halting, thickly accented English, "God bless you" and I nodded, not knowing the proper reply. They indicated I should eat, and I started with the peeled and quartered orange, spearing each piece with a fork, which seemed more civilized than using my fingers.

The nuns watched approvingly as each bite disappeared into my mouth. When I put down my fork to indicate I was done eating, they protested and vigorously shook their heads, and pushed a little bowl of peanut butter closer to me. I lifted a spoonful to a piece of bread and spread it on, careful not to drip, and cut off a corner with my knife. It tasted good, but I wasn't really hungry, and after a few bites I felt slightly queasy. This was the most I'd eaten in days.

I looked up from my plate and tried to tell them how good everything was, and how much I appreciated their kindness. I felt an urge to kiss the young nun on her cheek, or hug her, but I was too dirty to be touched. I smiled at her instead and pushed back my chair, said thank you one last time, and walked out into the cool night air.

CHAPTER TWENTY-EIGHT

A rooster crowed on the other side of the compound wall - it was the only sound in the silence before dawn. The smell of burned wood hung in the air, though the fires had all gone out. Every so often an arm or leg stirred sleepily, and before long people woke up and started preparing for another day of travel.

I ate a small bowl of cold millet porridge along with everybody else. It was watery, and the grains tasted like wood shavings – there wasn't enough sugar to sweeten the porridge of so many people. But it filled my stomach, and I wouldn't be hungry for many hours.

I looked at the thin, dented aluminum spoon I was holding, and it occurred to me that I had no idea what had happened to the cutlery Dennis had given me back in Kampala, which he made me swear to keep with me at all times. I must have left it behind at the house, or maybe it got mixed in with the general stockpile.

No doubt this was going to be a long day of sitting in the lorry, since we would be on the road much earlier than yesterday. When everything was packed and the evidence of our invasion cleared away as best we could, we took our places. One by one cars started their engines and turned back onto the main road. An uneventful day followed - there was little along the way to provide entertainment and time crawled. By late afternoon, word trickled down to us in the back of the lorry that we would not make it to the village as our progress had been slower than expected, mostly because of the terrible condition of the road. We would be setting up camp along the road - we were now far away from any potential unrest and it was safe to do so. We were scheduled to reach our destination by noon the next day.

I was relieved not to have reached the village yet. As long as we kept moving down the road, I could avoid facing the reality of the funeral – my heart shrank to the size of a pebble at the thought. I looked around and tried to get some sense of where we were. The land was dry as dust and nothing but the scantiest shrubs and leafless trees grew on it. I could see forever in all directions, the view cluttered only by our own presence and a small village nearby.

"Sara!"

I thought I heard Dennis call my name... I whirled around and saw him walk toward me with his telltale long stride.

"Dennis, where did you come from? You must be the last person I thought I'd see here - how'd you know where to find us?"

"When you people didn't show up like expected, I was thinking you probably weren't going to make it all the way up to the village today. So we just drove down this one road until we found you. And here you are..." Dennis started to say more, but his words became disjointed until he stopped altogether and hiccuped with laughter. I didn't get the joke, but it was good to hear him laugh. I grinned and waited for him to get his voice back.

"Ah, Sara, what have you done to yourself? You look like a beggar, too disgusting to touch with even a ten foot pole."

"Yes," I said sheepishly, "I know. I am a little dirty. Traveling in the back of the lorry is really dusty."

"So why are you in the lorry? Didn't people offer you a more comfortable seat?"

"Yes, but I didn't want it."

Dennis looked at me and raised a single eyebrow almost like Sam used to, only his face didn't quite have the required fearsomeness, and he just managed to look cute.

"I don't want to be different, Dennis."

"And then, did no one provide you with a piece of soap and some water after arrival?"

"Well, I guess what I thought is, I would like to respect the traditions and not wash until after the funeral."

Apparently I had made another joke. Dennis laughed even more loudly and bent over to slap his knees as if I had just told him the funniest thing he had ever heard. It was hard not to feel a little hurt and I wondered why my good intentions were so humorous.

"What?" I asked, sounding as cranky as I felt.

"Sara, you are too, too funny, *kweli*, I swear. Now who put you up to this, eh? It must be my little sisters, am I right?"

"So what?"

"Look, they mean well, of course. But they are just little more than *totos*, you must not place too much stock in the things they tell you. OK, so there is some truth in it: back in the traditional communities this kind of thing with not washing in times of grief was considered proper, maybe it still is, but in the city we don't do that kind of thing. How smelly would the place get, eh? Man, am I glad I got to you before you wandered off to shave your head." This image apparently tickled him enormously and he spent another minute or so howling with laughter.

I felt stupid. Here I thought I was doing the right thing, and now it seemed I had been too eager to embrace customs I didn't understand. Suddenly what I wanted to do more than anything was wash, and nothing seemed more appealing than water and soap and clean clothes.

"Tell me the truth, Sara. Wouldn't you like to clean up?"

I nodded.

"Alright, just hang on a minute, and I'll see what I can arrange."

I went to find my suitcase and saw it standing in the thin

shade of the single bare thorn tree, together with all the other gear that had made its way this far north. I pulled out a fresh blouse and lifted it to my nose, inhaling the clean, freshly laundered scent. I was flooded with memories of my mother, of home. The well-ordered, safe, familiar routines of my family seemed incredibly far away, and I was stabbed with regret. Things had changed, and I would not be stepping back into the same life again.

Dennis walked up to me carrying an empty bucket, a bit of ragged yellowish towel and a new bar of soap. He pointed at a structure about half a kilometer away that stood between us and the village in the distance. It looked like a small parking garage with a flat roof made of corrugated metal, and what seemed to be three windowless walls and one open side. A cow path led from our camp to it and beyond to the huts.

"What is it?" I asked.

"A place for some privacy, and protection from the heat of the sun during the day. Do you see the pump there very close to the building? Go to it and fill your bucket with water and then take it inside so you can wash without being seen. Can you manage the pump, or should I come to do it for you?"

I looked at the pump standing on a low cement block, seeing even from this distance that it was nothing but a tall cylinder with a spout and a long handle for pumping. How hard could it be?

"I'll be fine." I took the things from Dennis and started down the cow path. I walked slowly, not in a hurry, happy to have something to occupy my time. Shadows were growing long, outlines less harsh. As I put more distance between myself and our group I heard... silence. The quiet soothed me.

"Don't drink the water," Dennis yelled at me.

I waved my hand at him high over my head without looking back. *Yeah, yeah, I know, little brother.*

I reached the pump and stood close by it, inspecting it. A fat drop of water dripped from the spout at even intervals, leaving a wet spot on the cement, a tiny lake with neon green moss growing on the surface. Or maybe it was algae. It looked slimy and strangely out of place against the dryness all around; the only green thing in a landscape of reds and browns. I placed my bucket beneath the spout and positioned myself beside the handle. I grabbed the smooth rounded metal with my right hand, warm but not hot to the touch, and pushed the handle down, leaning into it with my full weight. Nothing but the same single drop fell from the spout. Was I doing this right? There didn't seem to be any other way to approach the pump, so I tried again. With all my strength and both hands I pushed the handle down, then up, then down again. After a few more energetic pumps, a gush of air and water spattered around, followed by a slender waterfall that dropped straight into the bucket. Delicious, cool, crystal-clear water. I stopped pumping when the bucket was full almost to the brim, and clamped soap, towel and clean clothes underneath my arm. I lifted the heavy bucket by its thin metal handle, careful not to slosh water over the sides, and walked awkwardly into the building. I stood still for a minute and waited for my sight to return in the sudden darkness.

I was not alone. In the far corner, about twenty steps away from me, stood a girl washing herself with water from a bucket similar to mine. She looked to be about my age. She was completely naked. I quickly swung my eyes away from her.

"Jambo," she greeted me, her voice sounding amused. I brought my eyes to her face and found her looking straight back at me. She smiled knowingly.

"Jambo," I replied. I was thrown for a minute - it hadn't occurred to me that I might not be the only one here. I put as much distance between us as I could by shuffling into the corner diagonally across from hers, and set my bucket and belongings down on the ground. I hesitated, but knew the only way I was going to get a good washing was to strip down, and there was no way I was going to let this girl laugh at me for prudishness she was obviously untroubled by. I took a deep breath and tore off all my smelly clothes. I stole a quick glace at the girl, hoping for a hint as to how to bathe without a shower or running water - I had never tried to get clean using such a small amount of water. Nor had I ever been this dirty. I saw her use a cup to scoop water over her body. I didn't have a cup. Instead I used my hands to lift the water and splash it over my legs, then my belly and finally my arms, cringing at how cold it felt on my sun-warmed skin. Soon I was damp from my shoulders down. I crouched next to the bucket and washed my face first. I dipped the soap into the water and slid it back and forth between my hands until a fluffy lather rose, and rubbed the soap in circles all over my skin. The white foam turned pink from the dust in which I was covered. After I had soaped every part of me, I scooped up the rest of the water to rinse away the suds.

The girl had stepped away from her bucket and briskly toweled herself dry. She picked up a small jar from the floor and carefully rubbed blobs of white cream into her skin, putting a glossy finish on her body. Her back was turned to me and I examined her unnoticed. Her beauty was riveting. Her skin was the color of shiny burnt copper, smooth and unblemished. Her body was hard and strong, and I glanced enviously at her perfectly rounded butt and breasts, fuller and firmer than mine. Her head was completely bald. I wondered whether she always wore her hair that way, or if she had any particular reason to shave it all off. Could it have something to do with Sam?

She started dressing and I turned my eyes away quickly, afraid to get caught in my shameless staring. She walked right by me as she left the building and looked at me, a slight smile on her lips. I wondered who she was; I couldn't remember seeing her before. Maybe she lived in the village on the other side of the path.

I would have liked to wash my hair, but had no idea how.

Obviously I couldn't walk out to the pump naked and I didn't want to put on my clean clothes only to ruin them with runoff from my filthy hair. How was I going to pump water and stick my head under the tap at the same time? Or should I pump the cold water into the bucket and pour it all over my head? I shivered at the thought and besides, I didn't have shampoo and conditioner. I gave up on the idea and decided my hair would have to wait, one last filthy tribute to tradition. I put on clean underwear, clean clothes, and felt like a new person.

Dennis and I sat side by side on a rock and relaxed into the end of another day, and I was happy to have his familiar presence nearby. He reached inside his pocket and pulled out a joint. We shared it and a comfortable calm settled over me, eyelids heavy. I turned inward to my thoughts.

"How is your mother?" I asked after a while.

"A wreck, Sara."

"Oh, man." I wondered what tomorrow would bring.

Small plastic containers of *waragi* appeared, just like they had every night. I wasn't sure what kind of booze it was exactly, only that it had a lot of alcohol and no flavor to tone down its bite. The way it was bottled in reused plastic juice containers and jerry cans made it pretty likely this stuff had been brewed in somebody's bathtub, and not bought in a shop. Dennis wandered off to score some.

"So, girls!" I called out to the sisters.

"Hello, Sara," they wandered over cheerfully and sat beside me.

"You look nice, I like this blouse you're wearing," said Adela, the middle sister, the bubbly girl.

I looked down at my Indian tunic-style blouse, its delicate fabric already stained with dirt. One of the buttons dangled by a thread and looked like it was about to come off. I had worn this blouse to the disco once, back when it was in better shape. It had been a mistake; as soon as the black light switched on for a slow dance, I saw I might as well have been wearing only a bra. Even Sam, whose first reaction was usually to laugh away my insecurities, was surprised at how undressed I suddenly appeared, and held me to him protectively as we shuffled around the dance floor. I giggled at the memory.

"It's yours, Adela. I want you to have it. I'll leave it for you when we get back to the house in Kampala. In fact, I will leave all of my things for you girls to share, so you will have at least a little something to remember me by."

They were grateful, so happy - it was too much for such a little thing. I changed the subject.

"So, today I washed," I said.

"Yes."

"Well, you know, Dennis said it would be better. I didn't wash my hair, though," I said, wanting to avoid offending anybody. "Anyway, while I was out there washing near the pump, someone else was bathing, too. I wonder who she was, do you know? She was about my age, a little shorter than me and slender with her head shaved. I got the impression she knew me somehow."

The mood among the girls shifted. They exchanged quick glances. No one spoke.

"What is it?" I asked.

"Oh, Sara, I am so sorry. You should not have been confronted by her."

"She is a nasty tramp," Adela hissed in a low voice. "She would do anything to get a foothold in this family."

"What are you talking about?"

"Sara, listen, it is like this." Adela's voice took on a soft, soothing tone. "Now, try to understand, of course this was never meant in a bad way by anyone." She lowered her voice. "When Sam came home to Kampala and spoke of going to Europe to study and to be with you, our mother could not approve of his decision. She wanted him to take someone from our own tribe. She arranged for women, many women, to be brought to him, to try to change his mind, and he spent some time with that one you saw today. Not so long, just a week or two, and then he said he couldn't do it. You see? He told our mother to stop bringing him women, he wanted only you and no one else. He chose you."

My mind was clear as ice, but I could make no sense of the thoughts tearing through my head. This could not possibly be true. Sam with another woman, what did that mean? To try her out as a potential partner, a sexual partner, a *wife?*

I stood up and shook off the girls' hands. I saw Dennis squatting near a fire and strode to him. I looked down at him. "Did you know this?"

Dennis looked at me in surprise for a moment and pursed his lips when he understood. He calmly poured some *waragi* and stood to face me. He handed me the cup and closed my hands around it.

"He was a traditional African man, Sara," he said with a wistful smile. "You knew this about him from the start."

CHAPTER TWENTY-NINE

I had had too much to drink. I felt woozy as I climbed into the back of the lorry, but ignored Dennis' pleas to ride in a car with him. I was in no mood for company. The sadness that had kept my brain furry until now made room for a sharp, frustrated rage. I was incensed by jealousy of this girl. How could I compete? I was the outsider. And now I would never be able to face Sam and accuse him of being a total shit for betraying me. I put my feet on the coffin. *You asshole, Sam.*

The lorry slowed, then stopped. We had arrived at the village. The sun blazed almost directly overhead and the air shimmered with desert heat. It must have been early afternoon. We were at the outer edge of the village, a dozen or so meters short of the first house. Cars that had arrived ahead of us stood scattered around. There was no clear demarcation between the end of untamed nature and the start of the village - no roads or fences or gardens to mark civilization. The women came. They ululated and wept and beat their breasts. They called on God with outstretched hands. I stood quietly and let hot, angry tears drop from my eyes.

The girls led me to the women and a circle of soft flesh closed around me. Beefy arms reached out to me, patting and squeezing. Voices clucked in their own tongue. The smell of heat on cloth and sweating bodies was heavy in the air. My scent was the same. I was gently shepherded into one of the small cinder block houses standing haphazardly on the cracked red earth. The air inside the house with its thickly plastered walls was surprisingly cool. The women left. I walked to the wall and leaned my forehead against it; little bumps of cement pushed pleasantly into my skin. I pulled up my sleeves and stretched the length of my bare arms against the coolness of the stone. I kicked off my shoes and felt the grainy cement underneath the sweating soles of my feet. A deep weariness settled over me and I went into the next room and dropped onto the unmade bed.

"Sara! Sara!" I was lying on my side with my back to the wall, covered by a scratchy blanket that had not been there when I fell asleep. I opened my eyes to see Anna's face close to mine; she was tapping my shoulder and calling my name softly. I looked at her - the oldest sister, the sensible one - and did not move.

"Sara, it is time to wake up. We came for you yesterday, but you were fast asleep. You slept all through the night."

Good: the less waking time, the better.

"Please get up. There are people who are waiting to see you."

I didn't want to see anyone.

"My mother is asking for you, Sara."

Fuck. The woman who told everyone I was not good enough for her son, even though she had never met me. The woman who had gone out of her way to force pretty girls on Sam.

"And the archbishop is here. He will be leading the funeral service himself, it is quite an honor," she said, her eyes bright. "He has come to talk with the elders today to prepare."

"When is the funeral?"

"Tomorrow."

I mulled this information over for a minute. I had to get up; I didn't have a choice. "Let me get dressed, OK?"

"Of course... I will find you some breakfast and come for you in a little while."

Anna skipped out the door. I did not move. She came back carrying a mug of tea and a bowl of porridge.

"Sara!" the child spoke to me sternly. "You haven't gotten out of bed. You promised." She put the mug on the floor next to the bed. I watched steam rise from it, tea no doubt cloyed with milk and sugar. Anna pulled the blanket off me and I sighed. I pushed myself up to sit cross-legged and drew the blanket around my shoulders like a cloak. I sipped tea, but had no appetite for porridge. My teeth felt gummy and I dipped the toothbrush in the cup of water that stood next to my bed, and brushed them with what little energy as I could muster, and rinsed my face with the handful of water that was left. I pulled on a clean t-shirt, but didn't bother to change my jeans. There was no point. With the hem dragging through the dust and the seat soiled from sitting on rocks and tree stumps, the new pair would be just as dirty as the old one before the day was done. I followed Anna to a nearby house.

The hum of women's voices floated out through the open door. Anna knocked on the wall and called *hodi*. Voices called back. We walked inside. Women sat on the few chairs available and on the floor with their backs leaning against the wall and their legs sticking straight out with one ankle crossed on top of the other. A wide cement berth was built into the wall below the glassless window. On it, curled on her side, lay Sam's mother. She looked younger and more vulnerable than the pictures I had seen, draped in a pale yellow dress, wide and silky, that floated lightly around her soft curves. She did not sit up, but reached for my hand, her eyes hurt and sad. A hint of alcohol whiffed up from her mouth. I took her hand but did not answer her squeeze of my fingers. My heart ached for this broken woman and the loss I understood all too well, but I could not forgive her. I would not let her comfort me.

I found myself a place to sit further down the wall. Time passed. Abigail walked in and spoke to her mother in low tones. She had come to collect me, saying it was time for me to pay my respects to the archbishop. I wondered what would be expected of me now - Anna had mumbled something about kissing his ring and I really hoped this instruction was not to be taken literally. I should have spoken up sooner to banish the notion that I was religious, but it had seemed an unnecessary complication with God so clearly on everybody's mind. Now I had to face the consequences of my little deception, because here I was expected to be thrilled by the prospect of kissing the archbishop's ring.

All three sisters escorted me – apparently this was a big deal. We entered the impressive main house belonging to Sam's father and walked toward the living room, pausing at the open door. I stood off to one side and looked in. The sitting area was more comfortably furnished than the other houses, with thick, velvet furniture in maroon tones. Two armchairs faced a sofa with an oblong, glass-topped coffee table between them. I could see only the legs of two men sitting on the sofa with their backs to me, but the archbishop was in full view, dressed in ample churchly splendor. His deep purple robe reached down to his shiny black shoes, and white lacy fabric peeked out from beneath his wide sleeves. The traditional Catholic collar stood around his neck. I noticed the chair he was sitting on was almost exactly the same shade as his clothing, like a throne made especially for him. The archbishop did not look up to acknowledge us waiting at the door.

I stepped back into the hallway, out of sight, clueless as to how to proceed.

"What am I supposed to do now? He's busy talking. Maybe we should come back some other time," I whispered.

"No, Sara, you can just go in now and pay your respects. It's all right. Of course he won't mind the interruption, don't be silly," the girls whispered back.

"How? Just barge in?" I asked desperately.

"Look, do you see his arm resting on the chair? Do you see the ring on his finger?"

I peered around the door and saw that the archbishop wore a huge gold ring with a large square purplish stone on his ring

242

finger. I turned back and nodded.

"You walk up to the bishop, and then you kneel, and he will reach his hand down and you can kiss the ring."

I rolled my eyes inside closed eyelids and sighed. There was no point in postponing the inevitable. I took two steps into the room, my eyes turned to the floor. Conversation mercifully continued and the men ignored me. I raised my head and scanned the room quickly, trying to decide what to do next. I'd have to walk around the coffee table to reach the side of the archbishop's chair, and somehow jam myself into the small space between him and the wall. Was I was supposed to drop to one knee or both? What if the archbishop had no idea what I was doing here - how would I explain myself? The archbishop finished his sentence and lowered his arm, displaying his hand, palm down, beside the chair. Was I supposed to hold his hand with my own, or just plant a kiss on the ring? Was I supposed to actually touch the ring with my lips or hover in the air above it? What if I made a smacking sound?

All eyes in the room had turned to me and nobody spoke as they watched, probably wondering why I was standing there. I almost took a step forward, but something held me back.

I bowed my head respectfully, and said the first thing that popped into my head, "Thank you for having me in the village."

The men nodded.

I smiled at them, relieved to be doing what felt right. I turned around and walked out of the room, past the girls, and straight out through the front door.

"Sara! Why didn't you kiss the ring? The archbishop was waiting for you to do so," Anna asked accusingly.

"Well," I said. "I couldn't do it. Because it made me too uncomfortable."

"It is an honor to kiss the ring."

"Yes. But it is not something I am used to doing."

I found myself a quiet spot a short distance down from the women busy cooking, and bummed a small cup of *waragi* from them, downing a sip of the disgusting stuff. Less thinking and less feeling, that was my goal for today. I looked up to see Dennis walking resolutely in my direction. *Now what?*

Dennis crashed down next to me. The rings underneath his eyes were deep and purple, his eyes hazy. I recognized the yellow t-shirt he was wearing, the one with cap sleeves Sam liked because it showed off his biceps. It was too baggy on Dennis.

"Are you hanging in there, Dennis? You look exhausted."

He rubbed his eyes, "With the many things already going on, now another problem. Matilda has announced she will not attend the funeral, nor will she allow her child to do so. It will be unacceptable if she is not present tomorrow, being Sam's stepmother. Such disrespect will not be tolerated, though it was well known she and Sam did not get along."

I couldn't imagine her skipping out on the funeral, where her absence would be so conspicuous. "She'll change her mind, surely."

"Let's hope so," Dennis said. He hesitated and turned around to face me. "Sara, there is something I am going to ask you to do. The family has decided you must say an official last farewell to Sam. I tried to spare you this, but there were many other voices."

I had no idea what he was asking me to do, but it was clear he was at the end of his rope. Anyway, I did want a chance to say goodbye to Sam one last time before the funeral. I stood up and a shadow of relief passed over Dennis' face.

He took my hand and we walked back to the main house, this time entering through the back door. We passed down a short, narrow hallway and Dennis indicated for me to enter a side room. He nodded at me encouragingly and gently pressed me forward with his hand on my shoulder. I stepped inside. The air smelled like death. Half a dozen women sat in the room, all kneeling on the ground. I dropped, too, with both legs folded beneath me, and leaned back on my heels like they did. One of the women wailed loudly without pause. I glanced at her, uncomfortably. She was an ancient crone, her face contorted, a few broken teeth showing in a wrinkled mouth open in a big O. Her earlobes, sagging low under the weight of massive copper earrings, swayed in the rhythm of her howls. She rocked back and forth in anguish. She scared me. I looked away quickly, and my eyes fell on Sam's coffin near the far wall, with a compartment, a small door, open to reveal his face. I stared in horror.

This was not Sam. His face was bloated to the size of a hideous balloon, his skin taut almost to the point of tearing. The silky chocolate of his complexion had faded to a horrifying purple, like eggplant, like no human being should ever have. I ripped my eyes away and knew then I would never see him again. The crone leaned over to me and poked a bony finger into my side, not breaking the rhythm of her howls. I didn't know what she wanted from me, and she poked me again and again. I looked up. She waved her hands: *come on, come on, come on.* I shuddered. I opened my mouth and from somewhere deep inside me, the sound of grief exploded from me. I wailed with the other women, an ear-splitting keening, on and on until I could no longer catch my breath and finally fell silent, slumped forward, drained of emotion and energy. One after the other, the women quieted down until only gasping sobs filled the room.

Suddenly a young woman sprang up. She raised both slender arms high above her head and tightened her hands into fists. Her sudden screeching screams had nothing to do with grief, and sounded more like terror, or madness; like a banshee. We stared at her with dread, paralyzed into inaction. She threw open the door and ran out of the house - we heard her screams grow distant, but not stop.

Dennis rushed in. He took my arm and pulled me to my feet, all the time shouting hastily over his shoulder to the others. I jogged out of the house beside him and turned to face him when he let me go.

"What just happened?" I asked, my eyes wide.

Dennis muttered, "That was Matilda. You see what I have to deal with."

I could no longer hear her screaming. "Where did she go?"

Dennis shrugged his shoulders. "I swear that woman has lost her mind. Amid all this, she is the one who craves to be the center of attention. The elders forced her to come pay proper respects, and this is how she does it, behaving like she an idiot."

"Behaving like she is possessed, you mean. Her screams just now made my hair stand on end."

Dennis grinned, "Yes, she is a demon witch, you are right. Let's hope she doesn't have any spells to put on us."

"Her, together with the other one - the old lady with the swinging earlobes," I shuddered, remembering her yellowed nails in my ribs. "She scared me half silly."

"I know the one you are talking about. She is the professional mourner, actually. She's paid to weep loudly so everybody else feels free to express their own suffering. And so there will be a proper atmosphere of grief."

"Really? Don't you think people are sad enough, without needing encouragement?"

Dennis shrugged again, "It is the way things are done. Tomorrow is the funeral, and until it is all over, we will proceed according to the rules, without cutting corners."

CHAPTER THIRTY

The last night before the funeral passed peacefully. Since all duties and obligations to tradition and appearances had been fulfilled, I had time to listen to what was going on inside my own head. Tonight I found it easy to remember good times. Evening chill set in and I drew a blanket around my legs, tucking the grey wool beneath me so I was warmly wrapped from the waist down. I sat with Dennis and together we remembered Sam as the two of us had known him: the guy who could be a real pain in the ass with his bossy ways and red hot flashes of temper, but who loved us and looked out for us in his own tough-guy way.

"Remember, Dennis, when he drove my car into town to pick up *banghi* and he just left us sitting there in that sleazy parking lot? I nearly shit my pants. And then he hops back in and drives off like nothing's the matter." I laughed softly, also remembering that when I told Sam how worried I'd been, he took me seriously and apologized. And it had never happened again.

"How about all those times I would ask him to sponsor me some beer money, eh? I knew he would give me a hard time, it was just his way, glaring at me with that one eyebrow pushed right up high on his forehead. But it never meant a thing. He always bought me beer in the end."

"He took it on himself to look out for us, you know? Even if we didn't agree with him or like the way went about things, he always did what he thought was right by us. I'm going to miss him very badly," I said.

"Me, too."

The sisters came over and huddled around us. Stars glittered overhead, but the moon was just a sliver and the night was dark. People brought lanterns and flashlights and stayed outdoors as hours passed and midnight came and went. It seemed I was not the only one who did not expect to sleep. The girls, though, were nodding off. Before they gave in to their sleepiness and left to find their beds, they asked for stories. They wanted Dennis and me to confirm the memory of a big brother they had lifted high on a pedestal, and we were happy to comply. We wiped away blemishes, censored the rough patches, and tried to make sure the girls would remember him always as they did now. Hopefully we all would.

When I became too tired to keep my eyes open after all, I decided to catch a few hours of sleep before the funeral. The village was quiet. I could see the thinnest strip of light bleeding into the black sky along the horizon - a hint of the dawn that would be arriving soon.

I took a step without looking where I was going and the smooth sole of my sandal slid down the jagged edge of a rock. I felt the skin tear along the side of my foot, on the hard part just below my big toe, and I stood frozen for a moment choking back the urge to scream. After the worst of it passed, I tried to see how bad the cut was, but it was too dark to see. I could feel the wound bleeding. I limped into my unlit house and felt around in the darkness to discover something to mop up the blood with. My hand settled on a roll of toilet paper and I dabbed at the gash as best I could, trying to stem the bleeding. It hurt with deep fiery stabs and I thought I might be doing more harm than good. I gave up and pressed a fresh gob of toilet paper to the wound, circled the roll around my foot several times and tucked the end in to make a bandage. It would have to do for now. I curled up on the bed, back against the wall, and fell instantly asleep.

"Sara, what happened? There is blood everywhere!"

"'S nothing," I muttered. What was Adela talking about? *Let me sleep.*

"Sara!"

I opened my eyes.

"Look - look here, there is a whole trail of blood from your bed all the way to outside. What happened?"

I remembered. "I slipped. It's nothing. Really."

Last night's sense of peace had evaporated in my sleep. Today Sam was going to be buried. My foot throbbed unpleasantly.

Adela threw back my blanket and sucked in her breath when she saw the bloody clump of tissue attached to my foot.

"Wait here."

Much as I tried, I couldn't fall back asleep and remained suspended somewhere between wakefulness and unconsciousness in a terrible place where panic and half-formed fears kept me in a chokehold. I was relieved when Adela returned carrying a bowl of water pressed into her hip, and some band-aids and soap in her free hand. I sat up and shook the dark visions from my head. She started to unwind the filthy mess of toilet paper. I looked at the dirt caked around the bottom of my foot and under my toenails. *Yuck.* I flinched when Adela yanked off the last bit of tissue and bent closer to take a good look at the gash: a few jagged centimeters of skin torn deep, bleeding again now. Shreds of tissue and tiny grains of grey rock stuck to the blood. On Adela's instruction, I lowered my foot inside the bowl, but it didn't fit and I managed to lean just the front part in. At least the wound was underwater. I pressed forward slightly so my heel wouldn't tip the bowl over. The whole front of my foot hurt. Adela grabbed a piece of soap.

"What are you doing?" I asked.

"Sara, this looks so ugly, and we don't have anything available to disinfect the wound. It will go bad if we do nothing."

"Wait, just let me handle it." I couldn't bear the thought of anyone touching my foot. I swished water around the gash with my hand, trying to dislodge the debris. When Adela insisted I apply soap, I hesitated, then pressed the bar lightly to the wound. Surely only contact was needed for the soap to do its job. I pulled my foot from the water. Adela looked at me disapprovingly, but what did she know? I didn't want to fuss with this any longer. She gave me a piece of cloth and I patted the skin dry carefully, not touching the painful parts, and finished off with two giant band aids crossed tightly in the shape of an X. I used the damp cloth to wipe smudges of blood, dried black, from my sandal, and put my foot inside it gingerly, adjusting the straps to make sure they did not touch the gash. I would not be able to wear any closed shoe until this foot healed.

I dressed in my black blouse with pearl buttons and a clean pair of dark jeans, kept apart especially for today. Adela was ready in a neat conservative black skirt and blouse, looking much older than her twelve years. We joined the villagers and the people who had traveled up from Kampala. Some stood together in clusters with their heads bowed silently in prayer. We waited. Adela went to her family. I stood alone. The morning sun beat fiercely on my head and I felt sweat prickle my scalp.

A girl's voice, strong and clear, sang the opening notes of a hymn. She was joined by many voices weaving around each other in swirls of harmony, the sound sad and forlorn. People pressed back against each other to clear a path through the crowd. I looked behind me and saw the coffin propped on the shoulders of six men. Dennis walked in the middle on one side, his face crumpled with emotion. As they passed through the crowd, the path closed behind them and we formed a slow procession behind the coffin. After the final notes of the hymn faded away, a new one started up elsewhere and hands clapped in a gentle pulse. We walked, perhaps a kilometer, perhaps more. We stopped and found a place to stand, three and four deep, around a grave that had been shoveled and hacked from the barren earth, the innards of the hole piled beside it in a rocky hill. The coffin was carefully placed alongside the grave where it balanced, not quite level, slightly on a tilt.

The archbishop took up his position at the head of the grave. He looked oddly out of place in his purple finery, a stark contrast to the rest of our raggedy group. He opened his bible, read passages from it and spoke. The crowd responded tenderly and I breathed the *amens* together with everybody else. The coffin was lowered into the grave. I saw Sam's mother flanked by two women who grasped her arms tightly - she looked as if she might collapse to the ground if they loosened their grip. I saw Sam's father with his face hidden behind his hands, two guards standing discreetly on either side of him. I saw the girl who had once bathed beside me, her bald head gleaming in the sun. A shovelful of soil was thrown on top of the coffin. It was hard to accept that Sam's body was being covered by pebbles and dirt. I imagined my tears mixing with the soil and staying with him there, down below the earth, dust to dust. Finally, we turned away and left a small group of men to finish the job of filling the grave.

Back in the village, there was crying and laughter, and an unexpected lightness in people's moods. It was all over. Dennis returned and I went to him and hugged him tight, hoping he also felt for the first time since Sam's death that everything might be all right again, one day. Dennis pulled away from me and held me at arm's length.

"We leave now," he said. "You have a plane to catch."

CHAPTER THIRTY-ONE

"What do you mean?" I asked.

"It's Friday. You leave Kenya next Monday."

I had not realized what day it was and felt disoriented now that it was suddenly time to focus on my life-shifting journey into the unknown. "I'm not ready. Can't I stay here with you a while longer? What am I going to do over there in London all by myself?"

Dennis cocked his head to one side, his tired eyes sympathetic.

"Ah, Sara." He patted my cheek and I felt like a small child asking for a gift too large to hold in her hands. "Be realistic. What is it you are going to do here? There are no jobs even for Ugandans themselves, this country is all broken down and will not be fixed miraculously overnight. You have no papers, there is no future for you here."

He was right, of course. I had not had time to give the future any thought, and suddenly remembering the changes just around the corner overwhelmed me. What would I do in a world light-years removed from lorries bumping down red dirt roads, millet porridge and *matoke*, cold baths in plastic buckets and the buzz of people around me, tied to me, even if only through our shared loss? It felt like I'd been here forever.

"Also, you know I have to go back to school in Nairobi," Dennis said. "Sam will not be around for me, either."

I nodded. I was not the only one who whose life had been

completely stood on its head.

"When do we leave?" I asked.

"An hour or so. Time enough for you to prepare."

There was something I needed to do before I left this village. I took a deep breath and swiveled away from Dennis, scanning the small groups of people who stood talking until I found what I was looking for. I walked resolutely toward the bald-headed girl without knowing what I was going to say to her; only that she had the answers I needed.

She saw me coming and we locked eyes for a second, but she did not acknowledge me and deliberately turned to the people standing beside her. I stood right next to her long enough for the others to start looking at me curiously, but she continued to ignore me. Finally, I tapped her on the shoulder and said, quietly, my voice sounding almost like a whisper, "Can we talk?"

She hesitated, then lifted her head and looked down at me from the corners of her eyes, arrogantly. "We can talk," she announced.

She walked quickly ahead of me, stopping when we stood behind the farthest house where nobody could hear us. She turned to face me, but did not speak. Rays of late sunshine shone along her scalp, and lit a downy layer of new hair.

I wasn't sure how to put the things I wanted to know into questions. The thought crossed my mind that it would be so much easier to simply leave things alone. It was not as if anything could be changed, or fixed. I closed my eyes for a moment and remembered: *this is my last chance to find out.*

"You are the one who was seeing Sam," I said.

She nodded and said, calmly, "Yes."

"Didn't he tell you about me?"

"Sam and I did not speak of you. Of course, I knew he had a white woman, in Nairobi. Everybody did."

"Why would you be with him, if you knew he was already

with someone else?"

She shrugged her shoulders. "It was an opportunity. He and his family had a lot to offer. He was a good man, you know this."

I let her words sink in for a moment. I spoke the next question, the important one, carefully: "But what did he want from you?"

She smirked knowingly and said, almost laughing at me, "What do you think? You think a man can just go two weeks, one month, without being with a woman?"

I did think so, actually. If that man truly loved the woman he had left behind, and he was planning return to her.

Maybe she took pity on me, or maybe she just wanted to make a point. "It did not last. He broke things off quickly, wanting to have just one. You." She shrugged again. "It was for the best. What am I to do with a man who has forgotten our African traditions, and has chosen to live the life of whites?"

It was time to pack. I tried to remember where my stuff was and found my little suitcase, battered and torn, leaning against the wall of my room. The clothes inside were dusty and wrinkled. Food packed by my mother had been taken, the money paid out at roadblocks. My toothbrush stood in a cup next to the bed. None of it seemed worth the trouble of carrying to Nairobi where I had a closet full of clean clothes and a bathroom full of new toothbrushes. I took the shoe box with Sam's letters and my airplane ticket, tucked my passport into my back pocket, and left the rest of the things where they stood.

I went to look for the sisters and found them sitting dejectedly in the shade with their legs pulled up to their chins and their backs against the wall of their father's house. Their usual chipper energy had vanished. I sank to my haunches and told them I was leaving. They lifted red-rimmed eyes and said goodbye. There was not enough life left in them to face another farewell. I understood.

"We will write, OK?" I said. "We won't lose touch."

The girls nodded heavy heads. I hugged each of them and whispered goodbye into their ears, and went off to thank men and women who had been kind to me. They had taken me in when I dropped uninvited into their lives in the middle of a tragedy, even though I was a foreigner and a stranger. It was hard to express my gratitude and sadness at leaving – I shook hands and stumbled over my words. I asked them to pay respect to Sam's mother and father on my behalf; I had not seen either of them since the funeral and did not want to intrude on their sorrow now.

Dennis stood waiting near Susan's car and I went to join him. The three of us who lived in Nairobi were driving back together and Susan, Sam's Kenyan mother, was eager to get started on the long trip to return to her own children. Nobody took much notice of our departure - what a difference from the uproar our arrival caused just a few days ago. The crisis that bound us together had passed, and already everybody was stepping back into their own lives.

There was little conversation in the car. The air smelled stale with the windows rolled up against the dust, and heat sapped what energy I had left. When I could no longer hold myself upright, I stretched out on the narrow back seat. My bent knees dragged toward the floor, and my head weighed down my arm, with my neck angled like a broken branch. The stained beige seat cover beneath me smelled rank, and I edged my face forward until my nose dangled in the air. The car sped along in good time, considering the potholes and ever-present road blocks. We flew right through Kampala and did not stop at the house. We paused every so often for a quick bite to eat and a bathroom break. We drove on and on, right through the night. I slept in short snaps but even in my dreams, my mind would not stop churning.

The conversation with the bald girl looped persistently through my mind. How much would I have put up with just to hold on to Sam? Would I have been able to share him with another woman? No. Would he have expected it of me? We had never spoken of the possibility.

Time was running out, and I couldn't stay on the sidelines waiting for things to start making sense. London, Kenya, Rijswijk, Uganda. University, work, home with my parents, independence. Independence. What would I do? What would I do if I ignored Sam's advice to get a job, or my mother pressing me to learn how to keep a home, or my father pushing secretarial training?

University. I wanted to sit in a beautiful building like a Greek temple and study something that fascinated me, like life in Africa, or how things are between men and women. I felt a twinge of something vague and hopeful, almost like enthusiasm.

I was exhausted. Finally, just when I had become too tired to think and allowed myself to sink into apathy, we came to a halt in front of the gates of my parents' house. I sat up and blinked at the damp green lawn, the carefully arranged plants, and the crisply trimmed hedges. The white gravel driveway sparkled as though it had been shampooed.

I picked up my shoe box and stepped out of the car. Dennis also got out.

"I cannot stay now, Sara, I am sorry. But I will see you tomorrow. I promise." He handed me my passport and got back in the car. After a quick wave from him and Susan, the car reversed, turned, and disappeared from sight.

The dust kicked up by their tires drifted slowly back to earth. I took a moment to pull myself together. It felt good to be home. Surely my parents wouldn't be angry at me anymore - everything had changed with Sam's death.

I examined the passport I held in my hands. It looked shabby. The cover had lost its stiffness and become floppy like fabric; the edges were frayed and one of the corners curled in on itself. I wondered how many hands had touched these pages on my journey through Uganda and saw grimy fingerprints as I flipped through it. It fell open to the page where my picture was attached - the same one Sam had once given to a lecherous soldier.

I looked up and saw the gardener had opened the double gates wide, no doubt expecting the car to drive through, and now stood waiting patiently to see what I was planning to do next. I stepped through the gates.

"Jambo, Francis," I said.

"Jambo, *memsaab*," he said, not looking at me. I couldn't blame him. What a stinky spectacle I must be.

My Volkswagen was parked at the end of the driveway – someone had gone to pick it up from the airport. I was comforted to see it standing in the spot where I had parked it myself so many times, a reminder of easier times. I relived for an instant my eighteenth birthday, when I had been ecstatic at the prospect of earning my license, and had no reason to think beyond the freedom of driving my own car.

Plants flowered in the garden even though the dry season had started, and bright red and yellow buds poked up from dark green stems. Francis must have spent many hours watering the beds with the long garden hose that lay curled beside the house. I walked to the front door and gravel crunched loudly beneath my feet with each step. My mother's face popped up in front of the living room window. I waved at her but she didn't waste time waving back – she ran straight out the front door and down the steps of the veranda, only stopping when she reached the driveway. She came close enough to have a good look at me, and the expression of relief and joy on her face was replaced by alarm.

"*Mijn God, Sara, wat zie jij eruit,*" she said, clapping her hands to her face. "You look terrible," she repeated for good measure. "Look how dirty you are. Your hair! I believe I can smell you from here. And what in the world is that foul bandage on your foot? Where is your suitcase?"

"It's good to see you, too," I said.

"*Ach,* I am sorry, child, it is just to see you like this, it's a shock, but I am sure everything will be fine once we get you cleaned up. A nice hot bath will do wonders. But do come in, come in! Papa is out back repairing the washing machine, it has been making this very strange clunking noise and you know how he is, he will not call the *fundi* repair man until he has tried everything he can think of to fix it himself. He will be so relieved to see you home safe and sound! We were worried sick, Sara, all the time you were gone we never heard from you. I know, I know, you were not able to get to a phone, but still, it was very hard on us not knowing how you were doing and when we could expect you home. Papa kept threatening to jump into the car to drive off to Uganda and bring you back home himself if this uncertainty lasted a minute longer."

She waved for me to sit down as we walked into the living room. I was about to lower myself in my usual place in the corner of the sofa when she called out, "No, no, not there, can you sit in the old leather chair? It will be easier to wipe clean than the sofa, you know how badly dirt shows on the light corduroy." She bustled off to get my father and I sat down in the chair she'd pointed out.

"Sara, daughter, you have returned!" My father boomed. He was wearing his workman's costume – a pair of faded jeans and an ancient tie-dyed t-shirt.

"Hello, papa," I said.

"My, my, what an adventure, what an adventure you have had, to be sure. You certainly caused us a fair amount of worry. But here you are, it all worked out in the end, and so now everything is fine. Are you well? You look a little," he searched for the right word, "a little the worse for wear. Why don't you tell us what you experienced during your stay in Uganda?"

"Wait," my mother jumped up from her seat. "I'm sure Sara could do with something to eat and drink before we start. You look like you have lost some weight, I would not be surprised if you have not been eating properly while you were out there in the bush."

I nodded. Now that my mother mentioned it, I realized I was hungry, and thirsty as well. "A glass of water, too, please."

It seemed my parents were not going to revisit the argument we had before I disappeared into Uganda, and were not going to impress on me the details of sleepless nights they suffered on my account. Maybe my father regretted his harsh words. Maybe my parents could see I had made the right decision to go, and was capable of taking care of myself.

When my mother returned, she put out a tray of sandwiches and fruit, mugs of milk, and a pitcher of water. I ate a few slices of dark bread with cheese and a handful of grapes, but my hunger was soon satisfied. My thirst took longer to quench, but after a few sips from a third glass of water, I was ready to start talking. I made several false starts, not knowing how to describe what I had experienced to an audience who hadn't been there, or what words to use to capture the emotions. Grief, fear, love lost and hope found. Joy in unexpected moments. The strangeness of everything, yet feeling I belonged at the same time. Once I warmed up, a torrent of words tumbled from me. My parents asked questions and made one or two comments, but mostly just let me carry on. It was new to be the one doing all the talking in our family and it felt a little odd, as if I had been unexpectedly cast in the lead role.

"So have I concluded this correctly... the funeral took place only yesterday?" my father asked when I finally stopped talking.

"Yes."

Even I had a hard time believing it. Yesterday I buried Sam in a village in northern Uganda, today I was having sandwiches with my parents, lounging in a leather chair. I tried to suppress a yawn, but could no longer keep my fatigue at bay.

My mother jumped up and cried, "Of course you are tired, with all this you have been through! Poor child. No more talking now, I am going to draw you a nice hot bath and then you must take a long nap in your own comfortable bed, and you will see how much better it will help you feel."

She ran off, and soon I heard the soothing sound of water gurgling from a tap. I pushed myself up from the chair.

"We must discuss your future. After you have rested," my father said gravely.

"Yes."

The bath was full. The water in the large tub was so clear, so still, it was hard to gauge exactly where the surface was. I sat down on the edge and dipped my fingers into the water, enjoying its warmth. I hesitated, clear water seeming more appealing than suds, but decided to be practical – I needed all the help I could get to clean this body, and a soak in soapy water would loosen the film of dirt that covered me from head to toe. I poured a double dose of bubble bath into the water and breathed the sweet smell of lavender as I watched the water turn pale purple. Lavender was my mother's favorite scent and it found its way into our home in soaps, detergents and candles. It smelled like comfort. I whipped up a layer of foam with my hand.

I quickly stripped and threw my vile clothes into a corner of the bathroom floor – not even my mother, who took pride in her ability to ensure everything within the four walls of her house was immaculate, would try to bring these rags back to life. They were ripe for the trash bin. My reflection in the mirror was leaner than I remembered, and I admired for an instant my new concave belly. I stepped into the tub with one leg and my eyes fell on the filthy bandage on the other foot; I yanked it off and examined the wound. It looked ugly. Yellow puss crusted the gash and the skin around it was shiny and red. I carefully submerged my foot in the water and clenched my teeth, waiting for the burning to pass. When the pain eased, I slid the rest of my body slowly into the warm water until just my bent knees and face touched the air. I closed my eyes. Water sealed my ears and the only sound I heard was my own heart beating. My limbs felt light and my hair floated around my head like mist.

I was drifting off to sleep. It took real effort to rouse myself and pick up soap, and start scrubbing. My skin faded closer to its natural color with each back and forth motion of the washcloth, until I was clean. I washed and rinsed my hair twice and considered a third time, but didn't feel up to it. My razor lay behind the soap where I had left it and I shaved the long, tough dark hairs from my legs and armpits. With my good foot, I pulled up the silver chain and unplugged the black rubber stopper, releasing dirty bath water. I rose to rinse under the shower, stepped out of the tub onto the shaggy bathmat and wrapped myself in an enormous white bath towel, thick and fluffy, and folded a second one around my hair. A layer of grime caked the bottom of the bathtub between mounds of bubbles and I turned on the shower again, and rinsed every last trace away.

My mother had pulled down the corner of my cover for me. The sheets and pillowcase were pale pink and smelled newly washed and ironed. The curtains above my bed were drawn, and daylight was muted by the thick red striped fabric, flooding my room in rosy shades. I slipped between the sheets and closed my aching eyes. It was good to be home. For now, that was enough.

CHAPTER THIRTY-TWO

I peered out from between my lashes and took a moment to ground myself. I was in my own bed. The hands on the alarm clock pointed at almost 9:30 - I must have missed dinner. Was that the sound of a lawn mower? I lifted a corner of the curtain and saw the day was just as bright outside as it had been when I crawled between the sheets. I had slept through dinner and the whole night and breakfast, too.

A light knock sounded on the door and my mother's voice called softly, "Sara? Are you awake?"

"*Ja, mama.* I am awake."

My mother's smiling face peered into the room. "Well, there you are! I looked in on you several times but you were sleeping so soundly, it seemed cruel to wake you. You must have needed your rest very badly. Do you feel better? Are you hungry?"

"I feel better. No, not hungry."

"Well, I am about to make coffee for your father, so why don't you come out and join us. There are some things your father wants to discuss with you."

"OK. Give me a minute."

My mother stepped out of the room, then leaned back in. The cheerful expression slid off her face and she looked uneasy. She hesitated before she spoke.

"Sara – did you see the letter? It is the one that arrived just when you were leaving for Uganda. I put it up against the lamp and thought you would find it as soon as you woke up."

Her hand pointed and my eyes swiveled to a rectangular

white envelope leaning against the bedside lamp, with my name and address written unmistakably in Sam's hand. My mother left the room quietly and clicked the door shut behind her. I picked up the letter and placed it on my lap. I stroked the writing with my fingertips and held it to my cheek. I tried to bring back to life the man whose hands had so recently drawn a pen across this envelope, whose tongue had licked this stamp and stuck it neatly in the corner. Had his lips brushed a kiss on this paper?

I opened my eyes, held the envelope in front of me and turned it over, and worked my little finger into a space beneath the flap where the glue hadn't taken. Very carefully I pulled up my crooked finger and tore the top of the envelope in short spurts until it split apart along its full length. When I peered inside and saw just a single sheet of paper, I didn't know whether to feel disappointed or relieved that there wasn't more, only certain these were Sam's final words to me. I took the letter from the envelope and sat still, stalling for time, waiting to find calm. I unfolded the paper and lowered my eyes to the words.

Sara, my number one woman,

I picture you now reading these words the way you described. You sitting on the edge of your bed alone in your room with only my letter, and the door closed tight. So then, now stand up and put on that John Denver album of yours. You are surprised, right? I know, I told you many times how much I hate the dude and his soppy songs. But for today, his words will do in my absence. Listen closely to "I'm Sorry". Do you hear what I'm trying to tell you? I'm sorry for the things I didn't say.

Sara, I made a mistake. I got weak and distracted from what is truly important. It is you I love. I don't want a life repeating the same useless behavior of the men in my family. You know this is true about me. There is a better future ahead for us, one between you and me only.

I will be back in just a few days. We will talk and I will explain. Please do not worry. Everything will work out fine, I promise.

263

Love you always,
Sam

My eyes went back to the top of the letter, and I read it again. I read it two more times to squeeze every last bit of meaning from the words and from what wasn't written, between the lines. I stood up, placed the John Denver album on the turntable and dropped the needle into the third track groove. I turned up the volume and listened to the singer wail his sad tune.

I wondered if Sam had remembered how the song ended. The girl had walked away from her lying, cheating lover, and all the beautifully crooned *I'm sorrys* in the world couldn't make her stay. Did Sam worry I might leave him, once he confessed to being with another woman? A flame of anger flared at being left with questions I would never know the answers to. Just as quickly, I pushed it down, sick of the pointlessness of raging at my dead lover. Carefully, I folded the letter back inside its envelope, put it inside the shoe box, and closed the lid.

I pulled on underwear, ran a brush through my soft, clean hair and tied it in a ponytail. I opened the closet door and was bewildered by the tall, neat stacks of clothing: t-shirts, jeans and shorts in a rainbow of colors, clothes for every mood and circumstance. I had no idea what I felt like wearing and grabbed some things from the top of a pile. When I noticed my foot, I hesitated – the wound looked disgusting. I unrolled an old pair of tennis socks, the fabric worn and soft, and pulled them on, hopping first on one foot, then the other, and clumsily backed into the chair standing in the corner. Folded neatly across the back were the trousers I'd sewn for Dennis' choir performance. I stood still and remembered his mild complaints about green and red basting stitches. It happened a lifetime ago. The concert had come and gone and Dennis didn't care about pants anymore.

"Good morning, daughter," my father spoke as I entered the

living room. He folded his newspaper and put it aside. "You certainly look a great deal improved over yesterday, I must say!"

"I'm sure I do," I said and smiled. "Does this mean it's alright for me to sit on the sofa today?"

My mother looked embarrassed at my little jab. "Why, of course!" she said. "Sit where you want – wherever you are most comfortable."

"There are things we must discuss," my father said, crossing his arms in front of his chest and looking official.

"Papa." I didn't know where to start.

My father cleared his throat, and spoke first. "Before you left, we had a conversation. I'm sure you remember. You were quite clear about not wanting to return to Holland. And I believe I was quite clear about my position regarding your decision."

"Yes."

When he continued, his voice was quieter. "We cannot always predict the course our lives will take. Then we must deal with the consequences of our actions, and sometimes adjust plans. It is, after all, an inevitable step in the process of growing up."

My mother looked up with what seemed like relief. "Is that a car I hear at the gate? We'd better go see who it is, Francis has his day off today. Why, yes, it is a car. Papa, will you go to open the gate?"

My father stood up and went to find out who had arrived while my mother rushed off to the kitchen to prepare. It was not unusual for my parents' friends and colleagues to drop by unannounced, especially in the weekend – expats spent a lot of time visiting with each other. My parents would now transform into hosts, offering chitchat and coffee, and if the guests stayed long enough, whiskey and peanuts. Our talk would have to wait.

But when my father came back, Dennis was with him. I had forgotten he would drop by today.

"Dennis." It was good to see him in circumstances less

desperate than the ones we had been through together. It cheered me to see him, the one person I didn't have to explain myself to. I looked him up and down and smiled. "You've cleaned up well. I hardly recognize you."

"I return the compliment. That is your actual hair color, eh? I almost forgot it was not sticky bush red." He smiled back at me, his little joke rekindling the intimacy we shared in Uganda.

"Very funny," I said, "Though I admit a hot bath and a good long sleep do help."

"I'm glad to hear it," Dennis said seriously, and the moment of lightheartedness passed. He squeezed my hand, leaned toward me and said, "Can we talk?"

I shot my father a glance and he waved his hands, signaling that Dennis and I should go outside. We stepped out of the front door and onto the veranda, and lowered ourselves into the creaky wicker chairs.

"Are you well?" Dennis asked.

"Well enough, I suppose."

"I have something for you. I had to use all my charm to get things done quickly like this, let me tell you," Dennis said. "I explained to the Kodak guy the circumstances, how you are leaving the country tomorrow and therefore these pictures here had to be printed with greatest haste. Would you believe it, it turns out this guy actually knew Sam – not personally, but from watching him play rugby - he is a big fan of the team. He was happy to help after I told him of our loss."

Dennis handed me a thin stack of square black and white photographs. The edges were trimmed prettily in waves and the prints looked old-fashioned and formal, but the images were very recent. I caught my breath when I realized what I was looking at. The picture on top must have been taken right after Sam was lowered into the ground – the coffin lay clearly visible in the bottom of the grave, uncovered by soil. A crowd of people stood alongside staring down, anguished expressions on their faces. I saw my head small and white in a sea of dark faces, strangely conspicuous. How odd I never realized it. My hair fell down past my shoulders, distinctly different from the afros and braided styles around me. The features of my light face were invisible, bleached away by the glaring sun.

I slipped the picture to the bottom of the stack. The next one showed the top halves of Anna, Adela and Abigail standing together, shoulder pressed to shoulder. The girls looked into the camera bravely with something close to a smile, but there was no joy in their eyes. I flipped slowly through the stack. The last picture was of Dennis, taken from a distance and showing his lanky limbs right down to his shoes, but not the expression on his face. The photographer had apparently not held the camera straight and the horizon behind him was tilted, as if he might slide off the earth at any moment.

"*Asante sana*," I said. "Thank you very much, Dennis."

"It seemed you should have these with you when you go on your journey tomorrow, to remember."

"It means a lot."

"There is another thing you should know." He was quiet for a moment, gathering his thoughts, and I waited for him to continue. "I heard today from Susan - she has been in touch with our people in Kampala – that which was suspected has turned out to be true. Sam was poisoned. There has been a confession."

I stared at Dennis in horror and disbelief.

"It is certain. There were already many indications, and now the woman has admitted to her crime. It is the middle wife, Matilda, you remember? The day she ran away quite crazed after viewing the body - you were there. She was found hiding among her people, and confessed it was she who killed Sam by poisoning his food."

I could not comprehend what he was telling me. "Dennis, what are you saying - Sam was poisoned? Poison? How would she even get her hands on that?"

He glanced at me and hesitated before speaking again, quietly. "Rat poison. Readily available."

I threw myself back in my chair and covered my face with my hands.

Dennis sighed and spoke slowly, as if he was trying to make me understand. "Matilda hated Sam; everybody knew this. Many times she called him arrogant and said he did not give her proper respect as a mother. She felt she had rights to a bigger share of money and property, and more attention from her husband, and blamed Sam for thwarting her interests, and for blocking the way to better opportunities for her child. She complained all the time of being powerless. Because of Sam."

"Are you telling me those are reasons enough to make her turn to murder? To actually kill her own stepson?"

Dennis hesitated. Then he continued, "Apparently there was an incident that pushed her over the edge. Shortly before his death, Sam accused Matilda's son of behaving disrespectfully, and smacked him. Slapped him in the face, right there in front of the mother."

I looked at him in shock, recognizing this part of the story could only be true.

"It is an inconceivable thing, for Matilda to turn to poison for her revenge. But she has confessed, Sara."

"I just can't imagine she would..."

Dennis snapped impatiently, "Or maybe it is you who is in denial."

CHAPTER THIRTY-THREE

I looked at Dennis in surprise. Was he accusing me of wearing blinders, of deliberately ignoring unpleasant truths?

When he spoke again, there was bitterness in Dennis' voice I had not heard before. "There will be no way for you to move forward if you keep your eyes closed to truths you don't like, Sara. You cannot build a life on wishful thinking, imagining this world to be some sugary place where everybody just gets along. As if donkeys would ever be welcomed into a herd of zebras!"

"Actually, I am not as stupid about reality as you seem to think," I said.

He looked at me. "Did you seriously expect being with Sam would make you able to live an African life, as his woman?"

"Look, maybe he saw our relationship his way, and I saw it my way, and we hadn't really started dealing with how different some things were between us. But that doesn't mean we couldn't have found a way to make a life together, you know. We loved each other," I said.

Dennis snorted in disgust. "What makes you think love is enough? It is such European thinking. Here in Africa, we do not have the luxury of living for love. Even when we have enough to eat, we have more urgent things to worry about, like educating ourselves, and staying out of prison."

Dennis was upset and I put my hand on his arm, hoping to calm him down.

"Trying to make things better. That is what the purpose of life comes down to, here in Africa," he continued. "And it is also the purpose of marriage."

I would never know if Dennis was right about Sam and me.

We sat quietly, our eyes turned down, each listening to our own thoughts. The brute senselessness of Sam's murder was bewildering. He had been just days away from leaving Matilda and the family - maybe not returning home at all for years. Old wounds would have had time to heal, and new insights a chance to grow.

A car sped through the gates. Only one person would drive up to someone's house like that: revving the engine along the short distance up the driveway, raising a huge cloud of dust, and then stomping on the brakes so hard the back wheels skidded on the gravel. I wasn't surprised to see Rashid step out of his light blue Peugeot. I hadn't seen him since the day at the disco when Dennis threatened him for supposedly making a move on me. How freaked out we had all been.

I took a deep breath, and walked down to greet him. "Rashid, it's good to see you."

His words tumbled out before I got close enough to shake his hand. "I am so very sorry for your loss. I..." he looked at me helplessly and seemed unclear how to continue. "It will be a sadder place without Sam. For all of us."

"Yes. Thank you," I said.

Rashid handed me a small square basket with three mangoes in it, their ripe peach and pink sunset colors soft against the dark cardboard on which they were displayed. "Thank you," I said again.

"It is what we do," Rashid said apologetically, shrugging his shoulders. "Our people do not consider flowers appropriate in times of grief."

"It means a lot," I said.

I wondered whether I should talk to him about something that was still bothering me, and decided I'd give it a try. I lowered my voice to keep Dennis from hearing. "I almost hadn't expected to see you at all, you know, after the thing with Dennis at the Drive Range. Do you remember? It seems Sam had asked him to look out for me, though you know he never meant for his little brother to go bonkers and actually threaten you."

Rashid waved away my explanation. "Please, it was a misunderstanding only. I have forgotten all about it. It never happened."

"Will you speak to him?"

"To Dennis?"

"He is here, sitting on the veranda."

He hesitated, just a heartbeat. "I am pleased to see my friend Dennis again," he said. He climbed up the stone stairs with determination and Dennis rose to meet him. They spoke back and forth in low voices and gripped each other's hand tightly, shaking off the past. I was comforted by the sight.

I joined the guys and took the cigarette Dennis offered me. Rashid held up a flame and I leaned forward, lighting the cigarette and sucking smoke deep into my lungs. I sank into the round-backed chair with my face turned to the sun and an elbow propped on the warm stone wall next to me. Through the open windows of the living room, I heard the familiar sounds of a record being slid carefully out of its sleeve and placed on the turntable, followed by the first notes of a song.

My father played classical music every Sunday morning, as far back as I could remember. He stored an enormous collection of albums in the cabinet beneath the stereo, alphabetically arranged with the spines neatly on display. My father would lower himself onto the low, creaky stool that stood in front of the cabinet, and closely examine his records, hearing in his mind the notes of each before selecting the perfect one for that particular Sunday's mood.

Today, my father thought to accommodate me and my friends. The chirpy harmonies of ABBA's latest hit drifted through the window. How was he supposed to know my friends were not the ABBA kind?

"Thank you, papa, that's really nice!" I called inside.

"Today we play music for you," he called back.

"Cool."

My mother brought sandwiches sliced into triangles, neatly arranged in two rows on a tray, remembering to point out to Rashid the ones he should avoid because they had ham. Friends dropped by as the afternoon wore on. They came to find out if what they had heard about Sam's death could possibly be true, to express their grief, to say goodbye, to find Dennis. As the day passed and light faded from the sky, people left again. Dennis was the last to go. He hugged me close and when he loosened his grip, I saw his eyes were moist.

"Sara, I am sorry for what I said earlier. You know I didn't mean to upset you, eh? In fact, don't pay any attention to the words that come out of my mouth these days – I am not myself at all."

"I know," I answered. "This is very hard. I know how much you're hurting."

"I will miss you, my sister."

"One day, I'll be back," I said.

I sat alone, quietly taking stock. Sam had been murdered by his stepmother. Was this what life had driven her to, or was it a mistake to try to find sense behind her violence? Was this nothing more than the random act of an insane person?

The ache of loss had settled somewhere between my heart and throat. I guessed I would be feeling this way for a while. I also knew I would survive.

A small rust-colored gecko darted up the wall and stopped every so often to flick its tongue at tiny flies. Insects buzzed around the ceiling lamp. My parents sat down in the empty wicker chairs across from me, and my father placed a large brown envelope on the table between us.

"Did you enjoy having your friends over?" my father asked.

I nodded.

"So now we must talk; there is not much time." He paused. "Sara, your mother and I are not heartless people. We understand this is a very difficult time for you. You have experienced a lot, too much perhaps, certainly more than is normal for a girl your age." My father nodded in agreement with his own words. "You think your plans for the future have been destroyed, but we must not forget that you are young and will heal and move forward with your life, even if you cannot imagine such a thing now. There will be other men and one day you will find the right one and marry and settle down."

I waited to hear where my father was heading with this.

He cleared his throat and continued. "While you were away, I took the liberty of making arrangements. It is all set; you need not worry any longer. The apartment is ready, the secretarial college has admitted you, and here you have the last piece of the puzzle."

My father handed me the unsealed brown envelope. I pulled out a thick sheet of paper: it was my diploma, and a quick glace told me I had passed my A-levels. I even managed to scrape through Geography. *Thank you Mr. Vasudeva.* This meant I was eligible for university. I looked up at my parents and grinned.

"There is more," my father said.

I opened the envelope wider and saw a rectangular stack of stiff white paper on the bottom. I recognized it immediately, and drew it out. An airplane ticket made out to Sara Janssen. Destination Amsterdam. A journey that would take me back to Rijswijk.

I examined it in silence. I shut my eyes and imagined the future that had just been handed to me, like a bed already made, ready for me to sink into. One where I would not be asked to make the difficult choices.

It was how I had always lived. Why would it cross my father's mind now to consider what I wanted for myself? He could not see beyond the little girl I had always been: eager to please, eager to fit in, careful not to aggravate the lion.

My eyes rested on my swollen foot, the wound oozing yellow through the sock. I would never be able to squeeze it into a proper shoe. Tomorrow I'd board an airplane and step onto the unfamiliar soil of my new home wearing retread sandals, my foreignness on display from the start. Picturing it did not upset me. I had loved and grieved and grown, and inside me I felt a sweet new confidence that whatever lay ahead would work out, even if I could not quite see how, just yet.

It was early morning when the taxi stopped in front of the gate, and I moved quietly out of the house, careful not to wake my parents. We had said our goodbyes last night. I took my patchwork bag and slung it over my head and across one shoulder. With the other hand, I lifted my suitcase, the largest I could find among the dusty collection in my parents' garage. It was heavy, bulging with everything I could stuff into it, and I leaned against its weight as I opened the gates and locked them behind me. I dropped the suitcase into the trunk of the taxi, nodding away the driver's attempts to relieve me of it.

I sat down in the back seat and said, "To the airport, please."

"To the Jomo Kenyatta terminal? You are traveling internationally?" the driver asked.

"Yes."

The taxi made a three-point-turn ahead of the closed gates. I twisted around and watched the house grow smaller through the rear window. *Goodbye,* I thought, feeling my heart squeeze hard as we pulled away from the home where I had lived many happy and hopeful years, and from the parents I loved. But no tears. I had done enough crying to last me a good while. I turned around and faced forward, sitting quietly, watching the sun rise and bathe Kenya in golden light.

We drove past the green sign with the airplane silhouette, and I peered down the road, catching a glimpse of the airport in the distance. I took a deep breath and sat up straighter, strengthening myself for changes I would be facing soon.

I drew a small plastic pouch from my purse to check my documents one last time. Almost out of force of habit, I slid the passport into my back pocket. The ticket with its magical destination printed boldly on the front: *Heathrow Airport, London,* I carefully returned to the pouch. The postcards Sam had given me to spark enthusiasm about a life in London - worn now from the many times I had taken them out to soak up the promise they carried - I placed on my lap, one above the other. I gazed at them, imagining it was me strolling along the walkway of the university with a sunbeam breaking through the ancient stone archway to light my path; sitting on a weathered wooden bench on the quad to chat with fellow students; eating fish and chips straight off a greasy scrap of newspaper.

The taxi stopped in front of the terminal. I returned the postcards to my purse, drew out my wallet and emptied it of my last Kenya shillings, leaving the driver with a handsome tip. It was a good day for both of us.

ACKNOWLEDGMENTS

With deepest gratitude

to my husband, who didn't so much as blink when I announced that I was giving up a lucrative career as translator to write a book, and has been unwavering in his support through every good and bad writing day;

to my sons, who unanimously cheered me on without questioning (out loud) what weirdness had gotten into their mother this time;

to my parents, without whom I would never have led such a traveling life, and the seeds of this book would not have been planted;

to my sister, who always knows what I mean, and always lets me feel I'm right;

to the Highline Writers, support group extraordinaire;

to those first readers who bravely and uncomplainingly slogged through the early terrible drafts in whole or in part;

to Emily, who generously opened the door to her family and invited me in;

to my first editor Sandi, whose delicately phrased comments opened my eyes to possibilities I had not yet discovered, and whose insistence on "more conflict!" took the story to the next level;

to my African friends who made sure references to things Kenyan and Ugandan were credible. Any mistakes that slipped through are wholly my own.

ABOUT THE AUTHOR

After a lifetime of globe-trotting, Jo Alkemade is happily
settled in Des Moines, Washington with her husband.
Her four sons are grown and walking their own paths.
Jo continues to be emotionally attached to Kenya, and visits
whenever she can.

* * * * *

If you enjoyed this book, please spread the word!
+ post a review on Amazon and beyond
+ like Jo Alkemade on Facebook

Thank you for reading!

Made in the USA
Lexington, KY
26 January 2013